BETRAYAL IN CALUSA COVE

EVERGLADES OVERWATCH
BOOK FOUR

ELLE JAMES

JEN TALTY

TWISTED PAGE INC

Copyright © 2025 by Elle James and Jen Talty

All rights reserved.

No part of this book may be reproduced in any form or by any electronic or mechanical means, including information storage and retrieval systems, without written permission from the author, except for the use of brief quotations in a book review.

Without in any way limiting the author's [and publisher's] exclusive rights under copyright, any use of this publication to "train" generative artificial intelligence (AI) technologies to generate text is expressly prohibited. The author reserves all rights to license uses of this work for generative AI training and development of machine learning language models.

ISBN-EBOOK: 978-1-62695-664-3

ISBN-PAPERBACK: 978-1-62695-665-0

I (Jen Talty) want to thank Elle for going on this journey with me. It's been an amazing ride and I've absolutely loved working with her!

I also need to give a shout out to Kris Norris. Thank you for spending hours on the phone with me discussing, snakes, gators, sniper angles, posions, and other murderous topics. You are are my Huckleberry.

Thank you, Jen. You're a dream to work with and your dedication to the story is spot on. Betrayal in Calusa Cove turned out so wonderful, because of you. This story wrapped up so beautifully and brought the team together in the best way possible. I'm honored you chose to work with me on these projects. Forever a fan of your work...Elle

AUTHOR'S NOTE

USA Today Bestselling authors Elle James and Jen Talty join forces in an electrifying collaboration born from an author retreat in paradise. Inspired by the lush landscapes of the Florida Everglades, their latest venture blends heart-pounding suspense, sizzling romance, and gripping action. With their signature storytelling prowess, Talty and James weave a thrilling tale that will keep readers on the edge of their seats, proving that when two powerhouse authors unite, the result is pure magic.

Everglades Overwatch Series
Secrets in Calusa Cove
Pirates in Calusa Cove
Murder in Calusa Cove
Betrayal in Calusa Cove

BETRAYAL IN CALUSA COVE

EVERGLADES OVERWATCH BOOK #4

New York Times & *USA Today*
Bestselling Author

ELLE JAMES

USA Today
Bestselling Author

JEN TALTY

CHAPTER 1

Fletcher Dane heard the boots scuffing across the cement flooring. His spine stiffened in response. His muscles ached. His bones rattled. It had been at least a full day since his captors had visited his tiny cell. He'd gone without water, food, and thankfully, the screams coming from his teammates. He could do anything...but that. He knew no one had broken. Or at least, that's what he believed. If one of them had, they'd all be dead.

Only one concerned him, though.

Ken.

He was the only one with a wife and kids.

Not that the rest of them didn't have something to live for, but Ken had a family. He had people who depended on him for more than a phone call once a week to check in.

Ken also had one foot out the door.

He constantly talked about leaving the Navy, saying his days were numbered, and that he most likely wouldn't sign his re-enlistment papers. It hadn't come as a shock to Fletcher or the rest of the team.

Dawson had been the first to mention the words out loud, but Keaton had repeated them, and Hayes had nodded in agreement.

Fletcher just couldn't imagine it. He'd known Ken his entire life. They'd been best friends since he could remember.

The metal door rattled to life, and Fletcher did his best to mentally and physically prepare himself for the next battle. He wasn't afraid. He knew what was coming, and he'd endure. He'd been electrocuted, waterboarded, cut, burned—you name it, his captors had done it. All in the name of giving up the mission. But Fletcher would never talk. He'd die first. The men inflicting the torture seemed to know that line between life and death well and straddled it each and every time they entered this small room to beat Fletcher. He did his best to keep quiet. All the men did, but pain had a way of escaping no matter what.

He sat up on the grimy mattress his captors had provided and watched as two men entered the room. They hoisted him to his feet and dragged him through the door.

That was new.

He didn't protest. He didn't fight. And he sure as hell didn't say one fucking word. There was no point.

The men led him into a different room at the end of the hall. His heart hammered in his chest. Adrenaline pumped through his veins. He knew at any moment, this could be the time they put a bullet through his brain. He'd been on numerous missions where he and his team had been the ones charging in, coming to the rescue. But with every passing day, hour, minute, the resolve that his team would be freed...left his mind.

Not that he gave up hope that a team was looking. But he'd accepted they might never be found.

One of the men stuck a long, old-fashioned key into the lock, pushed open the door, and shoved Fletcher into the space. He stumbled, his muscles too weak to maintain balance and hold him upright. He fell to his knees. He blinked, staring at a pair of dirty, bloody, bare feet. He glanced up and gasped.

Strapped to a chair in the center of a room that smelled like copper and rot, Ken Mitchell looked nothing like the guy who'd once shot-gunned beers on a Florida beach or teased Baily for not knowing how to tie a proper boating cleat. His face was swollen and bruised, his eyes barely open. But when his gaze met Fletcher's, there was still something there—something sharp and defiant.

Something that told Fletcher this was a man who would not be broken.

Now, he felt like a real asshole for doubting his best friend. The one who had been by his side when his parents had died. The one who had followed him into the Navy, like it was the most normal thing to do.

The man behind Ken said something in a language Fletcher didn't understand. His tone calm, detached.

"You talk now," the man said. "Or he dies."

Ken shook his head and mouthed, No.

Fletcher lifted his chin, rocking back on his heels as the other man grabbed him by the hair.

"You have nothin' to say?" the man asked.

Fletcher swallowed the bile that smacked the back of his throat. He held Ken's gaze. Memories of childhood flashed between the two men. They'd shared hopes, dreams, and broken hearts. There might have been a distance between the two men over the last few years—a wedge that had been solidly placed between Ken and the team by marriage, kids, and a different set of goals.

But none of that mattered now. Ken was as solid as they came in battle, and Fletcher knew that.

Fletcher inhaled sharply and blinked.

"Speak, now, or this man will die, and it will be your fault," the man said, holding Fletcher's gaze before tilting Ken's head to the side.

"Fuck off," Ken muttered. "Neither one of us is saying a damn thing to you."

"I'll give you one last chance," the man behind Ken said. "Tell us what we want to know, and I'll show him mercy."

If Fletcher talked, they'd all be dead. If he didn't, Ken would die, and sure as the day was long, they would all be killed, one by one. This was just another tactic. Just another form of torture.

"I will—"

"Shut up," Ken interrupted him, glaring. If the tables were turned, he'd be doing the exact same thing.

Talk about a lose-lose.

The man behind Ken pulled a knife and pressed it against Ken's neck. A few drops of blood trickled down his skin.

"Take care of Baily," Ken whispered. *"And when she really needs help, you'll find it behind the bait—"*

"Last chance," the man with the knife said, pressing the blade deeper.

Ken looked at Fletcher—right at him—when the blade slid across his throat.

Blood squirted. Fast. Endless. Red over skin. Red on hands. Red that no amount of time could ever wash off.

Fletcher couldn't move. Couldn't scream.

He just sat there and watched the life drain out of the one man he'd sworn he'd protect.

Fletcher jerked awake, breath ragged, T-shirt soaked through. The whir of the ceiling fan overhead too slow. The air in his room too thick. His fists clenched against damp sheets as the image of Ken's face burned behind his eyelids.

Damn it.

He swung his legs off the bed and pressed his hands against his knees, trying to ground himself. Focus on something real.

The hum of the marina generators.

The distant cry of a heron.

The ever-present scent of salt and oil and old rope.

Over the years since Ken's death, the nightmares had lessened... fading into the background. Once he'd come back to Calusa Cove two years ago, they'd started again. Memories of his childhood mixed with the dream, which only made it worse, but soon, they disappeared into the fog, much like the steam burned off the Everglades in the morning.

However, ever since Tripp's journal had been found, and more of Ken's secrets had been uncovered—or more like the realization that he hadn't known his friend at all—the nightmares taunted him like an alligator waiting to attack.

He pushed off the bed and headed downstairs. He stuck a mug under the coffeemaker and waited for it to fill before snagging Tripp's journal. Then he made a beeline for the porch—barefoot, shirtless, sleep forgotten. The sky was still black, stars muted by the early morning haze. The swamp beyond the docks stretched silent and wide.

The hum of the first boat making its way into the Glades caught his attention. He could see Silas as he headed up the canal and into the opening like he did every morning. The man was a creature of habit, but lately, since his longtime friend Dewey Hale had turned out to be a serial killer, Silas took to the waterways much earlier—and stayed out longer.

Silas's wife had mentioned more than once that she was worried about the man. He'd always been a bit of a character, but now he was withdrawn and disillusioned by the world. Fletcher couldn't blame Silas, or half the town, because everyone had felt betrayed by Dewey, especially after what had happened with Paul Massey and his drug running a few months before. Having two of their trusted townspeople turn out to be criminals, well, that tended to change a town's perspective.

Fletcher checked the time. It was a little after five in the morning. Soon, the waters would be filled with boaters—people going about their lives, even though a lot had happened in Calusa Cove, everyone was still on edge.

His quiet little hometown, built on legends and myths, was turning out to be full of secrets—the kinds of secrets that got people killed.

He sat in his father's old favorite chair, which sorely needed some new cushions. He lifted his feet, propping them up on the ottoman, and sipped the bitter brew while staring at the ripples on the water created by the slight breeze. This winter had been unseasonably warm for South Florida, and his air conditioning wasn't working properly. He'd ordered the part, and it should be arriving today. That would give him something to tinker with on his day off while he did his best to keep the demons at bay.

But it wasn't hot enough to really care, and the humidity wasn't stifling. That was something.

He opened the pages, grateful that Dawson had let him have the damn thing for the next few days. Fletcher had told Dawson he'd make copies for everyone. They all had a stake in this now, as they planned to bid on the old Crab Shack as soon as the town put it up for auction. There was a scheduled town hall meeting next week. Anyone who had any inclination to purchase it from the town trust would need to file their plans and have them approved before the town would release the land.

It was a strange thing, and Fletcher didn't begin to understand how the legalities worked. They'd hired a lawyer for that, but outside of possibly dealing with Decker Brown, no one else in this town had their sights set on the old Crab Shack.

However, there was so much more that weighed on Fletcher's mind. Ken had been their brother-in-arms. They'd been on the same SEAL team for years. They'd been through some shit together and had nearly died together a few times.

Fletcher shook his head like a dog. The last thing he needed was to keep replaying that scene over and over again in his head all day.

A tap on the porch screen door made him jump, nearly sloshing his coffee all over his lap. He turned his head. "Jesus, Baily. You scared the crap out of me." He tried to rip his gaze from the gorgeous woman standing at the door. She wore a pair of loose-fitting blue and white shorts, which he suspected were pajama bottoms, paired with a three-quarter-sleeved matching top. Her hair flowed past her shoulders, and he knew for a fact she hadn't combed it.

This was the Baily he'd fallen in love with. The natural beauty, all sweet, but not completely innocent, who used to sneak over and climb into his bed after their parents had gone to sleep.

"Sorry. I saw the light come on." She held up a paper plate. "I brought you an egg sandwich."

He chuckled. "You really love that little sandwich maker, now, don't ya?" He stood, unlatched the door, and let her in. "Thanks. You didn't have to do that, but I appreciate it." He kissed her cheek. While things between them were still strained, they were better.

At least they'd come to an understanding about life in general and the fact that he was never leaving Calusa Cove, nor was he about to sell his parents' home.

Unfortunately, the turning point had been when he'd told her the truth about her brother's death.

Well, not at first. She'd been pissed. Furious, actually. As if he could have saved Ken. As if telling their captors the truth wouldn't have gotten everyone killed.

But then came...*Why Ken?* A question no one could answer. And every man on the team, at some point, had wished they could've changed places with Ken.

Then again, they had all wanted to trade places with Fletcher. But that was a nightmare he wouldn't wish on his enemies.

"I have a confession to make." Baily eased into the other chair—the one that used to be his mom's.

Fletcher just couldn't make himself get rid of a single thing in this house. He knew it was strange. Everything was old and uncomfortable. But to him, it represented a big part of his childhood—and not just because of his family.

"What's that?"

"I've been waiting for you to wake up."

"Interesting." He winked. "Seeing you first thing is always the best way to start my day."

"You are so corny, and I promised your buddies I'd come check on you." She waved her hand toward the end table. "Eat your sandwich. You've been neglecting yourself lately."

He frowned, but that wasn't a false statement, nor was he surprised that Dawson, Keaton, and Hayes had enlisted Baily to keep tabs on him. The nightmares had been coming almost every night, and that made his stomach churn. In the last two weeks, he'd lost five pounds. Most people handled stress by eating. He did so by starving himself. He'd always been like that. Lucky for him, most of his life hadn't been riddled by the kind of stress that affected him that way.

The pressure of his military career had gotten to him sometimes. Still, the only way it had ever manifested was by affecting his ability to digest food, especially after those damn flipping nightmares.

He leaned over, unwrapped the breakfast treat, and brought it to his mouth. It was filled with all his favorites. A warm, fluffy English muffin, stuffed with cheddar cheese, bacon, sausage, and a fried egg that oozed the yellow yolk onto his tongue, accompanied by a dribble of hot sauce while the butter melted into the nooks and crannies of the bread. "Wow, that's good. Thank you," he managed with a mouthful.

"You're welcome." She leaned back, folded her

arms, and cocked her pretty little head. "Did you sleep at all last night?"

He took another large bite. Honestly, right now, he could eat three of these things. "I got at least five hours, so better than some nights."

"Are you talking to anyone about the nightmares?" Baily kicked off her flip-flops and tucked her feet under her butt.

"I did before I moved here, but not since then."

"Have you thought about seeing someone here?"

"Yeah," he admitted. "But honestly, the doctor I saw before told me there might always be triggers." He pointed toward the journal. "Knowing that Ken lied to me—and you—is doing something to me that I can't explain."

"I get it. I do. But we might never know the answers, and I'm starting to come to terms with that, especially since I've got bigger problems than what Ken might've been doing." She pursed her lips. "He was always a bit selfish. Always wanted out of this town. Always wanted to have money in his pockets and to be treated like he mattered. He wanted to be seen in ways I didn't understand. It's exhausting trying to figure it out, and I don't want to anymore. Reading Tripp's thoughts drives that point home."

"You don't wonder if that loan is tied to something your brother might've done?" Fletcher asked.

She shook her head. "He never asked my father to sell—only me. I doubt Ken even knew about that loan. One thing my brother hated was being in debt."

"That's true." Fletcher lifted his mug and took a long, slow sip. "So, what are your plans today?" He raised his hand. "Outside of working."

"Trinity and Chloe invited me to get my nails done." She lifted her hands and stared at her nails, letting out a hefty sigh. "I don't know why women bother with nail polish. All it does is chip off, and that crap you have to buy to take it off smells horrible. I'd rather soak my hands in fish guts than spend an hour at the salon. Total waste of time and money."

Fletcher covered his mouth. Laughing wasn't an appropriate response, but he couldn't help it.

She reached for a magazine on the small table next to her chair and tossed it at him. "I have no idea what on earth is so funny."

He cleared his throat. "Have you ever been to a spa or a salon? I mean, doesn't Silas's wife cut your hair at her home?"

"And your point?" she asked softly.

"Dawson mentioned you didn't go with the girls to get your nails done before the wedding. Why not?"

Baily pointed out the door and toward the faint hum of the marina air conditioners. "I have a business to run, in case you've forgotten."

"You could've called me to help out, so you could've gone with the girls."

She lifted her right hand and stared at her nails. "I did a good enough job on my own."

He knew money was tight, but getting her nails done for a special occasion shouldn't have been something she'd skipped out on. He had no idea how much a mani-pedi cost, but it couldn't have been a lot.

"Don't look at me like that." She lowered her chin and scowled. "It's the same look I get from Silas when I won't let him slip me a hundred after I help him with a line when he comes in. He waves his wild hand at me and tells me that's what he tips the dockhands, but I know, besides Bingo, who's saving for college, he does no such thing."

"Maybe not, but you're a stubborn woman, and while being proud is a virtue I can get behind, there's no reason you can't accept a little kindness from those who love you," he said as the morning sun peeked out from the horizon. "Silas really does care about you and the success of this marina."

"I'm not a charity case, and Silas finds ways to slip that money right under my door." She shook her head and laughed. "I don't insult him. I keep it. I've started a little fund in case whoever owns that loan decides to force my hand."

Fletcher had people working on figuring out who actually owned that loan, but the names were buried under a labyrinth of corporations and LLCs. Not to mention, she'd have to come up with close to a million dollars. What had her dad been thinking by borrowing that kind of money from strangers?

Part of him still believed that Decker Brown had had something to do with it. That he was still watching and waiting for the right time to make his move. He'd approached Keaton twice and Hayes once, regarding the property on the canal, but he hadn't made an offer. Decker had only asked questions. They had been questions that made everyone wonder if he was interested, but he'd never made an offer, and when confronted, Decker had shrugged and said he was only trying to make friends.

No one believed that.

However, Decker had been coming around for the last four months, and he had shown great interest in Baily. He had occasionally mentioned the marina and sometimes pressed her about whether things were that hard, why hadn't she packed it up and done something else. He'd always raised his hands and told her that he was simply trying to be a good friend and that he had ideas if she ever wanted to hear them.

Fletcher and the team had thought long and hard about letting Baily entertain the conversation, but they didn't want to put her in that position. She'd been bullied before about selling the marina, and she had no desire to do it, no matter how tough things got. Fletcher stood by her decision. He understood the importance of holding onto family legacies. All he wanted was for Baily to climb out from under the mountain of debt her old man had left her, but that was a tall order.

That brought his thoughts right back to Decker. If he wanted the property, what was he waiting for? The only thing he'd shown real interest in was the Crab Shack. It all seemed so strange. None of the pieces fit, nice and neat. They couldn't connect anything—or anyone—to the loans.

Decker seemed benign, which pissed Fletcher off. He wanted to hate the man.

And then there was Ken and his secrets and lies, and Fletcher had no idea how deep they went. Or why Ken had kept them.

"You're deep in thought," Baily said as she moved to the edge of the ottoman. She lifted his feet and placed them on her lap. Her fingers curled around his ankles and rubbed gently. She'd always had magic hands. "What are you thinking about?"

"You." He leaned forward, lifting her chin with his index finger. He stared into her warm gaze, watching her lashes flutter over her damn freaking beautiful blue eyes. He could get lost in those pools. He pressed his mouth to hers, and a faint moan escaped her throat. Wrapping his arms around her body, he deepened the kiss. It felt so good to...

Knock. Knock.

He jerked his head back, breathless.

Baily stared at him with wide eyes, as if she'd just been caught with her hand in the cookie jar.

Dawson stood at the door, his fingers looped into his weapon belt, his stance wide, and a smile the size of Texas. "Real sorry to interrupt that. But I was driving by when Bingo waved me down because he couldn't find Baily." Dawson pointed his finger. "Did you spend the night here?"

"I did not." She folded her arms. "Not that it's any of your business."

Dawson chuckled. "Maybe not, but based on the way you're both dressed and that lip lock, it was a safe guess."

"Cut the crap." Fletcher stood, scratching the center of his bare chest. "Is there a problem?"

"Yeah." Dawson nodded, and his face quickly sobered. "Though, I'm not sure how big."

Baily jumped to her feet and grabbed Fletcher's arm. "What happened? Is Bingo okay? He was scheduled to open the docks and marina this morning. I'm usually down there pretty early." She turned, bent over, and snagged her cell, staring at the screen. "It's just six, so we're literally just opening now," she said. "Crap, my phone must be on silent because Bingo tried to text me twice and he called once."

"He also knocked on the upstairs apartment before he waved me down," Dawson said. "The lock on the pump wasn't secure when he got to the docks this morning, and now there's no gas. Bingo swears he locked it last night. I'd like your permission to look at the security cameras."

"Yeah, of course." She let out a long breath. "I can't function without gas going into the weekend, and I don't know if I can get a rush delivery," she said. "Much less afford it." She rubbed her temples. "Bingo might be a young kid, but he's one of the best, hardworking people I have. I can't imagine he'd just plumb forget."

"Are you still keeping the cameras running all the time?" Dawson asked.

"I check them every few days," she said. "It's not the most high-tech system, but it works, and Fletcher updates the software for me when necessary."

Fletcher pulled open the door. "Let's go take a look and see what it reveals." He had to agree with her assessment of Bingo. He wasn't the kind of kid who made a big mistake like that. However, things happened, mistakes were made, but even if he had forgotten to lock up the pump, it didn't explain how close to five thousand gallons of gas had vanished into thin air.

CHAPTER 2

THE MARINA OFFICE always smelled like salt, sweat, and engine grease. Normally, that scent grounded Baily. This morning, it made her stomach twist.

She leaned over Fletcher's shoulder, watching Dawson poke at the keyboard with the slow, deliberate energy of a man who would rather be wrestling a gator than troubleshooting outdated surveillance software. Dawson was a good man—a sarcastic man—but a decent and kind one. He was always there when you needed him, and sometimes when you didn't.

Baily thought that when Dawson and Audra had married, it might change Dawson. But it hadn't. Not one bit. He was still the easy-going, laid-back, not much rattled him, good-natured, with a wicked sense of humor guy she'd always known him to be. But at the same time, Dawson wasn't the kind of person anyone should mess with, and not just because he was a police officer, sworn to protect the good citizens of Calusa Cove.

Tension filled her muscles as each screen flickered with static or blinked to black. One feed glitched with a frozen frame from yesterday around midnight. Another offered nothing but an ominous blue screen.

"Well, crap," Dawson muttered. "Every file from last night is either corrupted, overwritten, or just... gone." He picked up his cell and glanced at the screen. "Hayes is down at the docks with Chloe. The camera by the fuel pump? Fried. Literally. Looks like someone took a blowtorch to the wiring."

Baily stepped back, heart hammering against her ribs. "You've got to be kidding me." She hugged her middle. The realization that someone had been lurking around her marina in the middle of the night made her shiver.

Fletcher looped an arm around her waist, drawing her close. Normally, this was the moment she'd push him away. When she'd resent him for just being there, as if she shouldn't rely on his strength like he hadn't broken her heart—more than once.

But right now, she needed something...she needed him.

"I'm not," Dawson said dryly, his voice like sandpaper wrapped in velvet. "I save my jokes for when five thousand gallons of gas aren't missing, and no one's sabotaged your security system—because this was done by someone who knew a little bit about how your system works and knew how to make my job nearly impossible."

"You're telling me someone broke in, stole fuel, destroyed my cameras, and left zero evidence behind?" she asked with a shaky voice. "All while I was sleeping."

"That's exactly what I'm telling you," Dawson said, swiveling the chair left and right. "I need to look around more. I need to get Remy out here. This is now a crime scene. Unfortunately, this doesn't feel like a couple of teenagers messing with the cameras. From what I've seen so far, it appears methodical. A little too fast and a little too clean. Not to mention, whoever did this knew that dumping the gas on a weekend when you'd have a lot of traffic could have the potential to bury you." He gave a soft snort. "Hell, if I didn't know better, I'd say they had inside knowledge. But your staff is local, loyal, and I ran the background checks on every single one of them during the last two big cases we had."

"I can't believe this is happening," she muttered. "If they just dumped the gas, wouldn't we see it in the water?"

"No sign of it there," Dawson said. "But you both would've heard a truck pull in here if they'd removed it that way."

"We might not have heard a boat if they came in at idle speed, or with engines cut all together," Fletcher said. "That almost happened once a long time ago."

"I remember that," she said. "It was about two years after you left for the Navy. My dad caught someone messing with the tanks. They'd come in by boat. By the time Tripp got here, they were gone, and the Coast Guard never found them. The marina up by Marco Island reported a break-in that week, but nothing about someone trying to steal gas." Her eyes burned as she did a mental count of the cash on hand and what she had in the bank. She might be able to cover a gas delivery, but it would be the rush fees that killed her. However, what was worse was the ripple effect. She was always stealing from one fund to pay for something else.

Her credit was maxed out. Her savings completely depleted. She'd had to admit she could no longer do this on her own, and that reality hit her like a bullet between the eyes.

Fletcher turned to her, gripping her shoulders, eyes narrowed, voice gentle. "You okay?"

"No," she said, sharper than she meant to. She forced a breath through her nose and softened her tone. "I can't afford this, Fletcher. Not now. Not after everything. I was barely staying ahead, and now this?" She gestured toward the blank screens. "This could sink me. I'm up to my eyeballs in debt. I'm still paying off the new docks and repairs to the launch. I had to take out a loan to do that. I didn't have a choice. The town... the fines... and then there's the..." She let the words trail off and turned away from them both, staring at the faded logbook on her desk like it might magically offer a solution. Shame crept up her spine, mingling with frustration. The marina was all she had. It was her father's legacy, her brother's history, and it was her daily battle. Every dollar she earned went back into keeping it running. Into keeping it hers. She barely had enough to buy groceries when all was said and done. She went without so many things, and she gladly did so, because she'd always believed that, one day, she'd claw her way out of this mess.

But this morning, as the sun appeared bright and sharp over the Glades, she wasn't so sure.

A few years ago, she'd sold the family home and moved into the apartment above the marina, but even that hadn't been able to save her from mounting debt because her father had refinanced that damn house so many times there hadn't been much equity left.

"Hey." Flether's hands ran up and down her arms like a soothing bubble bath. "We'll figure it out. You're not alone in this."

"You say that, but it's not true. This is my marina, and there isn't anything you can do to stop what's happening," she snapped, then instantly regretted it. She rubbed a hand down her face. "I'm sorry. I just—"

"You're scared," Fletcher finished. "I am also considering what just happened, but we're here to help. I'm here, and I've got you. But you need to let me do more than repairs around the marina for free, or pay for a few odds and ends that don't amount to much."

She nodded, throat too tight to speak.

"I'll skip the part where I say it's all going to be okay and go straight to tracking whoever did this," Dawson said. "Because I'm really good at my job, and my wife would kick my ass if I didn't figure it out. Or worse, she'd make me sleep with the alligator that keeps camping out in the yard behind the B&B."

"You really like saying the word *wife*." Baily huffed out a laugh—more a gasp wrapped in disbelief.

Dawson smiled, nodding like a bobblehead. He always enjoyed diffusing situations with humor. It was his superpower. "It rolls off my tongue like candy. Now, all I have to do is get Audra to call me husband. Ever since she found out she's pregnant, she's skipped to calling me Daddy, which wouldn't be bad, it's just the way she says it—like she's made it dirty. It's ruining becoming a father."

Fletcher bent over, grabbed his knees, and laughed. Hard. *"Daddy,"* he repeated. But he elongated the word and added just the right flare, as if he were asking *Daddy* to do something sexual in bed.

"Oh, my God, that's just gross." Baily shook her head.

"I know, right?" Dawson rose from the chair and stretched. "Getting back to the problem at hand. I'll get the official report filed and lean on anyone I can at the lab to prioritize your footage, even if there's nothing but scrambled pixels. Might get lucky with metadata. Remy will collect any evidence he can, and we'll do that as quickly as possible so you can remain operational."

"Thanks," she said, her voice quieter now. "But that doesn't help me with the gas situation."

Dawson ran a hand over his head, shifting his gaze to Fletcher, who nodded.

"What?" she asked.

"We want to help you with that," Fletcher said.

"I don't mind you guys helping out with fixing things around the marina, or even paying for some of the smaller stuff." She glared. "But that's a big expense, and I wouldn't be able to pay it back for a while. You know how I feel about loans and handouts."

"It's not charity. It's not us playing hero." Fletcher let out a long breath. "I'm going to say what I know Dawson is thinking, and that's this looks and feels targeted." Fletcher took a step back and leaned against the counter. "You said the locks were all secure last night?"

"I triple-checked before I left. Bingo was here, too. He always locks up behind me. He's a good kid and has worked for me since he was fourteen."

Dawson's brow furrowed. "Then someone tampered with them after the fact. Or they had a key." He waved his finger toward the door. "Bingo said he used his to get into the marina, and the door was locked. No forced entry. Nothing out of place. The only camera outside that was tampered with was the one down at the docks. The rest, I'm guessing, were tampered with from inside the system. You'd have to do that from behind that desk, or hack in. I'll have the geeks in the crime lab look into that, but I need a list from you of who has keys."

The words hit like a slap. Baily blinked hard, her pulse jumping. "Are you saying this could've been someone I know?"

"I'm saying it could be someone who knows you," Dawson said. "Knows your routine. Knows where your cameras are. And knew exactly what they were after."

"Jesus," she whispered. "The list is short. Me, Bingo, Fletcher, Silas, and Christian. That's it. None of my other employees have one."

"Okay." Dawson nodded. "I trust Bingo. Period. Christian's been working for you for how long now?"

"Going on eight years," she said. "He's loyal. He's good at fixing things. I always worry another marina's gonna snatch him away. He's my only mechanic, and I can't pay him what others might."

"That's not a reason to sabotage you," Dawson said. "But I'll have a chat with him." He rubbed the back of his neck. "Fletcher keeps his key in his kitchen, and the guys and I all have keys to his place. We've only had to get into the marina once or twice, but that's always been with your permission, and Fletcher's security system is…well…better than the one you have."

Shame filled her gut. Not being able to afford

essentials, such as protection for her business, made her feel like an utter failure. But she stiffened her spine, sucked in a deep breath, and took it on the chin, like she always did. What choice did she have? She was drowning, and she knew it. She'd wave the white flag and accept their help. It didn't come with strings. It never did.

Only, she hated the way it made her feel, like her brother and his bitch of a wife had been right all along.

"I'll have to put out a sign that I don't have gas. That's gonna force everyone driving around for that damn boat parade this week to go down to—"

"We'll talk to the fuel supplier and see how fast they can get here," Fletcher said, placing a hand gently on her lower back. "I'll also ask if they can waive the rush charge. If it comes to it, we'll all pitch in to help on the docks until this gets sorted. You have to stop saying no to us." He lowered his chin. "You opened your books to me and the guys for a reason."

She sighed. "That's not going to keep the lights on forever. It's just another Band-Aid like everything else I do."

"You've kept this place running through storms, floods, and two hurricanes," Fletcher said. "You'll get through this, too. You have to trust us and let us help."

Her chest squeezed. "Not if this keeps happening. Not if I can't replace that gas. And if I can, I'll still have to cut corners somewhere else, like payroll. I can't do that. People rely on me. But if I don't have the gas, I won't have the money to pay my employees either. So, I'm screwed anyway I look at it."

"We're not going to let you go under," Fletcher said firmly. "You're not doing this alone, Baily. Not anymore. It's time to let us do the heavy lifting. I know you're proud, and I honor that. I'm the same way. But I know what that marina means to you, and I'm not gonna sit back and watch you lose it."

She swallowed. The emotion sat heavy in her throat, but she refused to let it break her. "I just don't get why anyone would target me," she whispered. "Why now?"

Silence settled over the room like a thick fog.

Dawson broke it with a slow exhale. "You run the last piece of commercial waterfront in this town worth anything, except for the land the old Crab Shack sits on, and that will be up for auction soon. You have a legacy that someone wants, and a developer is sniffing around like a gator in a fish barrel. That's the only thing that makes sense."

"So, are you going to haul Decker Brown down to the station, stick him in an interrogation room, and question him?" Fletcher asked with real venom dripping off every syllable.

Dawson lowered his chin. "No," he said. "I don't have any legal reason to do that. No probable cause. He's made no threat and no offer. He's just kind of here, and all I have is suspicion. But I am going to stop by his cabin that he's renting from me and have a little chat."

"Come on, Dawson," Fletcher said, pushing off the counter. "The man's a slime. We both know he's gonna make a play for the Crab Shack. That he's gonna try to outbid us. The next logical grab is the marina. If he can put Baily more at risk by—"

Dawson held up his hand. "I hear you, but as the police chief in this town, I have to set aside my personal feelings and investigate. Let me do my job… the right way."

Baily inched closer to Dawson and curled her fingers around his thick biceps. "Thank you," she whispered. She understood Fletcher's disdain for Decker. She had her own set of reservations about the man. She certainly didn't understand Decker. He'd come around, hung out at the marina, flirted a little, but never too much, never in such a way that made her feel as though he was all that interested, but just enough to make her wonder.

But he had also asked questions about the marina. Not hard ones. Not ones that were too deep, too personal, nor had he dug into her finances in a way that made her think he had that kind of an agenda. But ever since he'd shown up at the town hall meeting after the Crab Shack had burned down, her perception of Decker had changed.

If he wanted that piece of property, he might want more. Building something next to a rotting old marina wasn't a smart move. She understood why

Fletcher and his band of merry men wanted to do it. They all had savior complexes born out of when her brother had been murdered by the same enemy that had captured and tortured them.

They wanted—in a way—to atone for his death. They thought that, if they could save the marina, it would make the world right again.

But nothing could bring her brother back.

"Anything for you." Dawson nodded, glancing at his cell. "Remy just pulled in. I'm gonna miss that man when he retires, but I'm sure as hell looking forward to having Chloe on my team."

"When does she start at the academy?" Fletcher asked.

"Next month," Dawson said. "Kind of sucks that this state is requiring her to jump through that hoop to be a cop when she's spent years as an FBI agent, but local laws are different from federal ones."

"Is she going to be your second?" Baily asked, needing to talk about anything other than broken security cameras and stolen gas.

"That's a tough one." Dawson swiped at his brow. "I've got three men under me who are all great cops. Love the job, but not a single one of them has asked me about the position. Chloe has. She wants it. And she'd be damn good at it. But she'd be a rookie, regardless of her FBI training." Dawson moved toward the door. "I might not name one right away and see how it all plays out." He waved a hand over his head. "I'll let you know when we're done out there."

"Thanks, man." Fletcher made his way to the coffee station, stuck a pod in the machine, and pressed the button.

The door slammed shut with a resounding thud, and Baily's chest tightened. She scurried around to the other side of the counter and opened the ledger, glancing at the numbers. Her business account was pitiful. The marina operated on a month-to-month basis, especially during the winter. Even South Florida, with temperatures ranging from the fifties to the eighties, slowed down in the winter.

But with a big boat parade and a fishing tournament, well, that meant business. Big business. The kind of business that would keep her operational for a month or two. At least until the warmer temperatures brought more than a trickle of tourists back to the area.

Fletcher set his coffee on the counter, whipped out his cell, and tapped on the screen.

"What are you doing?" she asked.

"Texting with the gas guy."

She let out a long sigh. She didn't have any fight left in her to argue. "Okay."

He glanced up. "No argument?" he asked with a furrowed brow.

She shook her head.

"Good, because I'm paying for it, too."

She planted both her hands on her hips and

glared. She opened her mouth, but the only thing that came out was a mangled gasp.

"Whether you like it or not, I have a stake in what happens to this marina." He paused for a moment, looked at his screen, tapped angrily, then tucked the cell in his back pocket. "I have boats for Everglades Overwatch that need gas. I can't run a business without full tanks. Not to mention that, right now, I'm the only residential house left on this road." He waved a finger. "However, if it's not me writing a check to the gas man, it'll be Hayes because he and Chloe are about to build a house on Keaton's old land. They don't want some land developer in here changing things, knocking this place down and doing God only knows what. We don't want to live next to that. And we want the Crab Shack. We want to build something this town can be proud of, and guess what?" he said. "We're proud of Mitchell's Marina. It matters. It means something to us, too." He ran his fingers through his hair. "The gas truck will be here in an hour. I'll let Dawson know, and hopefully, this place will be clear by then so you can open the docks. Kirk from the gas company already has my credit card. It's handled. I don't want to hear another word about it. If you want to pay me back, fine. We'll talk about it later." He turned and marched toward the door, pausing after he curled his fingers around the handle. "I'll be home all day working around the house and going through Tripp's journal if you need me." With that, Fletcher ducked out of the door and disappeared.

"Ugh." She dropped her head to the counter. He could be so infuriating at times. She resented that, this time, she really did need his money, that she'd said yes, and he was the one storming off all angry. She could no longer afford to let her pride get in the way. If she didn't take Fletcher's help, she'd surely have to either sell or close up shop, and that meant someone would come in and buy the place anyway.

If her dad and brother weren't already dead, she'd strangle them herself.

CHAPTER 3

THE DOCK CREAKED beneath Fletcher's boots as he dropped onto the Adirondack chair, the weight of the afternoon heavier than usual. Sunlight glinted off the water, and gulls squawked overhead, but peace was a lie today. Fletcher lifted the cold brew sweating in his hands and took a long, slow draw. He'd spent the day tinkering around the house, doing his best to keep his hands busy while his mind worked through all the notes in Tripp's journal.

He'd memorized the entries word for word. The ones from when they'd been kids, from when Ken had been dealing drugs for Massey. Fletcher had reconciled that in his mind. It was the other ones that tickled his brain and made him pause.

Journal Entry One:

Ken's back in town. Something's different about him. He's polished in the way he talks. Educated. Almost like he's above everyone in Calusa Cove, and he's only been gone two years. But he's also jittery, especially around me. He's always been a bit frightened of me, but that's a normal teenage thing. Now, he's a man. Something feels off. It's like he's waiting for something to go wrong.

Journal Entry Two:

Had a beer with Ken. He's still twitchy. Doesn't want to look me in the eye. I asked if he'd heard from or seen Audra. He got defensive. Thought it in poor taste since he'd just gotten married, and then quickly added he'd seen her once about a year after he'd joined the military. Then I switched to asking about his new bride and her family. He smiled. Mentioned they had some manufacturing business, but brushed it off as if I wouldn't understand. However, it felt more like he didn't want to talk about it.

Journal Entry Three:

Ken and Julie stopped by the marina while I was there. He kept asking Baily about dock permits, contracts with fishing charters, and stupid stuff he already knows. Julie barely spoke, but when she did, it was a whisper in Ken's ear. Strange, if you ask me. Later, I asked Ken about the conversation, and he just said, "Just trying to get a full picture." A picture of what? He should already know.

Journal Entry Four:

Spotted Ken in the back corner of Massey's Pub with a guy I didn't recognize—business casual type, not local. They weren't drinking, just talking close, heads down. When I walked by, Ken shot me a look that said, Don't bother me, I'm busy. *I tried to say hello, but he shot his hand up dismissively. I would've expected that from his ex, Audra. But not him.*

Journal Entry Five:

Ken and his entire team are here for a visit. But Ken, he's hiding something. I don't know what, but it's eating at him. I asked him straight up if something was wrong. If it had to do with Baily and her problems. He actually told me to mind my own business.

Journal Entry Six:

Ken snapped at Baily today over nothing. She brushed it off, but I saw the look on his face. Not anger. Panic. Like he thought she'd figured something out. But what?

Journal Entry Seven:

Ken and his wife Julie are in town. I've come to distrust them. Something's not right. Julie has an unusual, polished smile. I heard her asking Baily about a slip "for a friend." But she seems to hate this town, and I have no idea why she'd recommend a friend keep their boat here. She's asked numerous times why Baily doesn't just sell the damn place. But what was weirder was Ken. He came slinking out of Fletcher's place, and I know damn well Fletcher wasn't home. Nor were his parents. I mentioned it to Fletcher, and he shrugged, saying he was probably looking for me or dropping something off. But when Ken saw me, he had that, Oh, shit, *I just got caught look.*

The problem was that Fletcher didn't have dates for when the entries were made. And then there were the scribbles about Ken, finances, and money. They weren't really entries. Just question marks regarding her father and his decisions.

"You look like you've had a day." Hayes leaned on the railing, nursing his own beer, while Keaton brought over a small cooler and dropped into the chair beside him.

"I have," Fletcher admitted. But it was more than a bad day. Ever since Baily had been honest with him about how tough things had gotten with the Marina, his life had been riddled with more worry than he knew what to do with. He could handle bullets flying. He'd been trained for that. Missions, even ones that went sideways, had been a way of life.

But dealing with a failing business and wondering if he could put food on the table? That had never been something he'd had to think twice about. Baily was one bad season away from folding, and that was something Fletcher couldn't let happen. Not if he had the power—and the means—to stop it.

"Wanna talk about it?" Hayes asked.

A lazy gator floated by near the reeds, its knobby head barely above water, indifferent to the humans watching from the dock. The marsh grasses swayed in the light breeze, and dragonflies skimmed the surface of the inlet. The distant whine of a trolling motor echoed across the water.

Down by the fuel dock, Baily moved with precise, practiced ease, tying off a center-console boat. Her braid was tucked under a faded baseball cap, her posture tense even from a distance. She barked a laugh at something Bingo said, but Fletcher could see the tight set to her shoulders, the way she double-checked the lines like she didn't trust the knots—or herself.

Fletcher watched her a moment longer than necessary. He hated that her life had become so... hard. All he'd ever wanted was to take care of her. To be the man in her life.

Boy, had he screwed that up. He'd known joining the Navy would be hard on their relationship. But when he'd made the decision, he'd never believed it would be a forever one. It had been about an education. About possibility. About getting out of this town for a beat. About doing something other than what he'd been born into...which hadn't been much...and should've been enough.

The Navy had turned into so much more, and he'd been the fool who'd believed love would be enough. That maybe she'd follow him to whatever base he'd been stationed at, and that, for a few years, they could enjoy that life, returning to this patch of land...someday.

But then her father had died, and Baily did what she'd always done and dug her heels firmly into the Everglades and her family's legacy.

He couldn't blame her for that.

But damn, his fucking heart took a big hit.

"I can't tell if Baily's pissed at me for paying for the gas or not. Last we talked, I explained how I gassed up all our boats, putting that money right back in her pocket, but she grunted something, rolled her eyes, and walked away."

"Her pride gets the better of her," Keaton said. "I understand that notion, but also, I don't think you needed to explain anything. She's not stupid, and I'm sure she understood that concept."

"I suppose. She does have a lot on her shoulders," Fletcher murmured, more to himself than the others as he watched her shuffle her feet across the lower dock and up toward the marina.

Keaton followed his gaze. "She always has. But something about this feels different. Everything before has been about bad decisions her dad made, but this is cold and calculated. A direct hit meant to sink a battleship."

Fletcher nodded slowly, pulling his gaze back to his friends. "It is. That LLC behind her marina loan? It doesn't trace clean. Chloe's been digging—quietly. Off the books. She's working some of her old Bureau contacts to see if anything pings."

Hayes turned slightly. "I still struggle with Baily's dad signing a loan that ties the deed of the marina to it like that. There's almost no way to come out from under it."

"Yeah. At first glance, it looks normal, but Chloe said it's wrapped in layers. Two shell corps deep, and the registered agents are out of state and don't match up. The deeper she goes, the more it smells like someone doesn't want to be found."

Keaton's brow furrowed. "Any ties to Decker?"

Fletcher shook his head. "Nothing concrete. But the timing is too clean. His development company was circling the drain until Tessa Gilbert backed him, but that alone tells me nothing."

"Except before Tessa did that, he was accused of stealing plans from the firm he used to work for," Keaton said.

"According to everything we found out, he denied that. And he's been damn squeaky clean ever since." Fletcher took another sip of his beer.

"Chloe has quietly talked to people who have worked with him, and they have nothing but good things to say," Hayes added.

"You think Tessa's involved in any of this?" Keaton asked.

"Only thing we can confirm is that Tessa was the one who funded Decker's rebound. Outside of that, she's just some rich socialite who he screwed around with for a few years, but now that seems to be over," Fletcher said.

Keaton leaned back in his chair, tapping his beer against the arm. "So, what now?"

"Right now? We lay low," Fletcher said. "We keep our eyes open. Chloe's helping, but obviously that's not official now. She's walking a tightrope, especially with the police academy starting next month."

"And Baily? What does she know?" Hayes asked.

Fletcher glanced over his shoulder at Baily, now standing at the front door of the marina, looking like she didn't know what to do next. He exhaled slowly. "Everything I know. I'm done keeping her in the dark. Not after what happened with Ken. Not after what that cost her. I told her about the LLC and how

Chloe was helping. Everything. I'm not making that mistake again."

Hayes nodded in approval. "Good. She deserves the truth."

"She's been fighting for that marina tooth and nail—alone—for too long. It's not happening anymore." Fletcher's voice dropped. "Not while I'm still breathing, and if it costs me losing her for good, well, then so be it. At least she'll have that marina. That's what matters to her most. If I can give that to her, then I'll be happy."

"You won't be truly happy until that woman is in your arms again." Keaton smiled faintly. "You really think she's going to let you help this time? And I'm not talking about putting a few nails into wood planks."

Fletcher gave a wry snort. "She'll fight me. She always does. But what happened today…it changed everything. It's not her buried in debt because her dad screwed up. Someone's coming for her, and I'll be damned if I'm going to sit on this dock and watch anyone destroy her."

"Why don't you tell us how you really feel?" Hayes chuckled and pushed off the railing. "Like how much you love that girl."

"I've never denied that truth," Fletcher said.

"Well, if someone's planning something, they're gonna need paper to move dirt," Hayes said. "Dawson will hear about that, and you'll be the first to know."

"Appreciate it," Fletcher said.

A heron lifted from the shallows and soared overhead, wings slicing the sky. The gator drifted closer before silently disappearing beneath the surface. In the distance, a thunderhead loomed above the mangroves, a reminder that calm in Calusa Cove never lasted long.

"We're going to figure this out," Keaton said.

Fletcher looked back toward the marina, where Baily was laughing again with Bingo, a little more relaxed now, like she didn't realize people were watching out for her. His chest tightened, but not with fear. "We have to," he said. "For her."

His heart would deal with the consequences of it later.

* * *

THE SCENT of lemon and garlic wafted through Fletcher's kitchen as Baily chopped fresh herbs, the rhythmic sound of her knife grounding her. Chloe sat on a stool at the island, sipping a glass of wine while flipping through a dog-eared cookbook. Audra had taken over the sink, rinsing vegetables, and Trinity stood by the stove, one hand resting lightly on her just-visible baby bump as she stirred something in a cast iron skillet.

"I swear," Audra muttered, holding a hand to her mouth. "If I so much as smell bacon one more time, I'm going to hurl."

"Hey, bacon is sacred," Trinity said, grinning.

"Don't go insulting the only reason my husband pretends to cook."

Chloe laughed, reaching over to steal a cucumber slice from the cutting board. "Didn't he make eggs last weekend and nearly set your entire house on fire?"

"Not exactly what happened." Trinity waved a wooden spoon in the air. "And the eggs, they weren't…horrible."

"At least Keaton tries," Baily said, shaking her head.

"Yeah, but he can't roast a marshmallow without setting it on fire." Trinity laughed. "Hayes keeps trying to show him how, and Keaton keeps shoving the damn stick all the way in the flame, as if he doesn't understand the definition of insanity." Trinity leaned her hip against the counter, her expression softening. "Baily? I hate bringing this up on our fun night, but are you doing okay? With the marina and stuff?"

Baily shrugged. "Define 'okay.' There's a giant question mark hanging over my livelihood. I'm sitting around waiting for some loan shark to call in my debt and steal my marina, just because they can, and someone fried my security cameras. But sure, let's call it okay."

Audra handed her a towel. "You're not alone, Baily. You've got all of us, and Dawson is so dialed in. He's been a man on a mission all day. He came home from work, barely shed his uniform, sat in front of the computer, and was researching and looking for clues. Gotta love that man of mine."

Chloe nodded. "Hayes has been making timelines. He's trying to pinpoint all Ken's trips to Calusa Cove and how it might be connected to your dad's poor decision-making. He's been going through all his finances, looking over the notes he kept from Ken, which is a total shocker that he had any of that, because Hayes keeps nothing. Can't even call him a minimalist. He's simply a guy who holds no sentimental value in anything."

"But people," Trinity said. "People matter to him, and that's what counts."

Baily smiled. These women had become her family. Her lighthouse in a world filled with thunderstorms, chaos, and grief. "Fletcher printed me off a copy of the parts of Tripp's journal with all the scribbles about Ken. I remember some of the things in there. Like arguing with Ken over marina things, over things he already knew about, and those things were all the reasons why he started pushing me to sell. And then there was the one about Julie and the boat slip. I remember that one like it was yesterday. She asked me all sorts of questions about seasonal and annual rentals. How I manage the boats for owners who don't live here, which was weird because I don't have a single person who isn't a local, except those who used to live here and come back often for family. It was the oddest conversation ever because it was the first time Julie ever seemed engaged or excited about anything in this town. But the second it was over, she was back to being bitchy."

"Did you ever get along with her?" Audra asked. She leaned against the counter, snagged her fruity non-alcoholic drink, and slurped. "And before anyone goes and makes a judgment that I might be a little jealous of my late ex's wife, I'm not. I've got my man, and he's the best. The only thing that bugs me about Julie is the way Ken treated me when he found me, and only because I think he already knew her. Looking at it now, he hadn't tracked me down to win me back. He'd done it to make sure I wouldn't return. There's a small part of me that believes he knew what Paul Massey did to my dad."

"Jesus," Baily muttered. "I've never heard you say that before. Have you mentioned it to Dawson?"

"I have." Audra nodded. "He grapples with the notion. Says Ken was as solid as they came regarding being a SEAL. That he never thought twice about him on a mission." She raised her hand. "But the last few years he'd been alive, Ken changed in the friendship department. He became distant, secretive even. They all blamed it on Julie, who treated them like they were a problem in hers and Ken's marriage."

"That's because she looked at them like they were the enemy." Baily sighed. "She was all sunshine and unicorns when we first met. Kept telling me we'd be like sisters. That lasted for a few months. Once they got engaged, it was as if a switch flipped, and she became someone else. Someone who saw me as a fly that needed swatting. About the only time she was nice was when her boys were around, or she was trying to offer me a job with her family's business, so I'd sell the marina. Occasionally, Ken would stick up for me, but that didn't happen often, and when it did, Julie really laid into him."

"I don't understand the part about why she'd care if you kept or sold the marina," Chloe said. "What difference did it make in her life? Your dad left it to you. He left both debt and any potential income to you. Not Ken. The only thing he got was profit if you sold, and I'm sorry, but even back then, you were upside down and wouldn't have had anything left at the end of a sale. She had to have known that."

"Unless Ken lied to her." Audra arched a brow.

"Even just a year ago, that statement would've had me either kicking you out or me storming off," Baily said. "But I'm seeing so many cracks in my brother's personality these days, I don't know what to believe. It was like he was Dr. Jekyll and Mr. Hyde."

"Well, as your brother's ex-girlfriend, I'm telling you, as lovingly as this crazy redhead can, that man wasn't always truthful, not even when we were teenagers." Audra eased into one of the chairs at the island. "I understand that he lied to me because he was dealing drugs for Massey and was looking for a way out without fucking up his life. But there were other little lies. Subtle ones. The biggest thing I can't reconcile in my mind is how hard he fought to have me believe that those dreams about my dad I used to have, right after he went missing, were just crazy nightmares about a traumatic event, and that I was starting to act just like my father…a nutty conspiracy theorist with an ax to grind."

"Are you thinking he never stopped dealing for Massey?" Chloe asked.

"I don't know. He quit working for Massey's Law firm, so there's that. He also avoided him, but he didn't avoid his son, Benson. Always a bone of contention with me. I hated that guy. Ken and Benson weren't great friends, but they were friendly. It just makes me wonder what Ken really knew because the one thing about Ken was that he always knew the right buttons to push with me to set me off. That last couple of months of our relationship, he constantly hid them, causing so many arguments. When he found me a year later, under the pretense that he loved me and wanted me back, he didn't say those words kindly. It was more like, *you love me. Now do what I tell you or be stuck in the miserable cycle you built for yourself and end up like your dad.*"

"That's not nice," Trinity said. "Kind of sounds like my mother."

Audra nodded. "Anyway, reading Tripp's journal only drives those points deep for me."

"I didn't know Ken, but I have to say, what I'm learning does have my hackles up," Chloe said, growing serious. "But Tripp, he talked in circles, and his journal doesn't make much sense."

"It's really affecting Fletcher. He's not sleeping,"

Baily admitted. "The nightmares are back. He told me that since the journal surfaced, they're coming every night."

"Keaton's had a few, too." Trinity stirred the pot one last time and turned off the stove.

"Same with Hayes. He wakes up in a cold sweat, shaking," Chloe said.

"Dawson flies out of bed sometimes at two in the morning with what sounds like a strangled scream. He can barely breathe," Audra said. "He calms down pretty quickly, but the first time it happened, it scared the crap out of me. At least they're all talking about it."

"It just sucks, because they're not only reliving what happened to my brother," Baily said. "They are reliving their own torture, and I hate that for each of them. And now, I feel like a bitch for being so stubborn about all their generosity. It's just I had no idea about the fine print on that loan until Fletcher pointed it out. It stunned me, and my pride has gotten in the way because all I've ever wanted was to be able to prove I can do this on my own." She wiped away the few tears that fell.

Audra slipped off the stool and wrapped her arms around Baily. "You are doing it," Audra said. "But there's no shame in accepting help from those who love you. Especially in what matters—and especially after what happened this morning."

"I know," Baily whispered. "I'm not fighting

Fletcher...too hard. I need help, but I can't bury him in debt either."

The kitchen fell quiet for a beat, then Chloe stood. "Let's go. The guys are outside, probably ruining a perfectly good fire without us and terrorizing my sister in the process."

They stepped out onto the back deck, carrying all the food they'd prepared, the scent of burning cedar curling in the air. Fletcher and Keaton stood near the fire pit, beers in hand. Hayes poked at the flames with a long stick, like he was testing fate.

Fedora, Chloe's half-sister, waved as she walked toward the group, cheeks flushed from laughter. Baily caught Chloe watching her, a soft smile tugging at her mouth.

"How are things going with you and Fedora?" Baily asked softly.

"Not as awkward as I thought they'd be. We've settled into a nice relationship. More friends than sisters, but we have a closeness that can't be explained. I like it." Chloe smiled. It was the kind of smile that softened the heart. "Fedora's wedding is coming up fast. Hayes is walking her down the aisle and panicking like she asked him to deliver a eulogy."

"Well," Audra said, flopping into a chair beside the fire. "He did use to date her mom."

"Oh, that part is not being discussed," Chloe said with mock horror. "I like Betsy, and I'm not jealous. At least not of her. Or of their past. But they do have a bond, and I have boundaries."

Everyone laughed.

Fletcher glanced over his shoulder and stepped away from the fire pit, inching closer. "How are you holding up?"

"I'm doing okay," Baily said. "The morning was a little slow, but Silas, bless his soul, once he heard I had gas, he told everyone. A few boats even turned around, coming to me instead of going to the competition." She laughed. "I think he told them I was cheaper."

"Silas has always gotten a bad rap in this town, but he's a good man." Fletcher nodded.

"So are you," she said barely above the crackle of the fire. "I'm sorry I gave you such a hard time earlier. It's hard for me to accept help. My dad raised me to be independent. Lately…no, ever since he died…I feel like a failure."

"Baily, you're the complete opposite." He wrapped his strong arms around her waist and tugged her gently to his chest.

She didn't pull away. She'd grown tired of fighting of him. Of fighting this thing between them. Of fighting what had always been between them. She'd loved him since she was a teenager. That love had never died. Not even when she'd blamed him for… everything that had gone wrong in her life.

"Thank you for calling Kirk and arranging for a rush delivery—and for paying it." She pressed her hand on the center of his chest. "I will pay you back when I get out from under this mess."

"The only payback I need is for that marina to stay yours." He pressed his lips against her mouth in a soft, gentle kiss that lasted only a second. "But I won't insult or offend you by telling you that you can't. Just know I don't expect it anytime soon. Other bills are more important. Other things need to be handled first." He arched a brow. "And please don't tell me and the boys we can't offer assistance anymore. Things changed the second someone stole five thousand gallons of gas."

"I can live with that as long as it's not more than what I need to stay afloat."

"Deal." He smiled.

"Can I ask you something?"

"Of course," he said.

"Do you think maybe it might be a good idea to try Julie again? Possibly ask her questions about Tripp's entries, without her knowing anything about the journal?" she asked.

"Dawson and I've chatted about that." Fletcher shifted, taking her hand, tugging her toward the fire. "But first, we'd have to get her to answer the phone, and she hasn't, not for any of us. And second, we'd need to find a way to formulate those questions in a manner that would elicit meaningful responses. The problem with that is we don't know what we're looking for outside of what Ken knew about the loan, if anything. Why the bad investment advice? And why was it so important for you to sell, because Ken just wanting you not to have to deal with it because he all of a sudden decided it was no place for a woman, well, that doesn't track."

"Not to mention, would she even be honest about any of it?" she said.

"And there's that, too."

The distant hum of an outboard motor cut through the chatter. All heads turned toward the water as Silas guided his skiff toward the dock, his expression tight. He waved his hand wildly over his head. "Hey," he called.

"Wonder what he wants," Fletcher murmured, already moving toward the edge of the dock. "He's been edgy, moody, or really quiet lately."

Silas climbed out, his gaze scanning the group. "Sorry to crash your night. Just needed to talk."

"You okay?" Baily asked. She'd known Silas her entire life. He'd been like this grumpy old favorite uncle. Quirky, a little left of normal, but he came in with smiles, hugs, and the best campfire stories.

Silas nodded slowly. "Yeah. Thanks for asking. Just—Dewey being the Ring Finger Killer…it's still so hard to believe. He came to my wife's birthday party last year. It's just… I don't know. I can't… I should've known."

"We all feel that way, Silas," Dawson said as he leaned against the post. "He was the last person on an interesting list of possible suspects. Kind of made me look like an idiot."

"You are no fool," Silas said. "Outside of Tripp, you're the best cop this town has ever seen."

"Means a lot coming from you." Dawson gave Silas a nod.

No one said anything for a moment. The crackle of the fire filled the silence. Calusa Cove had a way of taking quiet, contemplative moments like these and stretching them out for as long as possible, prompting people to ponder what was truly important in life.

Silas ran a hand through his hair. "That's not why I came, though. I was down by the Crab Shack. Saw Decker Brown walking around like he owned the place. Measuring distances, taking notes. Looked like he was surveying it."

Fletcher's jaw tightened. "Damn it. I knew that man was up to no good."

"I don't trust him as far as I can spit," Silas said. "I know you boys are planning on putting in a bid when it goes up for auction. I think that would be good for the town. You're all good for this place. You…just fit."

"Was he alone?" Fletcher asked.

"He was," Silas said.

Baily's stomach churned. Decker had been hanging around for months. At first, she hadn't had the same disdain for the man as everyone else, though his profession did give her pause. Developers were not welcome in Calusa Cove. Their town might be a little dated. A little run down. A little backward and old-fashioned. However, the people were solid. They enjoyed their life. While they knew change was necessary, a facelift here and there, they didn't want to redesign the fabric of their world.

"Perhaps we should take a walk and see what he's up to," Dawson said. "We can even bring him a beer." He chuckled.

Baily didn't see the humor in it, but Dawson sometimes liked poking the bear. She supposed it came with the job.

"Didn't you speak with him earlier about what happened at the marina this morning?" Baily asked.

"I did." Dawson shifted his gaze, catching Baily's and holding it. "He appeared shocked. Rattled even. Said he was in the cabin all night. I checked my security cameras, and his fancy Range Rover never left the parking lot."

"Doesn't mean he didn't have a hand in it," Fletcher said with a clenched jaw.

"You believe he stole Baily's gas?" Silas asked with his arms at his side, fists clenched. "Why, I have half a mind to go back down there and shoot—"

"Silas," Dawson said with a low growl. "Don't be saying things like that in front of me. That's a threat. And as an officer of the law, you know I have to take that seriously if you finish that statement."

"But we're talking about Baily. She's like a daughter to me. And someone threatened her." Silas ran a hand across his scruffy face.

"I know. And I'm dealing with it. Now, let me handle Decker." Dawson waved his finger. "Go home to your wife. Have a nice glass of whiskey. Watch a show. I promise I'll fill you in on what happened."

"Thanks." Silas climbed back in his boat. "I'd sure hate it if you boys didn't win that bid." He fired up his engine and idled down the canal.

Keaton sighed. "Well, there goes our quiet night."

Chloe crossed her arms, her eyes lit up with something that Baily couldn't quite understand. "Might not be quiet, but it could be fun."

Baily wasn't sure how eight people confronting Decker regarding the Crab Shack could be seen as enjoyable, but she'd follow their lead…quietly and in the background.

CHAPTER 4

THE PATH to the old Crab Shack was overgrown with palmetto and sea grape, a reminder of how quickly the Everglades reclaimed what man tried to tame. Fletcher walked ahead, boots crunched against the sand and crushed shells, and the warm, humid air clung to him like a second skin. Behind him, Keaton, Dawson, and Hayes moved in a loose formation, quiet but alert, each carrying the weight of what they were walking into.

It wasn't a battlefield. They weren't going to war. There were no bullets to dodge. No clear enemy to fight. But they certainly felt as though they were under attack.

Fletcher slowed his pace as the old structure came into view.

The Crab Shack had been a fixture of Calusa Cove for as long as Fletcher could remember, first as a bait shop, then a dive bar, and most recently, a half-hearted attempt at a seafood joint before it burned. Fletcher could still smell the charred wood if he let himself. Could still see the outline of the taped-off area where a body had been found.

Dewey Hale. Their friend. Their neighbor. The man they'd shared beers with, trusted with secrets, and who had turned out to be a monster.

Now, the skeletal remains of the Crab Shack sat at the edge of the inlet, fire-blackened timbers leaning like brittle bones, sun-bleached boards curling at the edges. A wind chime made of bottle caps jingled mournfully from a warped beam. Fletcher stepped over a sagging porch plank and scanned the property.

Decker Brown stood near the far edge, notebook in hand and a pencil tucked behind his ear. He was dressed in designer slacks and a long-sleeved button-up that looked too crisp for the Everglades, like he'd stepped off a yacht and not into a swamp.

"Afternoon," Fletcher called, voice even, even though anger coursed through his veins. Decker was up to something, and it smelled like danger.

Decker turned, surprise registering in his eyes, like he'd been caught doing something he shouldn't. He smiled that smooth, salesman's smile, the kind that looked like it belonged on a billboard. "Gentlemen. Didn't expect a welcome committee. How are you this fine evening?"

"That depends," Keaton said, stopping a few feet back. "What are you doing with that notebook, because from where we're standing, it looks like you're surveying the property like you've got plans for it or something?"

Decker tapped the notebook closed. "You boys know how this goes. A property like this, even burned out, has potential. View of the water. Close to the main road. I'd be a fool of a developer if I didn't assess its value and consider my options."

"I don't know. It's also got the stench and lingering memory of a murder," Hayes said bluntly. "That doesn't factor into your resale value?"

Decker shifted his weight, eyes narrowing. "Right, because you boys aren't considering that, too."

"What would you do with this place?" Dawson asked.

"I don't know quite yet. That's why I'm out here. But whatever it would be, it would be something shiny. Something new. Something this town can be proud of, because regardless of what any of you fellas think of me, my goal is never to destroy the heart of a town. Only make it beat a little faster."

Fletcher doubted that. "So, you're planning on putting in a bid."

"I'd be an idiot not to consider it." Decker's tone remained neutral, but there was a tightness at the corners of his mouth. Something defiant. Defensive even. "I keep my eyes open for opportunities. And this one just kind of fell in my lap, you know?"

"Any other properties catch your eye?" Dawson asked, watching him like a hawk.

"Not particularly," Decker said.

"What about the marina? Or the empty lot down the street? Or even Dewey's old place. His estate, once that's all figured out, is gonna have to unload it," Keaton said.

Decker tucked his notebook under his arm. His jaw flexed. "Marina's not on the market, and Baily's not interested in selling. Ever. That's what she says. The empty lot? I hear Keaton's selling it to Hayes. As far as Dewey's place is concerned, well, I've walked the property, but there isn't anything I can do with it. That land is zoned residential, and that's not something I do anymore—at least not on a regular basis. Besides, I don't go after anything that's not on the market. That's not how I operate. You can ask anyone I've ever done business with. I'm not a predator."

"Funny," Hayes muttered. "That word came up earlier."

Decker cocked his head, as if he'd been slapped. "Look, I didn't come to Calusa Cove looking to scoop up half the town, or any of it for that matter. I came here because I needed space. Quiet. A little distance from the job site, that's not far from here. I do that a lot. Another thing you can ask people about."

Fletcher studied him for a long moment. He found it interesting how Decker had to justify and qualify his decisions. That smelled like guilt...but of what?

Even so, the guy said all the right things. But Fletcher had learned a long time ago that the devil didn't come dressed in horns and fire. He wore a smile. Carried a clipboard. Promised renovations. Florida contractors sucked in general.

Decker spread his hands. "You think I'm trying to screw someone over? Say it now. Otherwise, I'd like to go back to my walk without feeling like I'm being interrogated for the second time in one day."

Dawson gave a half-shrug. "Just a chat. No need to get riled up."

Decker chuckled without humor. "In my line of work, being defensive is the difference between making money and getting sued. But I get it. Tight-knit town. Outsiders stir suspicion."

"Especially ones who keep showing up around properties that've been through hell," Fletcher said. He let the words hang between them, then stepped back. "Enjoy your walk."

Decker nodded slowly. "You guys take care."

They walked away in silence, boots kicking up grit and the occasional bottle cap embedded in the sand. When they reached the shade of the palms, Keaton spoke first, "I don't trust him."

"Me neither," Dawson said. "But he didn't say anything incriminating. Nothing I could use to even legally dig. He's just an asshole we might have to bid against."

"He's smart," Hayes said. "And he knows this game better than we do."

Keaton kicked a chunk of charred wood. "We need to get ahead of him. If he puts in a bid, we need to make sure ours is better. Outside of people liking us and rooting for us, the town will need to do what's best, and I'm sure he's got more money."

"He may have money, but we have something he doesn't," Fletcher said.

Hayes glanced over. "What's that?"

"This place is in our blood." Fletcher tapped his chest. "I might be the only one of us who was born and raised here, but you three have become part of this town. Money might talk, but it's not what this place was built on."

* * *

FLETCHER'S HOUSE had emptied slowly, laughter trailing off into the night as the others headed home. Now, the soft hum of cicadas filled the stillness, mingling with the occasional splash of water against the dock pilings. The scent of smoked wood lingered in the air, curling through the open windows and mixing with the citrus tang of the candle burning on the kitchen counter.

Baily stood barefoot near the sink, hands braced on the edge of the countertop. She wore one of Fletcher's sweatshirts, sleeves pushed up, the hem brushing the tops of her thighs. His clothes always smelled like pine and the Everglades. But more so, they felt like home and reminded her of simpler times.

She tapped her fingers, waiting for her cell to power back up. She desperately needed a new phone.

Another thing that would have to wait since she didn't have the money to drop on one, and the damn things were so expensive.

Finally, her phone buzzed where it rested on the charger, screen lighting up with a new notification. She grabbed it, unplugged the cord, and stared at the voicemail icon.

Her brow furrowed. Her heart hammered in her chest. She gasped.

"What's wrong?" Fletcher asked as he walked into the kitchen, barefoot, wearing jeans and his favorite rock band T-shirt.

She didn't look at him at first. Just stood there staring at her phone like it might jump off the counter and eat her for lunch. "There's a message on here from Julie. I haven't heard from her since Ken died. Since she told me I couldn't see the boys, since everything from Calusa Cove was just…too raw. Of course, she then said if I ever left, we could…talk."

He shouldered in behind her, reaching for the phone and glancing at the screen. "I wonder what she wants."

Baily sucked in a deep breath. "I've wanted to talk to her—left messages for her—but she's the last person I ever expected to hear from."

Fletcher crossed to her slowly. "I hope the boys are okay."

"Oh, God. Don't put those thoughts in my head." She grabbed the phone from his fingers and tapped the screen, but didn't hit play. "It looks like it came in around midnight. So, just twenty minutes ago. My phone only holds a charge for about three hours these days."

He pressed his lips against her temple. "Don't bite my head off, but my cell phone carrier has this deal where I can add a second line for next to nothing. We can get you a new one tomorrow if you'd like."

She turned her head and glared. "It's not just the monthly bill, Fletcher. It's the freaking cost of the cell. Do you know how much an iPhone costs these days?"

"I just got a new one," he said. "And I didn't trade in my last one, which, honestly, was perfectly fine. You can have that one."

"Why didn't you trade it in?" she asked, not wanting to deal with the message from Julie yet.

"Honestly?" Fletcher asked. "I figured I should keep it as a backup in case I dropped mine in the water."

"You treat your electronics like they're a fine piece of art." She laughed. "I seriously doubt you'd do that." She leaned back into his strong frame, enjoying the moment, knowing she probably shouldn't, but couldn't stop herself if she tried. He felt too safe. Too much like the old days. Too much like she'd found a small piece of herself she'd forgotten. "I'll take your old phone," she whispered. "And I'll let you put me on your plan."

He jerked his head back. "Just like that? No argument? And I don't have to beg or grovel?"

"As much as I like sparring with you sometimes, no. Every penny right now I need for the marina. A cell phone plan isn't going to put much of a dent in my finances, but it will help." She reached back and patted his face. "However, you will let me do a few favors in return."

"I kind of like the sound of that." He inched to her side, leaning against the counter, and winked.

"Get your head out of the gutter, Fletcher," she said. "You're gonna let me help you clean this place out finally." She lowered her chin. "It's time."

He sighed. "Why? I like my house. I like all the things in it."

"Oh, my God. The wallpaper in this kitchen dates back to the 1970s. The one in your bedroom is worse. And don't get me going on the furniture. I know it sometimes reminds you of your parents and grandma, and it's your way of holding on to them, but there are other ways of doing that. So, if I'm gonna let you help me with some of the stuff around the marina, you're gonna let me help you purge some ghosts. No argument. No sparring. Just a 'yes, ma'am.'"

He nodded. "Yes…ma'am."

She smiled.

"Now, how about we listen to that message from Julie?"

"Ugh." Baily glanced at the cell. Her heart filled with a mix of dread and uncertainty. "Fine." She pressed the button and held the phone between them.

Julie's voice filled the room, chipper and clipped all at the same time.

"Hi, Baily, it's Julie. We were watching the news and couldn't believe what we saw about Calusa Cove. That's crazy. Anyway, my father learned that the Crab Shack is up for auction, and I told him that it was right near the marina. It got me thinking about how much Ken wanted you to sell the marina. I can't imagine that things are much better, and I suspect they'll be worse now that the news broke that a serial killer was living right there...for years. Ken always said Dewey had a screw loose. Anyway, I wanted to remind you that we've got plenty of career opportunities for you here, and it would give you a chance to reconnect with your nephews. Just a thought. Call me anytime between nine in the morning and seven at night."

The message ended, but the silence that followed roared louder than any thunder she'd ever experienced.

Fletcher let out a low breath. "Jesus. I'm not even sure how to unpack that."

Baily tossed the phone on the counter, where it skidded and stopped near his keys. "The timing of that call makes me suspicious, and I don't even know why, except I never liked her or her family. They're all a bunch of rich snobs who look down on me and my life here in Calusa Cove. Like I'm some redneck or something."

"Nothing wrong with having a little red on the collar."

"She's never wanted me in those boys' lives," Baily said bitterly. "Now she's offering me a career opportunity? In exchange for seeing my brother's kids? That's cold. It also doesn't make much sense. What difference does it make to her where I live or what I do with my damn life?"

"She always had opinions about me and the guys," Fletcher said. "In the beginning, she voiced them, though not too loudly. After she and Ken married, she just stopped being around us. When she was, she let us know that Ken would be leaving the Navy. But I don't like how she's dangling your nephews like bait." Fletcher squeezed her shoulder. "She's trying to manipulate you, and I don't understand why."

"She was different in the beginning," Baily said, voice quieter. "Or maybe I just thought she was."

"I know we've been through this a million times, but is there any part of you that remembers anything about a conversation with Ken or your dad about that damn loan?"

Baily stared at the tiled floor, then nodded slowly. "Maybe. I don't know. My dad and Ken argued a lot right before my dad died. However, Ken seemed tired the last few times I spoke with him. Worn out from deployments. From pressure. From being caught in the middle of things, and he was always so quick to fight with me."

"Are you okay if I forward this message to myself

and share it with the guys? And Chloe? Something about it feels like a warning, and it doesn't sit right with me, especially since the marina was broken into and your gas was stolen."

She stared at him, tears in her eyes. From anger. From frustration. And fear. "I'm so tired, Fletch. Of fighting for that marina. Of wondering what my brother got himself involved in. Of trying to hold everything together while the ground keeps shifting beneath me."

He reached out and tucked a strand of hair behind her ear. "You're not alone. I'm right here."

Her lips parted. "You say that, but you've left before, and I'm sorry, I can't forget that."

"I know." He closed the distance between them. "And I wish things had turned out differently with us. It's hard, because the Navy…being a SEAL…it wasn't a bad thing for me. I can't regret that part of my life but hate what it did to us."

She looked at him then—and as if she really saw *him*. The man who had once been hers. The one who knew her better than anyone. The one who still made her heart ache.

She stepped closer, rested her cheek against his chest, and let out a shaky breath as his arms came around her. "I don't know what I want," she whispered. "But I don't want to be alone tonight."

"You don't have to be." His hand splayed across her back. "You can stay here."

She nodded against him. "Okay."

They stood there for a long while, wrapped in quiet and the soft pulse of something that hadn't burned out—it had just been waiting.

He tilted her chin with his thumb and brushed his lips against her mouth, slow and deliberate. He tasted like marshmallows, chocolates, and memories.

Drawing back, she laced her fingers through his and tugged him through the kitchen and toward the staircase. Once at the top, she shed her sweatshirt, dropping it to the floor, and toyed with the hem of her tank top.

"Baily," Fletcher whispered. "When you said you didn't want to be alone, I just figured you wanted to crash here, not…" He tugged her to his chest, crashed his mouth against hers, and assaulted her lips like she was his last meal.

His hands slid down her back, pulling her flush against him, his body hard as iron. One hand grabbed the nape of her neck, angling her head. She sighed against his lips, melting into him. The world, with all its troubles and puzzles, faded away.

His touch turned fiery, his hands exploring her with an urgency that roused her from her long-held sleep. Quickly, and without warning, he stepped back, ripping off his shirt and tossing it across the hallway. His fingers deftly found the bottom of her tank top, yanking it over her head and tossing it to join his on the floor.

A soft gasp slipped through her lips when his hand cupped her breast over her bra—a lacy pink number that she'd splurged on a few years ago. His thumb grazed over her nipple, and she nearly came undone.

"Want me to stop?" he asked, his voice low and gravelly with desire. He didn't wait for her answer. Instead, he bent his head to take the lacy-covered peak into his mouth. The feel of his tongue against her sent a series of shocks down her spine.

"No," she whimpered, her fingers threading through his hair. "Don't stop, Fletcher."

Her plea must have sparked something primitive within him, as he needed no further encouragement, and he navigated the clasp of her bra, freeing her breasts from their confinement. His warm hands enveloped her newly exposed skin, sending electricity jolting through her body.

"Baily..." He groaned as she nipped at his neck playfully, making him shiver beneath her exploring hands.

His kisses grew hungrier, more demanding. That was until he picked her up effortlessly and carried her into the bedroom, their bodies never parting until he set her down on the bedspread. Standing at the foot of the bed, he stared at her. "You're so beautiful," he said. "I've missed you so much."

Slowly, she reached for his jeans' button, fumbling like she'd never undone one.

He batted her hand away, released the button, and unzipped his pants.

"I can handle it from here," she said with renewed confidence.

His breath hitched, and she felt a sense of satisfaction sweep over her as she watched the intoxicating play of emotions on his face. She lowered his jeans and boxers over his hips and to the floor. She took him into her hands, exploring him as if this were the first time she'd ever caressed him, and yet she still remembered every inch.

Holding him gently, she brought her lips to him… kissing, licking, tasting.

His hand dove into her hair as he let out a deep groan, and his head fell back. She savored every sound he made as she bathed him with her tongue, doing everything in her power to push him to the edge. And when she felt his control snapping, she pushed back onto her heels and looked up at him through lowered lashes.

"Baily," he said hoarsely. "Come here."

She had almost forgotten what it was like to be this close, this intimate with him. His rough, calloused hands mapped out her body, finally settling between her thighs. Fletcher nudged them apart, ripped off her matching pink panties, and stared at her with a smoky look in his eyes.

"This is a little different from the last time I was… here." He traced his finger down the landing strip and took a broad stroke across her as she fisted the sheets. "I like it."

"It's new," she managed between ragged breaths.

He arched a brow while his fingers danced circles over her sensitive skin, driving her mad. "Is there a reason?"

"Something to do in the shower?"

"Now that's a visual." He lowered his head, and then his tongue slid across her in a slow caress.

The sensation was too much, stealing her breath. Her back arched off the mattress as a moan spilled from her lips.

His fingers dipped lower, tracing the wet folds between her legs. When he slid one finger inside of her slick warmth, she whimpered and thrust her hips upward to deepen his touch. He moved slowly at first, sliding in and out, matching the rhythm of his swirling tongue.

Baily pressed her heels into the bedspread to bring him even closer, surrendering herself to the pleasure he was giving with no thought left for doubt or regret. "Fletcher," she moaned loudly when his fingers curled slightly as he increased his pace.

He growled against her skin at that, lifting himself long enough to say huskily, "Say it again. I like hearing my full name roll off your lips."

"Fletcher," she managed with a ragged breath.

With a final brush of his tongue against her hot center and a couple more skillful strokes from his fingers, he tipped her over the edge. She cried out in pleasure as wave after wave of ecstasy filled her. Her body writhed and twisted on Fletcher's bed until the rush gradually subsided, leaving behind a lazy tide of bliss.

Panting, she looked at him. Fletcher's face flushed and was animalistic—raw desire reflected in those dark pools she found herself drowning in.

He crawled his way up alongside her until their bodies aligned. His hand slid up her thigh, dragging goosebumps in its wake. "I need to get protection from my wallet," he whispered.

"Not necessary. On the pill." She tried to keep herself steady, but when he pressed himself against her, she lost all control again.

The moment he entered her, time seemed to stand still. They both froze, staring at each other in an intimate silence that spoke volumes more than words ever could. Then Fletcher started moving in rhythm to their pulsating hearts. The friction between them ignited a fire that had long been dormant but had now roared back to life.

His strokes began slow and deep, stirring the depths of emotions she'd kept hidden for so long. Her fingers curled into his back, her nails leaving fiery trails as she pulled him closer.

"Fletcher," she gasped out, gripping him tighter as their union grew frantic and rushed.

"Yes," he rasped. "God... Baily."

His movements picked up speed, sending pleasure coursing through her body until it reached a breaking point. Heat spiraled from deep within her belly and radiated outward as an earth-shattering climax overtook her.

From somewhere in the hazy distance, she heard Fletcher cry out a strangled version of her name as he found his own release.

In the aftermath, they lay enveloped in each other's arms—the only sound being their mixed heavy breathing and the rhythmic beat of Fletcher's heart against Baily's ear.

Her mind slowly drifted back to reality as he pressed his lips against her hair. As the quiet settled around them, she closed her eyes.

He rolled to the side, rustled the covers over their bodies, and pulled her close.

"I have to get up at six," she said with a heavy sigh.

"I do as well." He kissed her temple. "I have to work most of the day with Parks and Rec, and I have one airboat tour, but then whatever you need at the marina, I'm at your beck and call."

"I'd rather clean out your old bedroom closet. I have a feeling that might be amusing."

"Or embarrassing." He tucked himself in behind her. "Get some sleep."

She sank deeper into his body and let the soft rhythm of his breathing lull her toward sleep. Hearing the faint splash of water outside, she realized everything had finally fallen silent—their world outside and their war within.

CHAPTER 5

Fletcher adjusted the brim of his Parks and Rec ballcap as he stepped onto the wooden deck of Massey's Pub. The aroma hit like a rocket speeding through the sky right before it landed on its target, clean. It was the perfect blend of bacon, grilled meat, and a hint of something sweet. He'd heard that Mrs. Massey had given up trying to find a buyer, and because business was still booming, she continued, trying to forget her husband had turned out to be a drug and arms dealer.

He glanced around and smiled. He was glad she'd been able to rebound, and that the town had done its best to forgive. At least people weren't boycotting since the place was humming with its usual midday buzz—locals and tourists mixed like old friends and new stories, a playlist of Jimmy Buffett and Kenny Chesney underscored the clink of glasses and low thrum of conversation. It was

Florida through and through. Breezy, open-air charm with a warm wood bar, fans twirling lazily overhead, and faded nautical maps framed on the walls. Inside, the AC was humming, but most folks preferred the shaded tables on the wraparound porch, where the scent of grilled fish and lime from the kitchen rolled out with every swing of the screen door.

He caught sight of Keaton already seated at a high-top near the window, the man unmistakable in his Fish and Wildlife uniform—tan shirt, green patch, and mirrored shades he hadn't taken off despite being inside. Fletcher slid into the seat across from him.

"I heard something fascinating this morning before leaving for work." Keaton pushed his shades to the top of his wavy hair, which always looked like it needed a good combing, yet was perfectly styled at the same time.

"Did Trinity figure out how to have a baby without going through labor?" Fletcher smiled as he sat down, lifted his cap, and ran his fingers through his hair, wishing he had Keaton's mop.

Everyone wished they had Keaton's hair.

"She can't wait to be a mother." Keaton shook his head. "But at our last doctor's visit, she asked if it were possible to be put under, have the kid taken out of her body, but not by C-section because she doesn't want scars." He smacked his hand on the table. "But she also doesn't want any pain meds or anesthesia, which she mentioned in the same breath. The poor doctor blinked, turned to me, and said, *Good luck*."

"Trinity is a walking oxymoron," Fletcher said. "She's strong. Independent. Can weather almost any storm. But she told Baily that pushing out a baby is the most terrifying thing ever. Baily figures she'll have one contraction, and the baby will pop out."

"With my luck, it'll be forty hours of Trinity turning into a foul-mouthed princess." Keaton chuckled. "But that brings me to what has me so utterly amused."

"Dare I ask?"

"Baily called Trinity at seven and informed her of where she spent last night."

"Your wife has a big mouth." Fletcher's lips tugged into a smile. He swiped his hand across his face to try to cover it.

"Not really. She happened to be in the bathroom, putting on her makeup, and had her cell on speaker. I just happened to stroll in at precisely the right moment." Keaton grinned like a big kid. "So, you and Baily, eh?"

"What are we, Canadian all of a sudden?"

"Hey, I lived in Oregon for a little bit. It's kind of like Southern Canada."

"Not even close, dude." Fletcher took an ice cube from his water and chucked it at Keaton.

"Tell that to my cuz, Foster. He thinks he's all sorts of Canuck."

"I just can't with you sometimes."

Keaton shrugged. "So, Dawson's dealing with old man Jenkins and Cooney's chickens?"

Fletcher let out a sigh, flagging down the waitress with a nod. "I could hear Jenkins in the background blustering that if one more rooster crosses onto his side of the fence, it's gonna end up in a stew pot."

Keaton let out a hearty laugh. "That man needs a new hobby."

"What he needs is fewer bullets."

The waitress arrived, all smiles and long braids tucked under a Massey's Pub ballcap. They ordered quickly—two iced teas, smoked mahi tacos for Fletcher, a fried shrimp po'boy, and a side of fries for Keaton—which he got every flipping time. The man never ordered anything else. Ever.

"I take it we're here to watch and listen to those two over there and not discuss your love life?"

Fletcher leaned forward, his tone low. "Dawson got a call from Lilly. Said the guy Decker was having lunch with looked like he sweats mortgage deals and overpriced scotch."

"I sat with my back to them, pretending I didn't see Decker when the hostess sat me. But if Decker noticed me, he didn't even flinch." Keaton leaned back as the waitress showed up with their iced teas.

She placed them on the table and shuffled off.

Keaton lifted his tea and took a slow sip. "I can't say I heard much…some chatter about the development site on Marco Island, but that's it so far."

"Well, tune in those ears of yours," Fletcher said,

shifting in his seat to keep himself mostly blocked by Keaton, but if Decker saw him, so be it.

"They're talking something about plans, drawings." Keaton tilted his head slightly toward the right. Massey's had no barriers between the porch and the dining room—just open windows and a half wall. "Hard to make out all the words over the hum of lunch service and that woman over there squawking about the price of her cheap wine."

"The wine here is overpriced, but it always has been," Fletcher mused, wishing he were on the other side of the table.

"Okay. I've got a few more words. They're generic, but troublesome," Keaton said. "Fit the landscape...enticing package...drawings by Monday... And this is the best or maybe the worst piece...gotta be better than the other bid..."

"Is that Decker saying all that?" Fletcher asked.

"No." Keaton shook his head. "It's been the other guy. He's a chatterbox. His tone is clipped, like he's got a chip on his shoulder or something. About the only thing I've heard Decker say is, *yeah, okay, right, I'm on it.*"

The waitress appeared with their food in record time. The service had always been generally good. But the food, which had always been piping hot and absolutely delicious, along with the atmosphere, had been the reason this place had survived after the scandal with Paul Massey.

"Anything else?"

"Only that Decker's noticed you, and now all I hear is a few faint whispers I can't make out." Keaton dug into his food. "God, this shit is good."

"You know, there are other things on the menu."

"If it ain't broke, don't fix it."

"You're pathetic." Fletcher took a bite out of his Mahi taco.

"And you spent the night with Baily and weren't going to tell us about it." Keaton waved his fork around. "I'm a little butthurt over that."

"I don't kiss and tell, and it's none of your damn business." Fletcher eyed Decker's table. So much about that man bothered him, but so far, everything he'd said checked out.

However, he was still planning on bidding on the Crab Shack. That just pissed Fletcher off even more.

"Right, because when I had my head up my ass over Trinity, you didn't make that your business."

"That's different." Fletcher jerked his head. "Looks like Decker's friend is getting ready to bug out."

The slick man got up and buttoned his blazer with the sort of poise that screamed boardroom. As he passed the window, he glanced toward Keaton and Fletcher. His gaze lingered, just long enough to register awareness. Then he was gone, disappearing down the steps toward the parking lot.

A beat later, Decker pushed back from the table and made his way toward their high-top with the confidence of someone who believed he held all the cards. Or maybe a man who didn't care about anyone else but himself. Or maybe it was something entirely different. Whatever it was, Fletcher wanted to wipe the smug grin off the asshole's face.

"Well, if it isn't Calusa Cove's finest," Decker drawled, resting his knuckles on their tabletop. "Enjoying your little stakeout lunch?"

Fletcher looked up slowly and smiled lazily. "Not many places in this town to go for lunch, and I ate the sandwich Baily made me this morning over my break as a snack a couple of hours ago." Damn, that felt good to say. "Did you have the Mahi tacos? They're good. Fresh caught every morning."

Keaton picked up a fry and took a bite out of it. "Real crispy. Not too salty. Just right."

Decker chuckled. "Sure. Just two civil servants, talking shop. Coincidentally seated near me and my associate."

"It's a small town," Fletcher said easily. "Massey's only has so many tables, especially on a warm day like today. Granted, winters don't get too chilly in South Florida, but we can have some biting temps."

Decker shrugged. "I get it. Everyone and their brother are curious about whether or not I'm gonna put in a bid, and you boys are stirring up trouble about it, no doubt. Truth is, I haven't decided anything."

Keaton gave him a steady look. "Funny. Sounded like your friend had a few ideas."

Decker's grin didn't quite reach his eyes. "He's got ideas everywhere. Talks a big game. Rattles off a million and one things. His philosophy is you've got to toss five hundred darts into a black hole. One will land on something."

"So, what are you shooting your darts at?" Fletcher asked.

"You just don't quit, do ya?" Decker sighed. "Look. Yeah, sure, we both know I'm interested in the old Crab Shack property. That doesn't mean I'm going to bid on it. I'm not even sure I've got a workable idea. One that the town would even consider, which means I've got some thinking to do. Not to mention, I've got other projects lined up, and the timing could all be wrong."

"And you could be playing us right now. Trying to catch us off guard. Make us think we've got this in the bag, but then you swoop in and steal it out from under us," Fletcher said.

"Wow, man. You've got some serious trust issues." Decker tapped his fingers on the table. "I've got to get going. You two fellas have a nice day."

Fletcher leaned back, letting the chair creak. "You do the same."

"Maybe I'll stop by the marina. See how Baily's doing." Decker nodded once and walked away.

Fletcher pressed his hands on the wooden top and stood.

"Don't," Keaton said firmly. "Not worth having to call Dawson here because you let your fists get the better of you, especially because Decker only said that to needle you." Keaton leaned forward. "Just like you commented about Baily making you a treat this morning to see if you could rattle him. You're better than that."

"I know." Fletcher eased back into the chair. "But what I wouldn't give to feel my knuckles connect with his flesh."

"I don't doubt it." Keaton dunked a fry in ketchup. "That guy oozes snake oil and gym memberships."

Fletcher snorted, lifting his iced tea. "Yeah, but even snakes strike when the grass gets quiet. We need to find out who that other guy was."

Keaton wiped his fingers and tossed the napkin onto the plate. "On it. I'll call Chloe. If she can't get a line on him, she'll call her old partner, Buddy."

They paid their tab and stood, stepping off the porch into the Florida sun, the scent of saltwater and Spanish moss thick in the air.

As Fletcher made his way to his truck, he felt something settle uneasily in his gut. Like maybe the tide was turning—and it wasn't in their favor.

* * *

BAILY SAT with her legs dangling off the edge of Fletcher's dock, the soft ripple of the water beneath her toes lulling her into a quiet calm. The sky was painted in watercolor streaks of lavender and blush, and the sun slipped low behind the mangroves. The air smelled of brine and wild sage, the kind of scent one could only get living on the edge of the Everglades.

Fletcher sat beside her, knees bent, bare feet resting on the sun-warmed wood. He passed her a cold bottle of sweet tea and clinked his own against it. "To surviving the week."

Baily smirked. "It's only Wednesday."

"Exactly."

They sat in companionable silence for a minute, watching a gator slink lazily through the channel, its tail swirling gently above the waterline. A heron lifted from the reeds nearby, wings wide, its shadow stretching across the dock.

She'd always loved evenings like this. As a kid, she used to sit on the docks of the marina, watching the sunset, enjoying the quiet stillness that Calusa Cove offered. This had always been home. She'd never had dreams of seeing the world. Of being anywhere else. Her friends, including Audra, had spoken of venturing off into lands unknown. Having wild adventures. Careers that brought them across the globe, offering something that this patch of land couldn't.

It had been something Baily couldn't fathom. Still couldn't.

And it had broken her heart when the man she loved had walked away. They'd tried to survive it. Muddled their way through boot camp and a few years of writing letters, visits between deployments, which had turned into arguments about the future.

Not so much about her leaving, though there were talks about that, because Fletcher had always believed they could come back. That someday he'd leave the Navy. But he'd always pushed that date out. And then, of course, her father had died, changing everything.

"You're deep in thought," Fletcher said.

"Just trying to ignore the pending doom and enjoy what makes me love this place."

"It is magical," Fletcher said. "No place on earth like it."

"And yet, you left," she whispered, keeping her gaze on the alligator—the one everyone called Captain. She knew it was Captain because he had a big scar on his back, probably from a boat propeller. He was at least twelve to fourteen feet long and always minded his own business. The people of Calusa Cove joked that he watched out for their quiet little town. That he patrolled the waters, a point that seemed to be driven home harder lately, as Captain had been seen more often since Paul Massey and Dewey Hale had turned on the town. It was as if Captain had grown tired of being betrayed by its own.

Fletcher tilted her face with the palm of his hand.

She blinked.

"Are you really afraid I'm going to pack my bags and take off?" he asked, dropping his hand to his lap.

"That thought does cross my mind sometimes." At first, she'd kept Fletcher at a distance because she'd blamed him for her brother's death. She'd needed someone to point her grief and anger at, and Fletcher had been an easy target. But as time passed, and the truth behind Ken's death had been revealed, she hadn't been able to keep blaming a man who'd suffered, too. If she were being honest with herself, which she was now, she'd put walls up because everyone she'd ever loved had abandoned her either through leaving or death.

Fletcher included.

"You spent years in the Navy. Years seeing the world. I can't help but wonder when you might get bored being back here."

Fletcher drew in a deep breath and let it out with a sigh. "I don't know what to say to you to make you understand or to feel safe in the knowledge that I don't want to be anywhere else but here."

"It's not that I don't want to believe that. Or that in the last two years, I can't see that." She tapped the center of her chest. "Or even feel it. Maybe it's everything that's going on, and it's like I'm just sitting around and waiting for the other shoe to drop, kind of like the ripple effect that happened after Audra's dad went missing. You and Ken left for boot camp. Audra took off. And from there, it was just like one by one, I ended up alone."

"Oh, sweetheart." Fletcher looped his arm around her waist. "You're not alone. Can't you see that? We're all here for you. Me, the guys, Audra, Trinity, Chloe…all of us."

"I do know that," she said. "It's just hard to accept sometimes after years of feeling alone and doing it all by myself." She lifted her hand when he opened his mouth. "Ken was hard on me the last couple of years he was alive. I didn't understand him anymore. We'd been close as kids. Sure, we fought and often didn't get along, but he was my brother, and he wouldn't, for whatever reason, support me and this damn marina. His legacy. He was angry about it. And he said the most outrageous things to me. I often wondered if you supported him in that decision."

"I didn't know he was doing that. If I had, I would've said something." He pressed his finger against her lips. "And before you go and say anything about that, when most of that was happening, you would barely take my calls. You didn't tell me anything. That is a two-way street."

"I know." She nodded. "I just can't help these feelings and thoughts. Instead of bottling them up and snapping at you all the time, I decided to tell you, since you asked about what I was thinking."

He chuckled. "I appreciate that. As long as you don't regret last night or this morning." He arched a brow. "Because I still lo—"

"I don't regret it, and let's not go there, Fletch. I'm not ready for declarations. Let's just enjoy things and see what happens. Can you do that?"

He nodded. "But I hate being called Fletch."

"Why?" she asked. "It's who you were for my entire youth."

"I don't know. I think because when I joined the Navy, everyone called me Fletcher or used my last name, except Ken. But even he started calling me that a few years in. When I came back, and people here were calling me Fletch, it grated on my nerves. Especially when you were telling me I needed to grow up. Which was odd, because I had. So, I thought Fletcher sounded more like a man and not a stupid teenager."

"That's about the dumbest thing I've ever heard." She let out a little laugh. "But Fletcher is a nice *family* name."

He burst out laughing. "My grandmother always loved that I was given her maiden name. Thought it bonded us together somehow. She was a crazy old woman. About the only person Silas was afraid of. Then again, she once ran through town after my dad when he first started dating my mom in a housecoat, hair curlers, combat boots, and a loaded rifle. Silas saw the whole thing. He was just a kid, but said it terrified him. Thought my grandma was gonna shoot my old man right there in front of Harvey's Cabins."

"Your grandma was the best, even if she was a little left of normal."

"She sure was," Fletcher said.

A few moments of silence ticked by. The sun disappeared, casting an eerie glow over the Glades.

"So," Baily said, bumping her shoulder into his. "Anything exciting happen in the wild world of Parks and Rec?" she asked, needing something normal. Something to ground her in the present. Something that wasn't heavy and filled with worry. Something that felt more like her past than her present.

Fletcher grinned. "Exciting is one word for it. Had to mediate an argument this morning between two people from that boat parade about whether or not manatees are just fat dolphins. I had to wonder where on earth these folks were from and if they'd ever seen the ocean before."

She laughed. "Seriously?"

"Swear on my life. One of them was convinced the manatees were part of a government cloning project gone wrong. Said it with a straight face. Didn't even crack a smile or lift a brow. The man was dead freaking serious."

"Oh, Lord."

He chuckled. "Dawson wasn't too far away, so I told them to ask him. Said he was the town's marine biology expert. That he knew everything and would be honest about something like that. You should've seen the look on Dawson's face."

Baily tipped her head back, laughing harder now. Fletcher leaned closer, brushing a kiss to her temple. It was simple. Sweet. Intimate. Like old times and just what she needed.

"The Navy brought you some good people. Dawson's a special man. He's good for Audra. The woman's still not tame, but she's softer."

"They bring out the best in each other," he said. "They'll make great parents. It'll be fun to watch, especially if they have a little redhead just like Audra."

"I believe Dawson is secretly hoping that's exactly what will happen. If anyone can handle another Audra in this world, it's him."

"No truer words," Fletcher said. "But I don't think Keaton could handle another Trinity."

"Trinity couldn't handle another Trinity," she said. "When do you think Hayes and Chloe will get married and start pumping out babies?"

"Oh, that's a tough one." Fletcher sipped his drink before setting it aside. "Their timeline for all that might be a little longer. I'm not sure they're in a rush, but I'm guessing they may get married sometime next year. I couldn't even take a stab at the baby question. I know they both want a family, which is strange when it comes to Hayes. That's something he never wanted. Said he wasn't cut out for it. So, there might be some trepidation there."

"I bet once their house gets built, it'll happen at lightning speed. They just need to be grounded and have a little distance from everything that happened."

"Yeah. That was a lot, and I know Chloe is still grappling with the idea that her biological dad was a serial killer."

Baily shivered. "I can't imagine. But biology doesn't make the person, and Chloe knows that. And she got Fedora out of it. The silver lining."

"I like that girl," Fletcher said.

Baily exhaled and let her head fall onto his shoulder, the peace of the moment wrapping around her like a warm breeze.

But the peace didn't last, and other thoughts crept into her mind. "I haven't called Julie back yet," she whispered.

Fletcher's arm tightened around her. "You don't have to if you're not ready."

"I know." She sat up straighter, brushing her hair out of her face. "But maybe I need to. Maybe hearing her voice will help me figure out what the hell is going on."

He nodded. "I'll be right here. Whatever happens."

"No time like the present." She pulled out her phone, thumb hovering over the voicemail screen. Then, with a deep breath, she tapped Julie's number and hit call.

It rang twice.

"Baily?" Julie's voice chirped through the speaker, unnervingly bright. "Oh, my goodness, I wasn't expecting you to call so quickly."

"Hi, Julie." Baily's tone was guarded but polite. "I didn't want any more time to pass before returning your call."

"I'm so glad." Julie's voice overflowed with sugar and sunshine. "I've just been thinking about you so much lately. What with everything on the news—oh, Baily, I can't imagine how scary things must be down there. A serial killer? Calusa Cove's always been a quirky, strange town, but that's just awful."

"We're doing okay," Baily said, glancing at Fletcher. He gave her a slight nod and squeezed her hand. "It's been…a lot. But the community's rallying."

"I just hate that this is going to hurt your business. I know it's always been a struggle, hanging on by a thread. I'm honestly surprised you're still open. But with something like this... Well, people talk, word spreads. It's like cancer, and next thing you know, you can't crawl out from under it."

"Ask her why she's really calling now," Fletcher whispered.

Baily pressed her lips together. "Julie, what is this about? You and I haven't talked in years. You cut me out after Ken died. Told me I wasn't welcome in the boys' lives anymore. Why now?"

Julie's tone didn't falter. "I've just been thinking a lot. Ken wouldn't have wanted us to be so divided. And the boys—they miss you. They ask about you."

Baily's throat tightened. "I'd love to talk to them."

"Oh, they're...busy right now. Bedtime. You know how it is. But maybe another time," Julie said, still upbeat but a touch more clipped.

Baily's heart thudded as it crashed into her gut. "Just for a minute. I won't keep them. I promise."

"I don't want to upset their routine. You know how important that is. If I break it, well, it will be hard to settle them back down. They're at a tough age, and I'm a single mom with just my parents to help. Sorry. I hope you'll think about coming here. About giving up that hard life in Calusa Cove. It's not what Ken wanted for you, you know. He wanted something a little easier." And then, before Baily could respond, Julie said, "I've got to tend to the boys. Take care." And ended the call.

Baily sat frozen, the phone shaking in her hand.

"That was weird," Fletcher said quietly.

"Yeah." She set the phone on the dock. "Weird doesn't even begin to cover it."

Fletcher pulled her back against his side. "The timing of this has my hackles up. There's got to be a connection somewhere, but it doesn't make sense."

"A connection to what's happening to me now?"

"I don't know about the break-in and the gas. I still think Decker's involved in that somehow. But the timing of that loan. The shift in Ken's personality. The fights between him, your dad, and you—I can't help but think that's all tied together somehow."

"That's crazy," she said. "Julie wanted nothing to do with this town or the marina. And her parents aren't in the business of making loans. They own a manufacturing company. Not even sure what they make. Or even what they do. I just know they're rich. They're powerful. And they're mean."

Fletcher threaded his fingers through his hair. "But if Ken wanted this place gone, burying you in debt was one way to do it."

"But that would've just screwed him over because, if I ever did sell, I'd owe him some of the profit from that sale."

"You're forgetting that Ken didn't need the money. Nor does Julie or her family."

"Okay, but then why not call in the loan?"

"They can't call in the entire thing just yet—not unless you're late or miss a payment, which you haven't. You've got a few months before they force your hand, whoever *they* are," Fletcher said. "I'm going to have Chloe focus her efforts right now on Julie and her family."

"That just doesn't make sense. I get that they don't like me. But they hate Calusa Cove. They have no use for property in this area."

"Regardless, Julie's call doesn't track, and we need to look at all the angles. Leave no rock unturned."

"Since that payment is due next week, and I don't have the money, knock your socks off."

"We're gonna figure this out, Baily. I promise."

Baily leaned into him, the warmth of his body grounding her against the chill creeping in from the swamp. The water shifted below them, the last light of day slipping into dusk, but neither of them moved.

"After everything I've been through, I can't lose the marina, Fletcher. I just can't. It's my heart. It's who I am."

CHAPTER 6

FLETCHER TUGGED open the creaky door to his old bedroom and stepped aside to let Baily in first. When he'd first moved back home, he hadn't been able to decide where to sleep. The master…or here. It had felt strange to stay in his parents' room, but even odder to live in all the memories of his childhood…of Baily.

Everything about this room reminded him of *her.* The scent of lavender from her body wash still clung to the sheets. His mind filled with every kiss they'd shared. Every intimate secret that had passed between them in their youth filled his heart profoundly.

So, he'd opted for the master bedroom.

Baily stepped over the threshold with a familiar grin tugging at her lips. "God, every time I walk into this room, I feel like I'm walking into a museum to our youth."

He glanced around his old room. It had the same dark green carpet, sprawled wall to wall, that it had always had. The thick matching curtains sagged slightly off their rods, and the wallpaper—green and blue stripes—still curled at the corners. A lava lamp sat on the dresser like it had been waiting for someone to ask it to dance. The ceiling fan overhead gave a little rattle as it turned. As a teenager, he would lie in bed and watch the blades spin while Baily curled up in his arms.

"You'd think after all these years it would've faded out of memory," Baily said, brushing her hand over a stack of old books. "But it's exactly the same. Down to the smell—dust and citrus polish and whatever cologne you used to drown yourself in."

Fletcher smirked. "I was trying to impress you. Clearly, it worked."

She gave him a sidelong glance, amused. "Worked well enough. But this room? You were all about your pride back then."

"Still am." He reached into the closet and pulled out the old box labeled *FLETCHER*, his mother's loopy handwriting still legible despite the dust and time. "Found this not long after the accident. Never opened it. Figured it was just old junk."

"You haven't looked inside?" she asked softly.

"No. I wasn't ready. And then... I just never got around to it." He set it on the floor and sat cross-legged beside it. Baily lowered herself next to him, knees bumping. There was something grounding about sitting on that old shag carpet with her—it reminded him of simpler days, when the future had been just something you dreamed about, not something you carried on your back.

He peeled back the flaps.

The first layer was what he'd expected—faded report cards with red pen scrawled across the tops, a cracked plastic trophy from peewee football, a faded Polaroid of him in a Halloween costume made of duct tape and determination. A few letters and cards.

Baily leaned over his shoulder. "Oh my God, that's my handwriting."

He held up the envelope. "Ninth grade. Valentine's Day. You stuck it in my locker."

Her cheeks colored. "I remember that. If I hadn't made the first move, you never would've."

Fletcher opened it and read aloud, "'I like your smile. And maybe your arms. Don't tell anyone.'"

She groaned. "Kill me now."

He grinned. "Why? That's pure gold. Frame-worthy."

They dug deeper. Photos, mostly. One of them standing in front of the old marina sign. Another of Audra, mid-tackle, landing on a juvenile gator while Ken and Fletcher shouted in the background.

"She was wild," Baily said, laughing. "That gator never saw her coming."

"She screamed, 'This is for science!' and dove." Fletcher chuckled. "Ken nearly had a heart attack."

"But then he bought her that damn T-shirt about

how small her boobs were because when she surfaced with that gator, it was like a wet T-shirt contest, and all you boys were staring."

"Was not," Fletcher said.

"Right, like I believe that."

"I only had eyes for your…breasts."

She gave him a little jab in his forearm. "Your mom made Audra soak in bleach water after. Swore she brought home bacteria from the swamp."

They laughed until their sides hurt.

Then, nestled between a stack of baseball cards and a cracked compass, Fletcher pulled out a worn brown notebook with a band around it.

He stilled.

Taped to the front was a note in rough handwriting: *Please give to Fletcher.—Ray Mitchell*

Fletcher blinked. "That's your dad's."

Baily's breath caught. "Yeah. That's his."

Carefully, Fletcher opened the notebook. The pages were filled with frantic, looping handwriting—thoughts scrawled in the margins, half-formed sentences, as if Ray had been trying to make sense of something and couldn't.

Marina's bleeding money. I can't stop it. Every day's worse, and every day, something weird happens or breaks.

Ken said the loan was a sure thing. That he had a connection who'd fast-track it.

Paperwork's signed. But the money... Where is it? Ken says wait. Says it's a glitch. It's not. But Ken said he'd handle it. Said he'd make sure I'd get the money. He sounded nervous and angry at the same time. Something's not right.

I should've talked to Baily. Should've talked to Fletcher.

It's getting harder to keep this from her. From both of them.

Baily leaned closer, eyes scanning every word.

Called the bank again. No record. No transfer. Ken says it's just delayed. He's lying. I know it. But I don't know why. He often avoids my calls or tells me that he's working on the problem and that I need to trust him. I don't. Not anymore, and that's not a good feeling.

The marina's hanging by a thread. What have I done?

Fletcher flipped the page slowly. The final line was written with a heavy hand, the pen digging deep into the page: *I'm not sure I can fix this.*

Silence stretched between them. Only the low whir of the ceiling fan filled the room.

"I never saw this," Fletcher said. "I never knew he was struggling like that. I mean, my folks told me he was distant the last few weeks before his heart attack, but I honestly had no idea."

"I didn't either," Baily said quietly. "He was always...steady. Resilient. At least, that's what I believed."

Fletcher closed the notebook slowly. "He believed in Ken until he couldn't. That much is clear. And Ken let him down."

"But why?" she asked. "Why would Ken push him into a loan that didn't exist? One that was tied to payments I'm still making. One that put me in this mess."

"I don't know." Fletcher met her eyes. "But it lines up with the stories about the money. The missing loan. The pressure your dad was under."

"And then he died," Baily whispered. "And this is what gave him that heart attack. It's what killed him."

Fletcher wrapped an arm around her shoulders. "I'm not going to stop digging until I have all the answers."

She cried softly. "I feel like I'm drowning."

"We're going to figure this out," Fletcher promised, holding her tighter. "For him. For you."

The old bedroom—soaked in memories, decorated in outdated colors and thick with the past—suddenly felt more like a crime scene than a sanctuary.

And Fletcher knew this was only the beginning.

* * *

BAILY GLANCED down at her fingers intertwined with Fletcher's. Things were moving fast between them. Too fast. It didn't matter that he'd been her first love.

Her only love.

They'd spent more time broken up than they had as a couple, and for some reason, she believed that should matter.

But her heart told a vastly different story.

As they strolled down the shell path that led from

his house back toward the marina, she did her best to put all the thoughts of their latest discovery in a corner of her brain.

Her brother hadn't been the man she'd believed he was, and deep down, she'd known that to be true but hadn't wanted to face it. Perhaps it would've been easier had he not died in action. Not died a hero.

Not died at all.

But he had.

He'd also left her with more questions than answers.

The moonlight danced on the water, crickets chirped in lazy harmony with the distant hoot of an owl somewhere deep in the mangroves. It would've been peaceful—should've been peaceful—if her mind hadn't been a storm.

"You remember when Silas caught us skinny-dipping in Lester McCurdy's pool?" Fletcher asked.

Baily snorted. "Which time?"

He laughed. "Right after my seventeenth birthday. He threatened to call your parents and tell them all about it. I was terrified. It was bad enough that my grandma was living with us at the time and would catch you sneaking in, tiptoeing up the staircase, and slipping into my bedroom. She used to wiggle her finger under my nose, while giving me a lecture on the birds and the bees, and tell me I better not get you pregnant."

"I got a few of those lectures from your grandma, and she even once slipped me a box of condoms."

"At one point, I had so many, I used to think, even for a horny teenager, I'd never be able to use them all."

"You certainly tried." She grinned. "You spent the next month after Silas caught us mowing his lawn to buy his silence and avoid your grandma's questions. I wondered why you were being so nice to him."

"I still think he got off on that," Fletcher muttered. "Told every guy in town I was his 'personal landscaping technician.'"

They were still chuckling when they reached the marina.

The laughter died the second Baily's gaze locked on the door.

It was ajar.

Her heart hitched. "Fletcher…"

"I see it." He stepped in front of her, instantly alert. His hand went to his waistband, and he drew the sidearm he kept holstered under his shirt. "Stay behind me." He pulled out his phone and tapped out a quick group message to the team: ***Marina. Door open. Possible break-in. Being preemptive. Back-up requested.***

"Do whatever I tell you. Got it?" Fletcher said.

"Loud and clear."

Fletcher pushed the door open slowly, the hinges giving a soft groan that echoed like a gunshot in the silence.

They swept the main room first, and nothing appeared out of place. It was just as she'd left it when she'd closed up shortly after the end of the day. The overhead lights were off, the display racks of fishing supplies, maps, and souvenirs untouched. The T-shirt racks were fully stocked. Hats, sunscreen, and other things boaters might need—all there.

The front room—the little office and supply nook just behind the counter—looked mostly normal.

But something was…off.

Baily stepped around him and bumped into the chair that she always tucked in neatly behind her desk. "Shit," she mumbled as she hopped on one foot, grabbing the other, rubbing her big toe. "I hate when that happens, which is why I always push that chair in. This room is too small not to."

"You've always been a creature of habit." He held her by the forearms. "Are you okay?"

She nodded, setting her foot on the floor.

Papers on the desk had been shuffled. The ledger she'd closed was open. Her pen, which she always kept on the right side of the desk, was now on the left.

Fletcher crouched and checked the small safe. Still locked. "Open this for me, please."

"Okay." She leaned over, tapped the code, and the door popped open. "Passport, extra keys, loan paperwork, journal entries you gave me, and the cash for tomorrow. It's all there."

"That's good. Now, lock it back up."

She shut the door and hit the lock key. "But Fletcher, someone's been in here."

"I agree, and I think they wanted you to know they'd been snooping around."

"I don't see anything missing, but things have definitely been moved or looked at." She tapped her finger on the ledger.

"Probably looking for something specific." Fletcher stood and motioned toward the staircase leading up to her apartment. "Again, stay behind me, just in case."

They moved quietly, his back to her as he took each step like it might explode. The second they reached the top landing, Baily sucked in a sharp breath.

Her apartment door swung open. The frame cracked. The knob hanging by a thread.

Fletcher turned, voice low. "Stay here."

She wanted to argue, but the look in his eyes told her this wasn't the time. He slipped inside.

A beat passed.

Then two.

Then he called out. "It's clear."

She stepped in and froze. Her apartment—small but cozy, her sanctuary above the world—gutted.

Drawers yanked from her dresser and dumped. Clothes lay in shredded piles across the floor. Panties tossed about like trash. Her favorite dress, the one she'd worn to Audra and Trinity's bridal shower, shredded into a couple of pieces and hung on the back of the chair by the window. Her mattress—slashed from corner to corner, its stuffing torn out like spilled intestines. The comforter hung off the bed frame, stained with something dark she hoped to God was just coffee.

Every dish from her tiny kitchenette lay shattered. The chipped ceramic mug she'd had since high school? Broken. The glass dish from her mother's old casserole set? In pieces. Even the stupid plate Fletcher had made her in ceramics class—destroyed.

Books ripped from their shelves. Pages torn. Photos upended. A frame with a picture of her and Ken—lay face down, the glass spiderwebbed. The damage—surgical—violent.

And it felt freaking personal.

With her hands balled into fists, she walked to the center of the room, staring down at the carnage, and something inside her snapped. Her gut twisted as if a tornado swirled, hurling around her insides, and tossing them aside like they were simply in the way.

Baily let out a guttural scream and kicked the edge of her overturned ottoman so hard it slammed into the wall. She picked up the broken frame and hurled it at the closet door. The glass shattered, raining down like hail. "I want to bring my brother back from the dead and wrap my fingers around his neck and—"

"Baily—"

She spun toward Fletcher, but all she saw was red. There was no fear. No worry about bills. No concern over when or if she'd ever be able to climb out from the rubble her father had created.

He hadn't done this.

Her brother had, and he was reaching up from the grave and doing it all again. "I am done. Do you hear me?" Her chest rose and fell in quick, angry bursts. "I have played nice. I have smiled and stayed quiet and paid my bills and done everything I was supposed to. And for what?"

He reached for her, but she stepped back, waving her hands wildly. She'd always felt as though everything in her life was out of reach. Out of control. Like, no matter what she did, she couldn't fix it. Couldn't make it right. But she'd done what she always had, because she'd foolishly believed that tomorrow was a promise of a new beginning. That one day, she'd wake up from this nightmare. That if she put her head down, did the hard work, she'd be rewarded.

However, now she knew the truth. Playing nice would get her nothing but a trip to the bank to file for bankruptcy.

"I need you to calm down." Fletcher lowered his chin.

"I will not," she snapped. "I'm always calm. I'm always smiles, sunshine, and unicorns. I put on brave face and take everything on the chin. But no more. No more being careful. No more weathering the storm. No more waiting for the other shoe to drop or hoping people will do the right thing."

"Whoever did this—"

"Wants me afraid. Wants me to close up shop and

wither away into the Everglades." Her voice dropped to a dangerous whisper.

"Baily," Fletcher said. "They were looking for something." He waved his hand. "They tore through this place because they think you have something they want, and it's more than the marina."

"What makes you think that?"

"Because of where they went looking." He pointed toward her ripped-up mattress. "Hiding places."

She blew out a puff of air. "I can't imagine what they think I have, but I won't let them rattle me. Not anymore. I won't let this break me. All they did was make me want to fight for what's mine—*harder*." She pounded the center of her chest before she stepped over her slashed pillow and faced him. Her voice was steel now. "I'm not playing nice in the damn sandbox anymore. I'm coming out swinging."

The front door creaked behind them. Dawson's voice called out, low and steady. "It's us."

Hayes and Keaton filed in behind him, weapons holstered but expressions hard.

Fletcher nodded. "Looks like you've got another crime scene here."

And Baily? She stood in the center of it, rage shimmering off her like heat. Whatever game had started, it had just changed.

Baily Mitchell was officially done being the prey.

CHAPTER 7

THE CALUSA COVE coffee shop was already half-full by six-thirty. The smell of dark roast and vanilla syrup lingered out the front doors like smoke floating toward the sky, mingling with the salty morning air that drifted in from the marina. Fletcher pushed through the door. Since he'd been the first to arrive, he ordered three coffees.

He made his way to the pick-up counter and waited only a few minutes. Taking the to-go cups, he raced to the table by the door. The one facing the front window. The one where he could see who was coming in and out. Old habits died hard, and this one might never go away.

A few minutes later, Hayes and Chloe stepped inside, shuffling their feet across the floor before plopping down with a collective sigh.

Hayes sat with one arm draped over the back of

his chair. He reached across the table, snagging one of the coffees, and sipped.

Chloe took off her baseball cap and did the same.

"Morning," Fletcher said, cocking a brow. "Or are we struggling to use our vocal cords?"

"It's early," Hayes muttered. "You know the sun's not fully up yet, right?"

Chloe gave him a wry look. "Says the guy who ran three miles before breakfast."

"Running is therapy." Hayes raised his cup. "Caffeine is survival."

"Here's to that," Fletcher said, raising his cup.

They were quiet for a moment, just soaking in the hum of the café. The hiss of milk being steamed. The clatter of mugs. The low murmur of regulars catching. It could've been any morning, any town. But it wasn't. Not with everything simmering under the surface.

And Fletcher had barely slept between Baily tossing and turning all night, and him having another nightmare. He wasn't quite sure what was worse, especially since his nightmare had changed drastically. It was no longer Ken he'd watched having his neck sliced and his body being drained of blood…but Baily. It had shaken him to his core. He'd hated telling Baily that it had been the same old same old.

But she had enough on her plate to worry about. She didn't need to add him and his psyche to her long list of problems. He understood trauma. He'd been dealing with his demons for years. They didn't simply disappear because he'd chatted about them in therapy. Or because he'd accepted that he'd been in a lose-lose situation, and there'd been nothing he could've done to change the outcome.

The ghosts of his past would always lurk in the dark, ugly shadows of his mind, reaching out and tormenting him when he least expected them. The only thing he could do was not let them rule his present or his future.

"How's Baily?" Chloe asked, wrapping both hands around her paper mug.

"I really don't know." Fletcher exhaled. "She's furious. I haven't seen her like this since high school."

"I don't see Baily as being the kind of girl to ever have anger issues," Chloe said.

"Oh, we've heard of it a few times," Hayes said. "I guess, some dude once was picking on Audra about her dad and decided it would be fun to put dog shit in a paper bag, light it on fire, ring the doorbell, and run." Hayes smirked. "Baily had been there. She'd chased the guy down the street and actually caught him, tackled him, and punched him in the nose."

"Sounds like he deserved it," Chloe said.

"He did." Fletcher gave a half-grin. "But I can't say she was normally one to toss her fists around. However, she could cut you with words. Ask the cheer captain who said she couldn't pull off red lipstick."

Chloe snorted into her drink. "Oh, that's a bad move."

"She left that kid crying in the girls' bathroom." Fletcher nodded. "That's the version of Baily that's back. Fire and grit and ready to burn the whole damn thing down. It's scary and wonderful all at the same time."

"I've never seen her be anything other than sweet, except for maybe when she's had to deal with a few ornery customers, but even then, she's always done it with a soft hand and a heavy dose of kindness," Chloe said.

"It's always taken a lot to rattle Baily." Fletcher fiddled with his coffee mug. "But these last few years, she's been…different. A little broken and beaten down. While I didn't enjoy seeing her with that much rage, I'm not surprised she cracked. But she's holding Ken to the fire. She's blaming him for everything. She's not defending him or making excuses. She totally believes he's behind the problems with the marina."

"Based on the notebook you found from her dad, I blame Ken, too." Hayes leaned forward, resting both arms on the table. "You knew him the longest. He was your friend before the rest of us, but even I was shocked by that. It was cold, calculating, and honestly, I can't figure out the end game. It's one thing to want his sister to be out from under a pile of bills, but to create them for her? For his dad? And for what? Just the sale of the marina?"

"I know." Fletcher nodded. "We're missing something. Missing something big. I have to wonder if whoever broke into her apartment was looking for something. Something that incriminates them, or gives us answers, or both."

"Hopefully, they didn't find it," Hayes said. "Have you been able to go through everything?"

"Not yet." Fletcher shook his head. "Dawson couldn't release the scene until late last night."

Chloe's smile faded. "Baily might need some more of that edge she's pulled up from her past because I learned something this morning while Hayes was out on his run."

Hayes shifted his gaze. "And you didn't tell me?"

"I figured I'd kill two birds with one stone." Chloe lowered her chin.

Fletcher straightened. "I'm listening."

"I had an old friend over in Criminal, Cyber, Response, and Services do some digging. We haven't found much on the shell companies tied directly to the loan. Whoever structured this covered their tracks well. No addresses. No actual owners. Just layers of legal fog under mountains of paperwork that go in circles and down rabbit holes."

"So, what do we know?" Hayes asked.

"One name came up twice. Garrett Danvers. Small-time accountant. Used to be an employee at the Barbaro family's manufacturing business. Did the books for a plant near the Patapsco River in Maryland for about ten years before something happened. Not sure what, but it seems he left the company abruptly."

"Christ." Fletcher's brows lifted. "Julie and her flipping in-laws. They're circling the drain."

"Exactly. Now this isn't tied directly to the LLC that owns the marina loan, but there's overlap. Enough to raise questions. He still lives in Maryland. I'm reaching out, seeing if I can find out anything about him."

"I don't like coincidences," Hayes muttered. "And with Julie putting the pressure on all of a sudden, the stolen gas, the break-in… Well, something stinks."

"There are a lot of things that are floating out in the wind. We've got dots that don't connect, including Decker Brown. This is a thread, but we don't know where to pull it," Chloe said. "Might be nothing—or it might be the start of the whole damn tapestry unraveling."

Fletcher sat back. "You've always had a way with metaphors."

"I also called my friend Greer," Chloe added.

Fletcher blinked. "Greer Hudson? As in the chick Foster knows?"

"Yeah. She's the sheriff out in Raven's Cliff now. Small world that Keaton's cousin knows her. We worked together when we were both with the Bureau. Greer's cousin, Enzo—he's a corporate and securities lawyer on Marco Island. Greer said he's smart, aggressive, and knows how to dig through paper shields like this."

"Has Keaton ever met him?" Hayes asked.

"Not that I'm aware of, but Greer says he's solid.

That he's wicked smart. Top of his class, and that she tried like hell to get him to join the FBI, but he got married young. Had kids. Didn't want to strap on a weapon. She also mentioned he likes the art of the deal and is trustworthy as hell."

"I'll take trustworthy," Fletcher said. "Trustworthy's a hell of a commodity these days."

Chloe nodded. "I'll send you his contact information so you can get him everything. Let him sift through it and see what he can find. While I understand federal law, I dealt with missing persons and spent my career chasing a killer. He's got the mind to deal with the legal language and the ability to dance through what it really means."

"I can't thank you enough for all that you're doing," Fletcher said.

"You stood by me when the shit hit the fan and saved my ass." Chloe smiled.

Hayes finished his drink and stood. "I'd better get going. I've got a morning meeting with Silas about the Mangrove Action Project. Somehow, I landed myself on the hiring committee. I didn't even know there was such a thing."

"Dewey had been doing it for as long as I can remember," Fletcher said. "But I do recall that my old man was once in charge of that committee." He laughed. "Good luck with that."

"I'm gonna need it because, sadly, Silas is spiraling." Hayes sighed.

"Can you blame him?" Fletcher asked. "Dewey

living under our noses like that? Silas probably being his closest friend, even though Dewey didn't really do friends."

Hayes shook his head. "I keep thinking about all the times I had a random chat with Dewey about absolutely nothing. He was always just kind of there."

"And now we're back to trusting no one," Chloe said as she stood. "Just like old times."

They tossed their cups, exchanged nods, and stepped out. Fletcher leaned back in his chair and watched them go, not quite ready to head home. Baily had been wrestling with his laundry machine when he'd left, and she'd been in a mood. He hadn't been surprised by that. Her home had been violated. Her things had been tossed about and, in some cases, mutilated. Every negative emotion a person could feel was flowing freely from her skin.

"Hell of a morning," came a voice behind him.

Fletcher turned. Decker Brown stood there in a tailored blazer over a crisp, light blue shirt, with hair a little too perfect for six-fifty in the morning.

"You always lurk near exits, or just the ones I'm sitting by?" Fletcher asked, annoyed he hadn't been looking out the window, and hadn't seen him coming, or he would've bugged out with Hayes and Chloe.

Decker smiled without warmth. "Just dropped in for an espresso. This place has a decent roast."

Fletcher stood slowly. "You walk the Crab Shack property again yesterday?"

"Funny thing," Decker said. "Word travels fast in a small town."

"You know what else does?" Fletcher stepped forward, lowering his voice. "Bad intentions. And secrets."

Decker cocked his head. "You think I'm the big bad wolf, huh?"

"I think you blew into town talking fast and flashing cash. And now, you're sniffing around places with a lot of buried memories, and I don't like it."

"I'm a businessman, Fletcher. I don't chase ghosts. When I see land, I see potential. That's it."

"Then why all the backroom meetings? Surveyors. The guy you were with yesterday wasn't exactly subtle."

Decker's smile slipped. "You know what your problem is, Ranger? You think everyone's hiding a knife."

Fletcher's hand hovered near his hip. Not threatening. Just instinct. "Only when I feel a blade at my back."

The door behind them jingled. Dawson stepped in, eyes cutting through the tension like a blade. "We good here?"

Decker looked between them and offered a lazy grin. "Of course. Just a friendly chat."

He walked past Dawson, whistling, and stepped up to the counter.

"Let's go outside," Dawson said.

Fletcher blew out a breath and followed his buddy out the front door.

"Jesus," Dawson muttered. "He always that slick?"

"Like oil on tile."

"You okay?"

"I'm tired of being a step behind," Fletcher said. "I want to know what he's planning. I want to know if he's tied to Baily's loan and Ken's in-laws. Or if he's just a snake here to buy up land and put a condo on it. And I want to know all that yesterday."

Dawson clapped him on the shoulder. "It's gonna take time, but we're gonna get the answers."

"We'd better. Because the town hall meeting is next week, and Baily's either going to snag my weapon in my sleep and do something stupid, or she's gonna lose the marina. Both equally unsettling, but for different reasons."

"She's still that bad?"

"Let's just say she told my toaster to get off her dick this morning."

Dawson swiped a hand over his mouth and did his best to cover up a laugh, but it didn't help. "I'm sorry, but that sounds like something my wife would say."

"That was one of the milder things that has come out of her mouth in the last twenty-four hours."

"Audra said she's never been much of a swearer, and that she was always the one grounding her, but that when she's pushed too far, watch out. It's like someone stuck a stick of dynamite up her ass."

"That's one way of putting it."

Just then, Decker eased through the doorway, juggling a coffee cup, a pastry, and his phone pressed to his ear. He paused to adjust everything.

"No, I'm not doing it," Decker said, standing by the door, staring down at his shoes, not noticing the two men only a few feet away.

"I've done enough," Decker said. "And I can't keep doing this. I won't."

Another long pause.

"Then burn me. I don't care anymore." He took his cell and tucked it into his coat pocket. He paused for a moment, glancing at Dawson, before scurrying off down the street.

"I think that's the first time I've ever seen him look like he doesn't have all the answers," Dawson said. "He kind of looked constipated."

"Wonder what he meant by *burn me*."

"Not a clue." Dawson glanced down the street toward Decker. "But he's in a big hurry, and have you noticed that he hasn't been going to his job site over on Marco Island lately?"

"Everyone has. I also saw him at the Crab Shack last night with a surveyor and the guy he met with at Massey's. I didn't bother walking down there because there wasn't much we could do about it, and he wasn't hiding it since it was during sunshine hours."

"Yeah, I was on patrol and saw them, too." Dawson looked at his watch. "I need to get Audra her special fruity frappé something or other and a chocolate treat." He shook his head. "She doesn't demand much, but ever since she found out she was pregnant, these two things every morning are the only things that she says make up for the fact that guests always want bacon."

Fletcher chuckled. "Bacon used to be her favorite meal. Of all the things that could make morning sickness worse for her, I can't believe it's bacon."

"She keeps hoping that it'll pass, and she says when it does, she's sitting down and eating an entire package all at once." Dawson waved his hand over his head before yanking open the door and disappearing inside.

Fletcher would be lost without his team. After the mission that had killed Ken, and they'd all agreed they'd had enough, he honestly hadn't really expected they'd all migrate to his hometown. But damn was he grateful for his brothers-in-arms.

CHAPTER 8

FLETCHER PARKED his truck and eased from behind the wheel with his mind racing from the morning's events, and it wasn't even seven yet. But what really tickled his brain had been Decker's sudden shift in demeanor and his strange phone call.

Whatever that had been about, it had rattled Decker, and that man had seemed *un-rattleable*. He'd always seemed to have that slow city-slicker swagger that oozed confidence and arrogance. As if he were untouchable. That had always bothered Fletcher. He could understand confidence. The Navy had given him that in spades. He could tolerate arrogance, but generally only from someone who was a million times smarter than he was, and only in small doses.

But Decker had waltzed into town with a little too much of both, not a drop of humility, and what seemed like now, a few dozen secrets.

Fletcher needed to unravel those.

He rubbed the back of his neck, and the moment he stepped through his side door, he heard the pacing.

Not the rhythmic stroll of someone lost in thought.

No, this was agitated. Rapid-fire steps. The scrape of angry feet on tile. Muttered curses that got more colorful with every loop around his kitchen island.

He set his keys on the entry table and followed the noise into the kitchen.

Baily was in his Navy SEAL hoodie, hair scraped back into a bun that was already starting to fall apart. Her cheeks were flushed, her eyes flashing with anger. She didn't even notice him until he leaned his shoulder against the doorframe.

"I didn't realize my kitchen came with a treadmill," he said, trying to make light of whatever... this was.

She froze mid-step, shot him a glare, and held up her phone. "Julie."

Fletcher's jaw tightened. "Did she call again? Did you speak with her?"

"She sent me a text. Just a text. No call. No explanation. Just...links." Baily shoved the phone at him. "The flipping nerve of this woman."

He took it. Three links to job listings. All corporate positions. All in their parents' company. One in Delaware. One in Jacksonville. One in freaking California.

"None of these are even close to where she lives," he muttered.

"Exactly." Baily threw her hands up. "She spent the last conversation dangling my nephews like bait on a hook. Now she's implying I can only see them if I sell the marina and move states away? I tried to call her. Straight to voicemail. Then she texts me back, saying, 'Sorry, busy. I'll call another day.' And ends it with—wait for it—'Go ahead and apply when you're ready. I'll make sure you get a good recommendation.' Who the frack does she think she is?"

Fletcher shook his head. "That's ice-cold."

"It's worse than that," Baily snapped. "She wants me out of Calusa Cove. And I'm beginning to think she wants *my* marina. She's being subtle enough that if I go off, she'll say I'm overreacting. That *she's* simply being helpful. Offering options."

"Sweetheart, you're not overreacting." Fletcher walked over and took her by the shoulders. "But I need you to breathe. You've had one hell of a week, and I'm afraid you're going to burst into flames if you don't relax a little."

"I don't think I know how anymore." Baily's voice cracked, just slightly. "I don't care about the bullshit links. I don't care about Julie and her squeaky upbeat voice that sounds like a freaking Barbie Doll. But I care about those boys. I care that she's using them. I care that she's trying to erase Ken's life and rewrite it however she wants, even though I can't stand my brother right now."

"I know." He ran his hands down her arms, then pulled her close. "But you are not alone in this. And you're not the only one who sees it. We're going to figure this out. And when we do, Julie won't be able to hide behind those half-truths anymore."

Baily rested her forehead against his chest. "I'm so damn tired, Fletcher. I suck in a deep breath. And when I do, I feel like it's half full of water, and I'm drowning."

"I know, sweetheart. I know. And I wish I could make that go away for you." He kissed her hair, slow and warm. He wrapped his arms around her fully. Let her soak in the quiet steadiness he knew she needed more than anything.

"I feel like I've lost those boys. Lost them forever. She says they miss me, but they're so young, and I doubt she's even mentioned me in passing. I'm a long-forgotten memory to Todd and Chad." Her voice barely carried.

Fletcher's heart broke into a million pieces. He tilted her face up gently, brushing a thumb over her cheek. "Right now, you need to let go of all the noise. Just for a minute."

He kissed her, soft at first, then deeper as she leaned into him. It wasn't about passion—it was about comfort. About anchoring her. About letting her know she was loved. Valued. Cherished. That no matter what, she had people in her corner, and they wouldn't let her down.

Only, before he could pry his lips from hers, she

had her hands undoing the zipper of his pants. "Whoa," he managed. "What are you doing?"

"Getting rid of the noise." She yanked his shirt over his head and tossed it across the kitchen, before lifting her sweatshirt off, revealing the fact she had absolutely nothing on underneath but her boxers.

Her bare skin shimmered under the kitchen light, a subtle beckoning that sent ripples of anticipation through Fletcher. Her scent mixed with a hint of salt from the sea breeze that wafted in through the window. His hands instinctively sought the warmth of her skin, tracing the contours of her round breasts with a kind of reverence that made her gasp.

He leaned down, his lips finding the delicate curves of her neck, his stubbled cheek grazing against hers.

"Fletcher," she whispered his name like a plea, an invitation, or maybe both.

Fletcher didn't answer. He didn't need words just now. His hands spoke for him as they roamed over the expanse of her body, tracing a carnal map along the dip of her waist, the swell of her hips—promises of the intimate exploration to come.

Gently lifting her onto the kitchen counter, he stood between her parted legs. His eyes drank in Baily's form unabashedly, a predator eyeing its prey. A chuckle escaped past Baily's lips at his avid gaze, forcing him to glance up at her face and meet that laughing smile with his own bemused grin.

"Like what you see?" she challenged him.

"Do I really need to answer that?" He licked his finger before tracing a delicate circle on her tender flesh. He watched her face as her lips parted, and her eyelids fluttered.

Maintaining his gaze, he leaned closer, breathing in that familiar scent of salt and sunshine that was so unique to Baily. It landed somewhere close to addictive.

He lapped at her tender folds, sucking in all her sweet juices as she squirmed on his kitchen counter, her fingers digging into his scalp. He would never tire of pleasing her. She was the air that he breathed. The water he drank. She was his world, and all he wanted was to make hers right again.

"Fletcher," she moaned out his name like it was some sort of sacred chant meant for only him to hear. She tasted like heaven.

He glided a finger inside, and she immediately clutched around him, her hips rolling against his mouth, her moans coming louder, driving him crazy.

"Yes, yes, yes…" She dug one of her heels into his shoulder, leaned back on the counter, and tightened her grip around his finger as her climax spilled out. "Please. I need you inside me now."

As quickly as he could, he shimmied out of his jeans, lowered her to the floor, turned her, and bent her over the counter. He smoothed his hands over her round ass as he eased inside.

Baily's breath hitched as he filled her completely.

His hands gripped her hips, anchoring her against him as he sank in deeper, reveling in the pleasure coursing through him.

"Fletcher..." Her voice was a soft whisper carried on the morning air as she turned her head over her shoulder, catching his gaze with her feverish eyes.

With a slow, burning thrust, he withdrew, pausing near the edge before driving back into her welcoming warmth with a grunt. This wasn't about raw desire; it was primal yet tender—a silent promise inked on their entwined bodies.

Each thrust ignited their shared heat, a dance as old as humanity itself. Fletcher watched his reflection in the kitchen window. His brow screwed up in concentration as he pumped into Baily with all the loving force he could muster. The sight of her bracing herself against the countertop, her body accepting him so wholly, nearly pushed him over the edge.

But not yet. He battled for control against his own impending climax, wanting to draw this moment out—as if somehow time could ease their troubles away.

Baily's moans grew louder each time he buried himself inside her. Each gasp punctuated by his name was a testament sent straight through his core, confirming that this—she alone—was where he belonged.

Her body trembled against the counter, fingertips gripping at the surface. Her climax washed over him in waves, triggering his own eruption. He was falling over the precipice, tumbling into oblivion with her whimpered name on his lips.

He ran his hands up and down her back, kissed her neck, all while trying desperately to catch his breath.

She dropped her forehead to the counter and sighed. "Well, now. I think I'm hungry."

He laughed. "That's one way to work up an appetite." He turned her, kissed her tenderly, hopefully showing her just how much she mattered.

When they finally pulled apart, she gave a shaky breath. "Thank you."

"Anytime." He smiled and went about finding their discarded clothing. Once they were both decent again, he leaned against the counter. "And next time you need to curse someone out, I'll be happy to let you use me in every room in this house…or you can take out your aggression on the punching bag in the garage."

She laughed softly, tension melting from her shoulders. "Might take you up on that…the punching bag, that is."

"I kind of hope you're joking." He tugged her toward the living room. "But for now, you're gonna sit your ass down, put your feet up, and let me make you something that passes for food."

"You cook now?" she teased, with a softness that hadn't been in her voice fifteen minutes ago.

"For you? I'll even break out the fancy toaster."

The smile she gave him didn't fix anything. But it was a start.

And Fletcher would take that win—because they were going to need each other more than ever.

CHAPTER 9

BAILY STOOD at the first dock of the marina and took the line Silas tossed her, tying off the bow. "Good day out there?" she asked.

"Mostly floated, staring at the mangroves." Silas finished with the stern cleat and jumped to the dock. "I think the committee might have found the next trimmer for this place, which we sorely need. All we need is for Dawson to finish that in-depth background check. He promised he'd pull out the stops. Use all his connections. Even mentioned back-channel ones."

"He's tired of big cases. He wants to go back to stolen bikes and kids doing dumb things. He wanted small town life, not big city problems." She leaned in and hugged Silas. He looked like he needed one, and she kind of did, too.

"Here." Silas stuffed some cash in her hand. He squeezed. "Don't insult me by trying to shove it back at me." He lowered his chin. "I have a stake in what happens to this place, and I know the kind of trouble you're in. The whole town does."

"Wonderful. Just what I need. Gossip."

He touched her cheek softly. "It's not like that. The good people of this town care about you. We don't like what's happening. Honestly, some people fear what's next. Of what's lurking around the next corner. We want to prevent whatever's brewing, not simply prepare for what's coming. Let us help. It's not much. It certainly won't solve anything. But every little bit helps."

"Thank you." She stuffed the money in her pocket. She didn't have any fight left. Only rage and the desire to defend what was her legacy.

"Glad you're finally seeing things my way." He smiled. "Because some of us have taken up a fund if that loan ever gets called in."

"Jesus, Silas. How do you know about that?"

"The Everglades has ears."

"That sounds like speak for, 'Silas has been eavesdropping on conversations and decided to wander through town, chatting with everyone, making my business, the town's business.'" She folded her arms. "So, everyone knows about that loan?"

"No one knows about that. It's all about the fact that this place is struggling, when everyone already knew your dad left you in debt. That was no secret, especially when you sold the family home. But the 'Save the Marina Fund' took on a life of its own when the gas was stolen and your apartment was broken into." He squeezed her forearm. "Take the help, Baily. Everyone in this town wants this marina, and you, to stay exactly the way it is."

"That's funny. The place is falling down. It needs so much work."

"You've been doing some renovations when you can. The rest will come when Dawson and the rest of those boys' figure this all out." Silas smiled. "I have no doubt that they will. I know I gave them a hard time when they all rolled into town. But they're good men. Solid. And Fletcher, he loves you. He'd do anything for you. Remember that, because someone like him is hard to come by. I should know. I got that with my wife," he said. "Speaking of her, I need to get home. She worries about me these days."

"You haven't been yourself…since Dewey."

"I feel betrayed."

"I know that feeling well," she said. All these years, she'd believed her dad had simply made poor decisions in the wake of grief. Or just dropped the ball while trying to raise two kids by himself and holding onto a struggling business. But that's not what happened. Not at all. No. Her brother had betrayed her and her dad in the worst way, and she hadn't a clue as to why. "Come on. I'll walk up to the parking lot with you." She turned, resting her hand in the crook of his elbow.

"Has Dawson found any clues as to who broke into your place yet?" Silas asked.

"Nothing yet." She sighed. "Both he and Fletcher believe whoever did it was looking for something. They just don't know what, and I can't figure out what I'd have of value anyone would go rummaging through my apartment for."

"Dawson…he's a smart one. If he thinks they were there for something specific, then I'm sure he's seeing something in some way the rest of us can't. Let him do his job."

"I am, but it still sucks."

They walked the rest of the way in silence, and just as they reached the lot, Keaton's fancy pick-up rolled in with Hayes and Audra.

"Have a nice evening, Silas" she said.

"You as well." Silas waved to the Keaton and the gang before jumping into his dilapidated old Jeep and firing up the engine.

"Hey there." Audra raced across the parking lot and wrapped her arms around Baily. "How ya holding up?"

"I'm between wanting to wrestle a python or bring Ken back from the dead and hold him to the fire."

Audra nodded. "I've been where you are, especially when it comes to your brother."

Keaton and Hayes pulled out a few boxes from the truck.

"Mind if we get started installing the new security system?" Hayes asked.

"We'll need access to the computers," Keaton said.

"I just need to unlock the office. If you need anything else, Audra and I will be upstairs dealing with the mess that was made of my apartment."

"Thanks." Hayes nodded. "If you ladies need any heavy lifting done, let us know."

"Yeah, because Dawson doesn't want Audra... exerting herself," Keaton said.

Audra rolled her eyes. "My overprotective, overbearing husband is a pain in the ass." She looped her arm around Baily. "We'd better get started. I've only got a few hours before exhaustion will settle in. Who knew being pregnant would suck the energy right out of me."

"Wait until this baby is born." Baily laughed. "Midnight and 3 AM feedings. Crying all day. You're going to be—"

"Ridiculously happy," Audra said. "Besides, I have me a Dawson, and he'll be the best *daddy* ever."

"Jesus, everyone is right. You make that word sound so dirty," Baily said.

"I blurted it out once during sex. Should've seen the look on Dawson's face. It was too funny, and now I just can't stop myself." Audra shook her head.

"That's just wrong." Baily stepped into the main room of the marina, pulled her keys from her back pocket, and unlocked the office door. "There you go, boys."

"Thank you, ma'am." Hayes set a box on the floor. "We'll be a few hours, but I'm confident we can get this up and running tonight."

"Thanks, I appreciate it." Slowly, she climbed the stairs. When she'd first sold the family home, she'd been depressed about losing all her childhood memories. So much of her life had been wrapped up in that house. She'd thought she'd lose what little of her mother she remembered. However, she'd quickly learned that those memories would always be with her. They were in her heart, and no one could take that from her.

Besides, that house had been too much. Too big. She didn't need all that space.

She stood at the opening of what had been her sanctuary. Her private space. The place she'd end her day with a glass of wine, a good book, and thoughts of what her future might look like when the world righted itself.

"You okay?" Audra asked.

"Yeah," Baily managed.

The apartment still smelled like fear.

Not hers—at least not anymore—but something far more primitive. Like a warning left behind by whoever had stomped through her life and overturned the pieces. The scent clung to the walls like mildew…thick, sour, and impossible to scrub away.

Baily stood in the doorway, frozen, staring at the carnage left behind. She hadn't really cried. Not when she'd first walked back into the apartment. Not when she'd seen her dresser drawers dumped, her clothes cut into ribbons. Not when she'd spotted the framed photo of her and Ken shattered on the floor, glass shards scattered like landmines.

But now, standing there, basking in the knowledge that Dawson had no solid leads, that the crime lab had found nothing of use from the security footage, frustration threatened to crack her right down the middle.

"They didn't leave a single damn fingerprint we can use," she muttered, finally easing into the small apartment. She hadn't a clue as to where to start.

Audra looked up from the hallway, where she opened a garbage bag. Her wild red hair was pulled into a haphazard bun. "Dawson said there were too many prints downstairs and only yours and Fletcher's up here, so he's thinking they wore gloves, all careful like, and that's why he really believes they were looking for something."

"They weren't careful," Baily snapped. "They weren't even methodical when they tore through this place. But they knew I'd be gone. They knew what to break to hurt me."

"And yet, they didn't take a thing that we can tell," Audra added quietly. "Except the gas."

Baily's hand tightened around the mop. "And a piece of my sanity." She turned her back to the room and walked toward the window, flinging it open to let in the breeze. Below, she could see the marina docks glinting under the mid-evening sun. Hayes and Keaton were crouched side by side, installing the new security system—state-of-the-art, motion-tracked, facial recognition tech that probably cost more than she'd made last quarter.

She hadn't argued when they'd told her they were doing it. She hadn't even asked who was paying. Fletcher had just kissed her forehead and said, *We're not asking. We're doing. You've been targeted twice, and we're not playing games with your safety.*

How could she argue with that logic? She wasn't too stupid to live.

"Place still feels like yours," Audra said softly, stepping into the room with a box of torn books in her arms. "Even after all this."

"Sometimes, I'm not sure what's mine anymore." Baily gestured toward the couch cushions that had been gutted and tossed, like a fox had made a den in them. "Ken and I used to sit up here when we were kids. Eat popcorn. Watch cartoons while we waited for Dad to finish work, so we could do whatever. That's where I bandaged his busted knuckles after he got into it with some drunk jerk during the Fourth of July. And now…"

"Now you can't even picture him doing that," Audra said, finishing the thought for her.

Baily nodded. "It's like the Ken I loved, the Ken I grew up with—he vanished. Julie happened, and everything changed."

"I never met her." Audra crouched near a toppled photo album and started gathering loose pictures. "She came into his life after he joined the Navy. I thought it was after he showed up in that shithole I was living in a year after my father died, but I've since learned he'd already met her by then. He might not have been dating her. Or maybe he was. The boys are a little fuzzy on that timeline."

"I think they dated in secret for a while. Keaton told me that he always thought they knew each other better than Ken let on when he first started bringing her around. But he changed when things with Julie got serious. He stopped calling as often. Then it was just holiday texts. The occasional voicemail. When he did visit, it was quick. But he always had something to say about me selling the marina."

"I always thought something shifted in him before he left," Audra murmured. "Not something big…just subtle. Like he'd decided he was done with Calusa Cove. Done with all of us. Including me."

Baily sank into a chair. "You've said that before."

Audra looked up, eyes solemn. "I thought something was eating at him. I would ask him about it, and he'd brush it off like he was just worried about me. About us and him joining the military. But when my dad went missing, he was so different. I know I was a hot mess. I get that I made things hard for everyone. But I swear, Ken was acting off. He would get angry at me and demand I stop the insanity over my father's disappearance."

Baily swallowed. "If he did…if he knew Massey killed your dad…"

"I hate that I'm even thinking that he did. Some days I'd look into his eyes, and I'd see guilt. Like he wanted to unload something. But other days, all I saw was frustration and misplaced anger…at me."

A knock at the apartment door pulled them both from the conversation.

Fletcher stepped inside, face tight with something between wariness and focus. He was still in his boots, his jacket damp at the edges from the misty evening rain that had settled in the Glades.

"Sorry to interrupt, ladies," he said with a nod. "How are things going?"

"As you can see." Baily waved her hand. "We've barely made a dent."

"You don't have to rush this." He leaned against the doorjamb. "You know you can stay with me for as long as you like."

"Not the point." A smile tugged at her lips. Being in Fletcher's bed again had brought a small amount of peace. A tiny bit of calm in the wake of a hurricane.

"Did you come to help?" Audra asked.

Fletcher shook his head. "Just talked to Dawson, and he got an interesting phone call."

"From who?" Baily asked.

"Decker Brown, and he wants to meet," Fletcher said. "Said it was important. Dawson thought it might be a good idea for me to join them."

Audra straightened. "He might take that as an act of aggression."

"I don't believe your husband gives a shit what Decker thinks about me being there." Fletcher looked at Baily. "I'm headed to Massey's to find out. I'll text you when I'm on my way home."

Baily's stomach dropped. "I kinda want to be a fly on that wall."

Audra folded her arms. "So do I. I wonder if he's gonna talk plans for the old Crab Shack."

"He could be feeling the pressure. Everyone in town is talking about it, and they aren't being too welcoming to Decker anymore. People like Decker don't like pressure." Fletcher kissed Baily's forehead. "Finish cleaning. I'll be back soon."

As he left, Baily stood by the window again and watched the waves lap at the dock pilings. The water looked calm. Deceptively so.

But everything in her gut said the real storm hadn't even hit yet.

CHAPTER 10

THE PARKING LOT behind Massey's Pub was quiet, except for the low hum of the refrigeration units and the occasional call of a night heron overhead. Fletcher stood next to Dawson's unmarked SUV, arms folded across his chest as he leaned back against the bumper. A cold front had pushed down from the north, putting a chill in the warm Florida air.

Fletcher welcomed cooler temperatures. He'd never minded the heat, but it was always nice to get a reprieve.

"How's Baily?" Dawson asked as he stared at the pub, gaze fixed on...something.

"She's hanging in there," Fletcher said. "She's tougher than she gives herself credit for, but all this with Julie, the marina, Ken... It's wearing on her."

Dawson nodded, stuffing his hands in the pockets of his jacket. "Audra says she's barely sleeping. That she jumps at shadows now, but that she does so with fists at the ready. We need to get ahead of this before something else pushes her over the edge and she reacts with vengeance."

"Baily has never had much of a temper. Not like the short fuse her brother often had. But when she snaps, she goes off like a rocket."

"That's what I want to avoid. I've seen that in my wife, and we both know what it's like to be backed into a corner."

Fletcher's jaw ticked. "I'm guessing Baily and Audra won't find anything useful in Baily's apartment."

Dawson nodded. "I'd say whoever ransacked that place found what they were looking for, or they'll be back, and the latter part of that statement scares me, especially because we haven't a clue as to what they're looking for."

"My folks died a few months after Baily's dad," Fletcher said. "We were deployed. My folks never had the chance to hand off that notebook that Ray left for me. It makes me wonder if there might be something else hidden somewhere in my house." He arched a brow. "I've never really gone through the house. There are boxes and crap everywhere. Baily has been bugging me for months to clear the place out. I think it's time I do that. Maybe we'll find something."

"Have you gone through all the nooks and crannies of the marina?"

"We have," Fletcher said. "But it can't hurt to do it

again. Baily has inventory in the back room, so I'll go through all of that."

"Good." Dawson shifted his weight. "We're missing a big piece of this puzzle. Like we're sitting on something that could blow the lid off this, but we don't know what rock to overturn to find it."

"Needle in a haystack," Fletcher mumbled. "Did Decker give you any indication of what he wanted?"

"Nope." Dawson shook his head. "All he said was that he *needed* to meet. That he had something important to discuss, and it couldn't wait. His voice sounded strained. It cracked at times. But I had no facial cues to help me understand what that might have been all about."

"I don't trust this guy. He could be fishing for information about our plans."

Dawson nodded. "That thought did cross my mind, but why call the cop? Why ask for a meeting with the guy who makes a living asking questions and solving riddles? Why not Keaton or Hayes? Or even you?"

"He'd never call me for that. We're too combative with each other," Fletcher said.

"True, but I make even less sense. Hayes would be the one I'd call if I were in Decker's shoes." Dawson widened his stance and looped his fingers into his belt—typical of Dawson, even out of uniform. He'd taken to being a police officer like he'd been born wearing a badge. "Hayes has that cool, laid-back vibe that screams boy next door. He's all warm and inviting. People instinctively trust him and…" Dawson's let the words tail off as he stared up at the sky. "When we were captured, he was the first one they tried to break. They went at him hard. For hours. His cell was right next to mine, and I heard it." He rubbed both hands over his face as if to try to erase the memories. "I don't know what made them shift their attention to Ken."

"We'll never know," Fletcher said softly. "That mission was fucked before it started. We all knew it. Ken was freaking out long before we jumped from that chopper and had boots on the ground. He told me he hadn't signed the re-enlistment papers and that he had no intention of doing so. That he was done. That his life was with Julie, the boys, and working for her family's business. He couldn't wait to get out. He was gleeful about it."

"Had that mission not ended the way it did, would you have still re-enlisted?" Dawson asked. That was the one thing no one ever really talked about because it hadn't really mattered. What was done was done. That mission had destroyed them both emotionally and physically.

Hayes's shoulder probably couldn't have withstood the fitness test, and he would've been sidelined to a desk job. Keaton's injuries could've done the same. Fletcher and Dawson's bodies had recovered well enough, but their minds were still suffering the consequences.

Staying in the Navy after that, at their ages, hadn't been an option.

"It's hard to say," Fletcher said. "Baily wasn't talking too much, but you know I wanted her in my life, and that always meant I needed to come back here. However, the Navy—being a SEAL—had become part of who I was. I'm not sure. I guess it would've all come down to the same thing it always did before I signed those papers."

Dawson snorted. "A trip back here to see if Baily would have anything to do with you. If it was a no, the pen came out."

"Exactly. It was a never-ending cycle." Fletcher sighed.

"How are things going with the two of you?" Dawson arched a brow and cracked a smile.

Fletcher chuckled. "Well enough. It's comfortable. Like a favorite pair of slippers that are worn out at the toes, but you're never going to get rid of. But at the same time, it's all shiny and new."

"That has to be the weirdest thing you've ever said," Dawson said.

"I don't know how else to explain it, and I don't want to test fate, so I'm just following her lead. Doing my best to be there for her. Not push the wrong buttons and make damn sure she doesn't lose all that she holds dear."

"You're turning into an old sap, you know that?"

"We all are," Fletcher mused. "Are you sure you want me in there for this? He called you, not me, and

Decker and I... Well, we don't usually have nice things to say to one another. Just letting his name roll off my tongue makes me want to haul off and connect my fist with his ugly ass face."

"I wouldn't have called you if I didn't think it was a good idea." Dawson's gaze met his. "But you need to let me be the one to do most of the talking. No posturing, no chest beating. Let's find out why he called."

"I can probably behave," Fletcher muttered, pushing off the SUV. "As long as he doesn't say something that pisses me off."

Dawson chuckled dryly. "Come on."

The pub door creaked open on well-worn hinges. The familiar scent of fried seafood, spilled beer, and lemon cleaner hit Fletcher like a wave. It was early enough that the place wasn't too crowded. A few locals nursed beers at the far end of the bar, but there were still a few empty tables. But that would change.

They spotted Decker Brown immediately.

He sat in a booth near the back, hunched over a glass of whiskey. His usually perfectly styled hair was a mess, and his blazer looked like it had been slept in. He was twitchy, fingers drumming against the side of the glass, gaze darting around the bar like he wasn't supposed to be there, and he was terrified he was about to get caught.

He glanced in their direction, and his eyes went wide. He lifted his glass, brought it to his lips, dropped his head back, and drained the glass.

"Good evening, Decker." Dawson stood at the edge of the booth, while Fletcher hung back two steps.

"Dawson," Decker said, voice low. "Didn't expect you to bring backup."

Dawson slid into the booth across from him. Fletcher wasn't quite sure what to do yet, so he simply inched forward, trying not to crowd Decker, and yet, making his presence known…and felt.

"Is there a reason Fletcher can't be here? Is this official police business?" Dawson asked with a calm, even tone. It wasn't accusatory. Just a simple question, but it lingered in the air like thick fog.

"I wanted to speak to you. Alone." Decker's jaw flexed. "This is a…sensitive matter."

"Does it have to do with putting in a bid for the old Crab Shack?" Dawson asked.

"That's part of it, but not the sum total." Decker turned, waving his hand toward the waitress.

"If it's about that, then Fletcher stays. He's one of my business partners in that deal, not to mention his home is one lot over. This affects him." Dawson scooted further in the booth, motioning to Fletcher to sit. It wasn't a casual wave of the hand. It was more like an order. One that Fletcher wouldn't ignore.

Decker looked at Fletcher. His eyes were bloodshot. His shoulders were slumped and seemed to carry the weight of the world. "Fine. Might as well have a seat."

Fletcher was already halfway in.

The waitress showed up. "What can I get you boys?"

"I'll take another bourbon," Decker said. "Make it a double."

"Tequila on the rocks." Dawson nodded.

"Same for me," Fletcher said. "Food, anyone? Because I haven't had dinner, and I'm starving."

"Yeah, sure. How about we get the seafood appetizer platter?" Decker leaned back, raking his fingers through his hair. "That's enough food for all of us."

"You're going to share?" Fletcher asked, wishing he'd kept his sarcasm to himself.

"I'm even gonna foot the bill," Decker said in a hot, mocking tone.

"Let's settle things down a few levels." Dawson nodded to the waitress, who scurried away like she'd seen a snake dare a chicken to cross the gator-infested river.

A thick silence filled the booth. Fletcher decided to wait for his drink before saying another word. Not that pouring alcohol on this situation would be a good idea, but this wasn't his meeting. He was only along for the ride.

The quiet stretched, only filled in by the country music lazily playing in the speakers and the chatter of the other patrons. The waitress brought their beverages.

"I'll keep a watchful eye on these, and when you boys are close to the bottom of the glass, I'll bring another round," she said.

"Thanks." Fletcher lifted his tequila and sipped. He'd make it last. He needed to remain sharp around this slimy asshole.

"So, how about you tell us why you called this meeting?" Dawson raised his drink and took a long, slow draw as he eyed Decker.

"I'm not even sure where to begin." Decker exhaled slowly. "It's a long, convoluted story, and there are still some holes and missing pieces that don't make sense."

Fletcher glanced toward Dawson, but continued to nurse his drink, which kept him from saying—or doing—something he might regret.

"That's not helpful," Dawson said. "Why don't we begin with why you started coming around Calusa Cove four months ago?"

Decker stared into his dark liquid for a long moment. He sipped, scratched the side of his face, and sipped some more. "Have you ever heard of a private equity investment firm called Sea Glass Under the Stars?" Not once did he lift his gaze.

"We have," Fletcher said. "But what does that firm have to do with you, this town, and your bid on the Old Crab Shack?"

"It's a bit of a story." Decker leaned back, tilted his head, and swiped a hand down his face. "Please give me a little time to tell it. I promise most of it will make sense in the end."

"All right." Dawson nodded. "The floor is yours."

"But we reserve the right to interrupt and ask questions," Fletcher added.

Decker blew out a puff of air and nodded. "About five years ago, I was working for someone else. Someone who knew I had aspirations of going it alone and seemed to be supportive of my goals, even though that meant I'd leave the company and start my own."

"That's mighty big of your old boss, especially since you'd become the competition," Dawson said.

"Not in my mind." Decker tossed his hand over the back of the booth. Some of his confident swagger had returned. "The man I worked for did mostly new builds and neighborhood developments. That really wasn't my passion. I liked restoration, but definitely not remodels. I wanted to do things like remake old churches. And when I do new construction, it's about adding flair and flavor to what's already in the surrounding area." Decker shook his head and laughed. "My old boss used to call me a hippy. Said my ideas were too…out there. But take my project over on Marco Island. I'm rebuilding a couple of old warehouses and turning them into—"

"Restaurants and some local hangout," Fletcher said. "We heard all about it and can't say the locals were all that thrilled."

"Well, now that depends on who you talk to because I nearly walked away from that deal." Decker leaned forward, resting his hands on the table. "You boys think I don't care about people and community, when I know that matters. I understood that the county was torn. Afraid of change. I let them sit around and discuss it and figure out if it's what they…and the townspeople…really wanted. Sure, there are a few who vehemently disapprove. And that will always be the case. Change is hard. But I'm not destroying the fabric of the neighborhood. I'm not changing the feel of it either. I'm hopefully adding to it."

"I almost believe you." Fletcher raised his drink.

Decker let out a sarcastic grunt. "I suppose I'm either a really good salesman and liar." He took a good swallow of his bourbon. "Or I'm just fucking passionate about what I do."

"We're getting sidetracked," Dawson said.

But before Decker could say another word, the waitress showed up with their food. That was probably a good thing, because it allowed tensions to settle.

Fletcher loaded his plate and mentally prepared for the rest of whatever was going to come out of Decker's mouth. So far, he actually believed the man. At least about his passion. The gleam in his eyes couldn't be faked.

"So, you were talking about Sea Glass," Dawson said.

Decker nodded. "I made my move and left Tate Construction. Six months into putting a bid on my first project, Tate came after me, hard. Said I stole the plans right out from under him, which was utter bullshit because I didn't even know that Tate was all of a sudden moving into the restoration business."

"Is he doing that now?" Fletcher asked. "Because we did a little checking up on you and all that. It disappeared, and he went back to building track homes."

"He went far enough to make it look good and make me nervous." Decker polished off a shrimp, downed his drink, and waved to the waitress. "Can I get a Coke, please?"

"No more bourbon?" the waitress asked.

Decker shook his head, sitting up a little taller. "Tate made just enough noise that I struggled to get my business off the ground. I was considering leaving South Florida until Tessa Gilbert came strolling into my world. She was all glamorous and beautiful, and, at first, I was all in."

"All right. Let's cut to the chase," Dawson said. "We know she funded your business. We know she was your girlfriend. What we don't know is why this story matters."

"I'm not surprised you know all that." Decker wiped his fingers on his napkin and pushed his plate aside. The waitress set a tall, cold soda in front of him and he took his time slurping half that down. "For about five minutes, I thought Tessa was interested in me. The man. Two months in, when I was telling her about my problems with Tate, she offered to help. She'd give me the money I needed, and she'd smooth things over with all the people she knew.

And she knew people, let me tell you. I didn't think anything of it. She was my bed partner, and while I didn't love her—never loved her—it worked. Until it didn't." He craned his neck. "She started putting projects in front of me that I wanted nothing to do with. Things that would tear communities apart. Or didn't make sense to me."

"What about the Marco Island one? Was that her?" Fletcher asked.

"No." Decker shook his head. "As a matter of fact, she was downright pissed off when I agreed to take that one on. It's one of the reasons I ended things with her, although she didn't take that too well." He sighed. "Then one night, about five months ago, she came to me and told me she needed me to start coming to Calusa Cove." Decker arched a brow.

"Now, that's interesting." Dawson's expression didn't change.

"I wouldn't go that far." Fletcher rubbed his hands on his jeans. "Why? What does she want to do with this town?"

"It's not her, but I didn't know that right away." Decker closed his eyes. His chest moved as he took in a heavy breath. "I told her I didn't have time for whatever games she was playing." He blinked. "A week later, a packet came to my house. Inside it, there was information on all of you…and Baily."

Fletcher pounded his fist on the table.

"Relax," Dawson said softly. "Go on."

"Also inside were fabricated images of me taking

bribes from city officials. A couple of images of her face, beaten, with a note that stated that if I didn't do what she wanted, she'd ruin me—and that she had more dirt. More things on me that would not only bury me but put me in prison."

Fletcher glanced between Dawson and Decker.

Dawson rubbed his index finger and thumb over his chin, like he always did when deep in thought. "I gotta ask. Any chance these things are true?"

"No," Decker said. "But I was scared. I've worked hard to get where I am. Poor kid from Miami. Grew up with nothin'. I'd come here. I'd watch. Observe. And I'd report back, just like I was told. But then, the old Crab Shack burned down, and things changed."

"She asked you to put in a bid," Fletcher said.

Decker nodded. "I've been trying to find a way to claw myself out of this mess. And then, yesterday, I thought. Fuck it. I don't care. None of it's true. A good lawyer would be able to help me prove that, so I told Tessa I didn't give a shit. To go ahead and burn me."

"Ah, so that's what that phone call was all about in front of the coffee shop," Fletcher mumbled.

"I didn't realize you'd heard, but yeah," Decker said. "Only, now it's worse."

"Worse how?" Dawson asked.

"Tessa got someone else involved. Someone who doesn't just threaten. They call in hitmen to do their dirty work, and people don't ever find the bodies." Decker fiddled with his cup.

"That's a big accusation." Dawson leaned forward, elbows on the table, his cop attitude coming off his skin.

"But it's the truth." Decker held Dawson's gaze. He didn't waver. Didn't back down.

Fletcher was almost impressed.

"I know these people. I grew up in Miami trying to avoid people like them. People who took advantage of the less fortunate. I watched as my neighbors were offered things that were too good to be true. All they had to do was trust. Sign on the dotted line, and we'll solve your money problems. Before you know it, you'll be able to afford college for little Johnny. It's all a lie. All one big scam to control the streets of Miami and other cities like it." Decker exhaled.

"Are we talking a cartel?" Fletcher asked.

"Oh, they have connections to cartels." Decker cocked his head. "They work with them, building a stronger pipeline of drugs, guns, and human trafficking into the country."

"I'm starting to wonder if you're not connected," Dawson said.

Decker raised both hands. "I swear to you I'm not. I just know this shit because I've got two cousins and an uncle in prison because they worked for these people." He sighed. "They know the right buttons to push. And they've been pushing mine for years, I just didn't know it." He shook his head like a wet dog. "I couldn't believe it when they called. I mean, I knew they were behind everything the second I was sent here, and Baily was involved. Whatever made me think I could put them, or the hold they have on my family, behind me, I don't know. But Baily's not going to be able stand against them either. These people are powerful and—"

"Wait a second." Fletcher lowered his chin. "Who exactly are we talking about?"

"The Barbaros. Ken's in-laws," Decker said flatly.

"What the fuck?" Fletcher and Dawson stared at each other for a long stretch while that all settled in.

Hitmen. Drugs. Miami. It didn't make sense.

"Are you saying the Barbaros are running drugs through Miami?" Dawson asked. "They don't live there."

"They have a manufacturing plant there, and it's right near one of the bigger ports. They also have one in Jacksonville, Virginia, Delaware, and a couple in California, as well as Texas." Decker waggled a finger. "I grew up near that plant in Miami. I did my best to avoid it and the people working there. Only I had lots of family who couldn't. Money was tight. Jobs scarce. I got lucky. Or so I thought."

"Let me ask you this." Fletcher held Decker's gaze. "Did you steal Baily's gas? Break into her apartment?"

"Don't lie to us," Dawson added. "It will just piss me off."

Decker shook his head. "They know better than to ask an amateur to do something like that. I would've gotten caught. But I can guarantee it was someone who works for them. Someone who's watching." He glanced around, gaze shifting nervously.

"Are you worried they're watching now?" Fletcher asked.

Decker chuckled. "I was told to reach out." He shrugged. "Told to make my intentions with the Crab Shack clear, and that I've got more money and power than you. Thing is, I'd love to develop that land, but not as an owner. Not now. But I'd work for you, which is not what they want. They want me to work for them. To build what they want so they can run whatever through this town and launder money through small businesses that will quiet the noise in bigger cities."

"Now I feel like you're taking us for a ride," Fletcher said. "Why would you switch sides?"

"Someone's gotta draw up the plans, pull the permits, and oversee whatever vision you boys have." Decker held up his hands. "But that's a discussion for another day."

"So, what do you want from us?" Dawson asked evenly. "Why are you even telling us this?"

"I want out," Decker said. "I want protection. And I want to burn them down without destroying everything I've built...or without hurting anyone in this town."

Dawson leaned back. "You're suggesting we help you double-cross the Barbaros? Our best friends' in-laws. Based on your word?"

"I've got evidence on who they are. And I've got

some family willing to talk…quietly," Decker said. "I'm also willing to let you use me. I'll report back to them that this meeting went just like I told them it would. That you told me to fuck off and get out of town. That I told you good old boys that I wasn't going anywhere. Then I stick around. We act like we still don't like each other. I'll let you tap my phone. My cabin. I'll give you everything. The Barbaros destroyed my neighborhood in Miami. I watched them do it. They'll kill Calusa Cove if they get a foothold with even one business here."

Fletcher narrowed his eyes. "Why should we trust you?"

"Because I'm the only one who's dealt with them directly. Because I came to you instead of running. Because I like this place. I didn't think I would, but I do. I'm not your enemy."

Dawson drummed his fingers on the table. "If we do this, you'll follow our lead. You'll tell us everything. You'll wear a wire if we ask. You'll keep your nose clean." He leaned forward. "And if you fuck us over, I'll be the one putting cuffs on your wrists and locking you up in a cell. I'll also be enjoying that."

Decker nodded, taking the bill the waitress had left moments ago. He tossed some cash on the table. "I'll do whatever it takes to get out from under them and to make sure they don't ruin this place."

"Interesting that you don't seem to be afraid of the latter part of that statement." Dawson nudged Fletcher to get out of the booth. "Because if you screw us—if you lie again—there won't be enough lawyers in the state to protect you."

"It won't matter. The Barbaros will find someone to put a bullet in the back of my head and feed me to the gators." Decker eased toward the door.

Fletcher lingered a moment. "One last thing. If you so much as look at Baily the wrong way, I'll forget every promise I made to Dawson and make you disappear into the Everglades."

"You know what, Fletcher?" Decker said. "I like Baily. She's a good person. And she's damn lucky to have a man like you. Believe it or not, I mean that."

Fletcher watched as Decker headed toward his fancy Range Rover, all decked out with every bell and whistle. "What do you make of all that?"

Dawson had already pulled out his cell. His fingers flew across the screen. "I really don't know. Texting Keaton, Hayes, and Chloe…especially Chloe. I want her looking into Decker's…" Dawson glanced up. "You can't make this shit up."

"So, you believe him?"

"Trevor, Tripp's kid, he always said there was another group trying to muscle their way into Paul Massey's drug business. Mentioned the cartel was working on a deal, but could never quite come to terms, but managed to avoid a war." Dawson stuck his phone in his pocket and paced.

That was never a good sign. When Dawson paced, his mind was spinning. When his brain did that, shit was about to go sideways. "Trevor didn't have a name. The cartel? They ain't given one up. But what Decker's saying sorta tracks."

"What do you mean by *sorta*."

"I've heard chatter of a big-time crime organization looking for small towns to quietly buy or develop local businesses to launder money. It's all very *Ozark,* as in that TV show. But do it in a coastal town like this, they can also move small amounts of product and even human trafficking." Dawson raked his fingers through his hair. "Criminals like that think cops like me can either be bought off or are just stupid."

"Okay, but it's the Barbaros we're talking about," Fletcher said, folding his arms across his chest. "We've had dinner at their flipping mansion."

"I know." Dawson sighed. "I don't know what kind of game they think they're playing, but it started years ago. At this point, I'm sure we're simply collateral damage."

"Jesus, I don't want to have to tell Baily all this." Fletcher lifted his gaze to the sky. "There's no way Ken didn't know. Maybe he distanced himself to protect us, or maybe he did it because he didn't want to get caught. But either way, he screwed his dad and sister over. There's no way to reconcile that."

"But you have to admit that Ken was acting all weird near the end," Dawson said. "He was solid in the field, but when we weren't deployed, there was something lurking behind his eyes. I always believed it was because he was just done with the Navy. That he was ready for something else and had one foot out the door."

"That's what we all thought," Fletcher added softly. "However, knowing he knew about that loan, and that notebook Ray left proves that, changes everything. The question we have to ask ourselves, especially after that conversation with Decker, is if Ken knew what he got his father involved in before Ray signed that loan…or did all that knowledge come in after the fact? Because, as much as we're finding out that Ken did some shady things, I still struggle to believe that he willingly buried the marina in debt."

Dawson let out a long breath. "If the Barbaros were making a play for this town years ago, they might've seen Ken as a way in since he did once deal for Massey." Dawson arched a brow. "We don't know how or why Paul let him go so easily. I mean, Ken could've taken down that operation, but he didn't. Why?"

"I'd like to believe it's because Massey had something on him, not because Ken had some weird loyalty to the man."

Dawson nodded. "Like maybe the Barbaros were holding something over his head. Could've manufactured some bullshit like they're doing with Decker, or it could've been something as simple as, if you don't do this for us, we'll ruin your career because we have proof you used to be a drug dealer for the cartel. That'll get you kicked out of the Navy real fast."

"And once he had kids with their daughter, they

could've held those boys over him," Fletcher said. "But we're pulling in a lot of what-ifs with no real knowledge right now, except our gut feelings that Ken was hiding something. We need to dig more."

"Agreed." Dawson inched closer to his vehicle. "I better get going. I'll let you know if I find anything."

"I'll see you later." Fletcher headed toward his truck. His mind filled with questions and no real answers. He slipped behind the steering wheel. The only thing he knew for sure was that he hadn't really known his best friend at all.

CHAPTER 11

Baily crouched near the edge of the dock, tightening the hose fitting for one of the water lines while Bingo tossed off a coil of rope. The sun hung low behind a blanket of haze, casting a soft gray hue over the marina. The air was cool, which was pleasant, and the scents of salt, grease, and mangroves lifted from the earth and wafted in the breeze.

This had always been the dream. Sure, it was hard work. It often brought too little money. But the rewards—they were greater than any fat bank account, even in the midst of chaos, especially now that she had friends she could call family.

She'd always had friends in Calusa Cove. People who were not only loyal to the marina but also loyal to her and her father's vision. She couldn't imagine being anywhere else in the world. This patch of land had something magical. Something so special that when anyone dared to drift in the waters, they always wanted more.

"You think the tourists will ever stop asking if they'll see dolphins in the Everglades?" Bingo grunted, tossing another coiled line into a crate.

Tourists were an interesting breed. Many thought every stop on their itinerary, including a gas station, was meant for their entertainment, and Baily didn't understand them one bit.

"Not a chance," Baily said, crouching to help. "Yesterday, someone asked me if the manatees here were friendly enough to pet, like they're labradors or something."

"They're not fast animals, so people can touch them half the time." Bingo snorted. "But that doesn't mean they should, and we should get a big sign that says: 'This ain't SeaWorld.'"

"Well, you'll love this one then." Baily stood tall, stretching out her back. "A family stopped to gas up for the boat parade. A mom and her kid got off looking for some snacks. They saw a few gators and asked if there was a feeding machine so they could toss them some food."

"That is about the dumbest thing I've ever heard." Bingo shook his head. "I'll never understand why some kids think it's funny to feed them marshmallows." Bingo sighed. "Last year, one of them damn near got their foot taken off after their kayak flipped over and the gator went for the bag of treats."

"Gators aren't bright. They see food, they go after

it," Baily said. "All those kids are doing is training them to follow kayaks, paddleboards, and other small vessels in the water. It's a disaster waiting to happen."

"Agreed."

Footsteps echoed from behind her, heavy and unfamiliar. Baily stiffened, rising slowly. She turned to see Decker Brown stepping off the gravel lot and onto the dock like he had every right to be there. She straightened, wiping her hands on her jeans as a cold rush prickled down her spine.

Fletcher had warned her to tread lightly when it came to him. Not to say too much, to keep her cool, and when he showed, to point him in the direction of her office.

She still resented that last part of the sentence. Ever since Fletcher had told her about his drinks with Decker last night, her anger had coiled like a snake in the pit of her stomach. It was hot and ready to strike.

"You lost, or just looking to get thrown into the canal as alligator feed?" she asked with a kind, sweet tone.

Fletcher would be at least proud of the fact she hadn't raised her voice.

Progress.

Decker hesitated, clearly uncomfortable in his designer boat shoes and pressed polo shirt, which clashed against the working grit of the marina. He looked around before answering, voice low, "I'm guessing Fletcher told you. I'm sorry."

"It's a little late for sorry," she mumbled. "For which I'm not interested in hearing."

"I guess I can't blame you." He shifted his weight. "Is Fletcher inside?"

Baily narrowed her eyes, glancing around to make sure no one else was watching. "For the record, I don't like this game. Fletcher made a stink about you meeting here. About waving a white flag. Said it might be better if someone saw you walking into the marina and not a bar. He used the word *optics*. But don't think for one second I'm thrilled about playing hostess or even want to listen to this shit. You lied, and I don't care what the reason is."

Decker shifted awkwardly. "Look, I didn't come to cause trouble. I didn't know—"

She cut him off with a sharp wave of her hand. "You caused trouble the moment you rolled into this town thinking you could trade in your problems by creating them for someone else."

"I didn't know what I was getting into."

"Yeah, well, neither did the rest of us. You've been circling like a shark since the moment Dewey was exposed, and now suddenly you want a meeting? Fletcher might be willing to give you the benefit of the doubt. Me?" She shrugged, keeping her distance out of fear she might actually haul off and hit him, or shove him right next to that nice ten-foot gator hanging out in the reeds. "I'm still undecided."

Decker didn't respond, just nodded and kept his head down as she led him across the gravel, inside the marina, and into the back room, which was a little bigger than her office. She pushed it open and stepped aside, motioning him in like she was escorting a criminal.

Fletcher leaned against a folding table, arms crossed. The second he saw Decker, his jaw tightened.

"You're late," Fletcher said flatly.

"I stopped in town, just to see if I was being followed." Decker flicked a glance toward Baily, but she was already turning on her heel, heading back out. "She's not staying?"

"I heard enough of this bullshit last night," she muttered under her breath. "Fletcher will either call me if I need to be here or fill me in later." She glanced over her shoulder. "I can't be trusted in the same room with you. Fletcher's worried I'll use that pretty face of yours as a punching bag instead of the one in his garage."

"She's right." Fletcher smiled, giving her a wave. "Don't go too far."

"I've got her six," Bingo said and trailed behind her as she made her way back to the dock with long strides and her heart hammering in her throat. There had been a time, when she'd first met Decker, that she'd actually liked the man. She'd even entertained going on a couple dates. Coffee at first. She'd quickly learned she wasn't interested, but he wasn't a horrible human.

Or so she'd believed at the time.

Did all men betray trust?

She pulled her phone from her back pocket, scrolling through her contacts. She was about to call Audra—maybe Trinity, someone who would understand the boiling mix of frustration and helplessness clawing at her chest—but a car pulled into the lot.

Chloe stepped out, dressed in a pair of jeans and a fitted jacket, sunglasses perched atop her head, and a messenger bag slung over her shoulder. In some ways, she was the total opposite of Hayes. She was focused, direct, and often times, harsh when she opened her mouth—that was if she even spoke. However, once they'd all gotten to know her, she'd softened a bit.

Hayes could be quiet. He could blend into the wall and remain unnoticed. But everyone saw Chloe coming. She was a force to be reckoned with. Hayes was just this laid-back dude who made everyone feel good.

Yet, Hayes and Chloe together…were pure gold.

"Good evening, my sweet friend," Chloe called out, striding toward her.

"Nothing good about tonight, and I'm not sweet, not anymore," Baily said, forcing a smile. "Not when Decker Brown shows up wearing horrible designer clothes that mock boat attire and make me feel like I'm on a bad movie set for a remake of *Jaws*."

"Wow, that's a mouthful. You're starting to sound like Audra." Chloe stopped beside her, following her gaze toward the marina. "I take it Decker's already here."

"Unfortunately." Baily crossed her arms. "He showed up looking like a kicked puppy. Claims he had no idea what he was getting into when he was asked to come to town and keep tabs on me. That he didn't know the Barbaros were behind it, yet that family destroyed his town outside of Miami." Baily let out a whopper of a sigh. "If the Barbaros are behind my loan, then Ken knew. If Ken knew, I'm bringing him back from the dead and killing him myself."

Chloe's brow rose. "Yeah, I understand how you'd feel like that."

"I honestly don't understand anything," Baily muttered. "Nothing makes sense. Ken and Julie acted like they wanted nothing to do with this place. I feel like I'm walking a tightrope with no idea when or where it's going to snap."

Chloe exhaled. "I know. And I wish I could say I have all the answers, but it's still a tangled mess. I came by to go over some things with Fletcher. I think we're circling something. A name came up—Garrett Danvers. He used to work for the Barbaros' manufacturing business. His name's buried in one of the shell companies connected to the LLC that's tied to your marina loan."

"Garrett Danvers? That name doesn't ring a bell."

"He lives in Maryland. I haven't been able to get hold of him, but I've got an old friend heading to

Garrett's place tonight. I'm hoping we'll hear from him before this meeting with Decker is over. Meanwhile, I've pulled in a favor." Chloe glanced over her shoulder and lowered her voice. "My old friend Greer Hudson—she's a sheriff out in Oregon now. We were in the Bureau together. Her cousin Enzo is a corporate and securities lawyer on Marco Island. Greer said he's the best, and he's willing to take a look at everything we've got."

Baily's eyes widened. "I trust you, Chloe, I do. But do we want to bring in someone else?" Baily hugged her middle. "I've been screwed over too many times..." She let the words trail off.

Chloe curled her fingers around Baily's forearm. "Listen, I totally understand why you'd be concerned about me, or anyone, talking to some Joe off the street. Greer isn't just anyone. She's a sheriff and a former FBI agent that I would trust Fedora's, Hayes's, and my life with. She's as good as they come. If she says her cousin is solid, then I believe her."

Baily nodded. "What about this Garrett guy in Maryland?"

"My contact isn't going to bring you, or this situation up. All he's gonna do is ask some questions and find out if Garrett left on good terms or bad. See if there's dirt to be had and go from there. If there's a thread to pull, we'll find it. But we need to do the digging, and this is how it works. Sometimes, you've got to trust a little when trust doesn't feel like the right thing to do."

"All right," Baily said. "Fletcher has access to everything. The loans, the books, the bank statements. I'm not keeping secrets from him anymore."

"That's good, because we're running out of shadows to hide in. If we're going to bring the truth into the light, it needs to happen fast."

Baily looked back toward the marina door. "Let's just hope Decker decides to stand in the light, too."

Chloe gave her a steady look. "He's not the one I'm worried about. It's the people hiding behind him. The people who put him here. They're threatening him, too. Holding things over his head…things that aren't true. I did some homework on that, and so far, his story tracks." She tapped her bag. "This Tessa Gilbert chick, her company is a front for laundering money for the Barbaros. Can't quite prove it, but all the tells are there."

"What the hell was my brother involved in, and the bigger question is, did he know when he married her?" Baily whispered with a tight jaw.

"Hey, do you want to come with me to the meeting?" Chloe asked. "I know Fletcher won't care."

"I've chosen to stay away because I'm struggling to keep my anger in check. I say and do things that aren't conducive to that kind of discussion."

"Just breathe before speaking and stuff your hands in your pockets," Chloe said. "That's what I do. It's saved me more times than not from getting myself fired."

Baily chuckled. "Okay. Let's go." She was tired of

waiting. Tired of being one step behind. It was time to fight back.

And this time, she wasn't backing down.

* * *

Fletcher leaned forward, elbows on his knees, as tension thickened in the back room of the marina. The walls were thin enough to hear the quiet hum of the wind slipping past the windows, the occasional creak of the dock outside, and the distant sound of a boat engine starting somewhere on the water. But inside, the air was heavy.

"Mueller, he went back to Virginia. Or at least that's where I believe he went." Decker took a packet of paper out of his small backpack and laid it on the table. "He could be anywhere, lurking in the shadows, watching, especially after my little temper tantrum with Tessa. I tried to smooth that over. It's not like I haven't asked questions before or threatened to stop giving her updates over the past few months. But I never did."

"Why is that, if you didn't know about the Barbaros?"

Decker leaned against the table and sighed. "Tessa hinted about the plans I supposedly stole. How she made that go away, and how she could make them resurface and bury the project I've been working on over on Marco Island. I've always known she could be vindictive, and I thought maybe there was a man somewhere in this town she had her sights on…romantically." He ran his fingers through his hair. "I needed to protect myself. I put my heart and soul into that development. But also, I sank most of my equity. I lose it, I'm done in this game. Selfish, I know. But what would you have done in my shoes?"

"Not a fair question," Fletcher said. "And not because of the selfish comment. We all can be that. But since I joined the Navy, I haven't done a single thing alone. I haven't felt alone, and I haven't walked into danger alone. If I were you, I would've called my friends." He arched a brow. "But my friends come with assault weapons and backup plans, not pencils and drawings."

"Yeah," Decker mumbled. "And, thanks to Tessa, I don't have too many real friends." He shrugged. "I know I talk a big game. Walk and act like I've got swagger, but the truth is, all I've got is my work. My company. I thought when I broke things off with Tessa my life would change. That I'd be able to make a clean break, especially since I paid her back every penny I owed her. But she—and the Barbaros—they don't let people go. They put them down like dogs."

"That's a visual I could've done without, man." Fletcher lifted the papers. "What am I looking at?"

"Some early sketches and ideas for the old Crab Shack." Decker smiled, as if he were proud. "I haven't shown these to anyone. They're for you. If you want them. What I'd give to Tessa are bullshit drawings that I know this town would pass on."

Fletcher had no idea what he was really looking at, because some of what he was staring at didn't make sense. Blueprints weren't his thing. Hayes and Keaton had a mind and eye for such things. "Why are you showing me these?"

"I thought, since I'm here discussing everything, we could chat about an idea I had."

"Let's wait for Chloe." Fletcher glanced up over the paper. "Aren't these kind of plans usually on big sheets and pages long?"

"I didn't want to print out the plans, which I haven't done on my program anyway, just in case Mueller was still in town. Or if there was spyware on my computer. Chloe and Dawson were going to look at that later."

"I'm not a trusting sort, and you letting us peek into your personal things, well, that makes me wonder." Fletcher flipped a page. He might not understand all the details of the drawings, or even some of the verbiage, but he could see the bigger picture, and this concept wasn't bad. It also wasn't too far off the mark from what he and the guys wanted to do.

"Do you have any idea what it's like to grow up dirt poor?" Decker asked.

Fletcher laughed. "Have you looked around this town? At the majority of people who live here? Most are barely scraping by."

"Oh, I get that. I see it." Decker nodded. "But where I come from? People only have two choices. The first one is to take the money and jobs that the Barbaros of the world hand out and hope they don't end up in prison or at the bottom of the ocean. That somehow they'll be the exception to the rule, when they know deep down, they're feeding the beast and just another piece of the bigger problem." He held up his hand. "Or, they can dive into the dumpster for dinner. And I mean that literally. They can use that same garbage collection tin box to hide behind when the thugs come looking for people to do small errands. They promise you it's a one-time thing. No obligation. And they'll stay away for a little while, smile at you on the street, like they kept their end of the bargain. But then, they'll need another favor. One, only you can provide. They pay you well, and next thing you know, they're threatening your sister. Your mother. Your little mom and pop shop. People like the Barbaros take over neighborhoods. They do it slowly and methodically, until most small businesses are cleaning their money, and all the teenagers are doing their bidding and being groomed."

"How'd you manage to keep your nose clean?"

"I was a scrawny kid. A nerd. Not much use to them for dealing street drugs, but my uncle told me to be careful. That a man like me, with my smarts, they'd want me for something else."

"Your uncle, he works for them?"

"Most of my family did." Decker said.

Fletcher leaned back and cocked his head. "Then explain to me how you flew under the radar."

"I got beat up a lot, making myself appear to be not worth the trouble."

"That's smart," Fletcher said.

Decker shrugged. "It's survival in the streets of Miami run by the Barbaros and others like them. When I was in high school, there was a war going on between them and some cartel. Not the kind of battle done with guns. But the kind done with money. It was quiet, but we all knew it was happening. It came down to power and who controlled those in power. I didn't know the players because I just wanted out. I did my best to stay invisible, and I thought I'd been successful. But I guess, they always kept tabs on me."

"Does the name Mendoza ring a bell?" Fletcher asked.

Decker nodded, eyes wide. "Sounds familiar. Could've been the same cartel. There's more than one in Miami, and honestly, I try to stay clear of it all. I don't even speak to anyone in my family. When I went to college, my uncle told me to make a clean break. Just walk away and never look back. He told me it was better that way."

"That cartel used to run drugs in and out of here with Paul Massey." Fletcher arched a brow. "Do you live under a rock? You were coming around at the start of all that."

"I was." Decker nodded. "But I can't say I paid much attention to it. I try to avoid anything cartel-related. It brings up a lot of trauma, and I don't want to get involved in that shit. I was spending more time in Marco Island than here, and I was trying to…hell, I don't know. I had my head buried in the muck."

"You can say that again." Fletcher set the papers on the table. "What kinds of things did you report back to Tessa? And was it always phone conversations?"

"If I texted, she called." Decker nodded. "Honestly, there wasn't much to tell. Things like you all were living in town. She did take an interest in Dawson being a cop, and there were some questions about how the town reacted to you all."

"I would think she'd be really interested in the Massey case."

"I didn't bring that up. It didn't affect Baily. Not directly anyway. But she did ask a few questions. She wanted to know how Dawson handled the case—was he a good cop. Thought she was just shooting the shit with me, and I did my best to get her off the line because I wanted her out of my life." Decker rubbed the back of his neck. "Things didn't heat up until the Crab Shack burned down. That's when Tessa wanted more. Wanted me to turn up the charm and find Baily's weak spots, but I told Tessa no way. I wasn't that guy."

"We're gonna need you to pretend to be *that guy*," Fletcher said, cocking his head.

"Yeah, I can do that." Decker nodded. "I can lie to Tessa because I've been doing that for a while."

"Excuse me?" Fletcher blinked.

"I told you, I wasn't the enemy," Decker said. "I fed Tessa just enough information to keep her off my back while I tried to figure out my move. Only, I quickly learned I don't have one. At least not alone. I'd tell Tessa dumb things." Decker chuckled. "I will say she wasn't very pleased to learn that Hayes took up with a Fed."

"Does she know Chloe moved here and retired?"

"She knows they're living together, but I haven't said Chloe's left the FBI. Not sure that's public knowledge." Decker sighed. "Lately, Tessa's been hyper-focused on Baily, the marina, and the Crab Shack. My last conversation with her was right after our meeting at Massey's Pub. I told her that I informed you of my intentions. That I had more money and that there was no way you'd win the bid." Decker laughed, although it was sarcastic in nature. "Tessa told me I better not screw it up. I'll enjoy knocking the wind out of that woman's sails. I just don't like the way Baily looks at me now."

Fletcher chuckled. He shouldn't be thrilled that Baily was giving the old stink eye to Decker. But after being on the receiving end of it for years? Yeah, Fletcher would enjoy it for as long as it lasted. He didn't care that it was childish or that it made him appear a little jealous.

"I'm glad you find this amusing," Decker mumbled.

The door creaked open, and in walked Chloe with Baily two paces behind.

Fletcher stood, nodded to Chloe, and made a beeline for Baily. He rested his hands on her hips. This might be considered a dick move, but he didn't give a shit. He pressed his lips over her mouth and kissed her good and hard.

The room stilled.

That was until Chloe cleared her throat.

Fletcher pulled back. "Is everything okay?" He traced Baily's jawline.

"I'm fine," Baily said with an arched brow. "Chloe talked me into staying for this meeting."

"Good. I think you should be here." Fletcher pulled out another chair and opened it. "Chloe, why don't you start?"

Chloe sat cross-legged on the edge of the table, phone in hand, her brow tight with focus. Decker leaned against the wall near the corner, arms crossed, trying to pretend like he wasn't the most uncomfortable man in the room. Baily sat next to Fletcher, her eyes hard as steel, but Fletcher knew her well enough to see the worry swimming beneath the surface.

"I did some digging into Tessa Gilbert, hoping to find some cracks—something that ties her company back to the Barbaros—"

"I know she's working for them," Decker muttered, interrupting Chloe. "Even if no one can prove it, she's all but admitted it to me."

"Well, we need proof, and so far, I've got nothing," Chloe said. "She's third-generation rich. Never really had to work a day in her life. That company was her father's, and she's just pretty much lived off the dividends, not really working, just pretending to, and backing a few younger studs she's dated over the years." Chloe glanced in Decker's direction, who grunted. "Don't feel bad, you're not the youngest. Before you—"

"I'm well aware of Tyson Hughes. He was maybe twenty-five. Like I said, I was never in love with the woman, and I get that makes me look like a greedy asshole." He shifted his gaze to Fletcher. "Who did exactly what he'd been trying not to do his entire life."

"Don't beat yourself up," Fletcher said, holding Decker's gaze. "She's a Trojan horse. An unexpected enemy, and anyone could've fallen for it."

"You wouldn't have." Decker let out a big puff of air in one extended swish.

"I don't know about that." Fletcher tilted his head. "Everyone's got a weak spot. If she'd found mine, she might've been able to tug at the right string."

Chloe's phone buzzed. She lifted it. "My contact in Maryland." She tapped the screen. "Talk to me, Diego."

The speaker crackled, and then a low, gravelly male voice came through. "I'm with Garrett. He's jumpy but talking. We met in a park—neutral ground. I brought coffee, he brought years of fear."

"What did he say?" Chloe asked, sitting up straighter.

"He confirmed what your guy Decker said, and he's got some proof to back it up," Diego said. "The Barbaros have been running drugs and guns through their plants for years. That was bad enough. But a few years ago, they expanded. Started bringing in people. Women, kids. Young. Vulnerable. They're trafficking them through cargo shipments disguised as parts and equipment. It's not just moving drugs anymore. It's moving bodies."

Baily sucked in a breath. Fletcher's hand curled around her waist. They'd suspected this was what had been going down, and Decker had been the first to say it out loud, but again, he hadn't had any proof. No documents. Only his suspicions. But hearing it from Chloe's contact, well, that made it real. That drove the point home.

"Garret kept the books for their warehouse in Maryland. He started noticing things. Things that didn't settle right in his gut. He did some investigating. Next thing he knew, weird shit started happening. Things like he'd get blamed for stuff, but then his boss would be all like, 'Man, stuff happens. We know you're good. Now, how about we make this happen? Or that happen?' It all got very cagey, quickly," Diego said.

"Is Garret safe?" Baily asked.

"They haven't touched him in two years, but he hasn't done anything with what he knows," Diego said. "He's scared. Damn scared and with good reason. But he's got intel. Things like how they've been scouting small coastal towns. Places where they can bribe officials, buy properties under shell corps, and build infrastructure that'll support their ops. Garrett heard whispers—Calusa Cove's on their list. The marina? Perfect cover. Same with some new builds, investments in businesses that need a little help, and public land near the Glades. Overflow points. Storage and transport hubs. He's got a file. A few things that are concrete, others just notes and things that need to be tied together."

"Jesus," Fletcher muttered. "What's he going to do now?"

"Nothing that would get him flagged with the Barbaros or their people," Diego said. "He drives a rideshare and works at a local fishing charter. But every once in a while, someone from that organization comes poking around. Honestly, he thought I was one of them."

"You do have that look," Chloe said. "Why is he talking now? Why's he trusting you?"

"Because he's honestly got nothing to lose. He left too early to receive a pension. He's got no money. His wife died last year. Cancer. Real shame. No kids. No grandkids. He looked me square in the eye and said, 'Let's burn the mother fuckers down if it's the last thing I do.'"

"Gotta love guys like that," Fletcher said. "But he could be playing us."

"I doubt that," Diego said. "Man's broken. Until I walked into his one-room apartment, he hadn't even an ounce of hope. Now? He's got something to live for."

Chloe nodded. "Tell him to pack a bag. He comes to Calusa Cove, or maybe we send him to Oregon. We'll protect him. Maybe we can give him a reason to start over, after this plays out."

"You sure?" Diego asked. "Because he wants to see them pay for what they've done to his neighborhood. To his friends. It's not just him. It's this entire harbor."

Fletcher shifted his gaze, catching Decker's. The man looked as if he'd seen a ghost. As if he knew exactly what that looked and felt like.

"Set it up," Fletcher said. "I'll try to back channel this with Foster's team in Oregon and some fellas I know in an organization called The Aegis Network. Between the two, they can arrange transport and decide where to send him, for now."

Chloe nodded. "I'll call Greer."

"All right. I'll get him to a safe house," Diego said.

"Chloe will send you Foster's and a man by the name of Logan Sarich's contact information. Logan's out of Orlando," Fletcher said. "Between those two, we'll figure out the details."

Chloe hung up and exhaled. "So, yeah. It's worse than we thought. And now, we've got a guy on the run with a target the size of Florida on his back."

"Been there before." Fletcher arched a brow. "But

at least we know what it is they're doing, and sort of know what they want."

"And what's that?" Baily stood and paced in the small room. "Because they can't use this town," Baily said, voice tight. "I don't care what they think their money can buy. Or their muscle can push around and manipulate. We're not for sale. *I'm* not for sale, and I won't be pushed out of my family legacy by fear." She folded her arms. "I guess I know the sick game Julie's been playing. Dangle those boys, get me to sell, and then it's her and her family that set up some dummy company to… I just can't even think about it or the fact that my brother probably knew all this." Baily rubbed her temples. "It's like a bad mob movie, and I'm the chick that's too stupid to live."

"You're not stupid, Baily," Decker said, then he pushed off the wall. "You're one person doing your best to make it. The Barbaros? They've got a network of criminals in at least five major metropolitan cities at their beck and call. Not to mention, they've got billions of dollars. And we can't forget, they've probably been planning this for years."

"Can't believe I'm going to say this." Fletcher waved his finger toward Decker. "But what he said."

"Agreed." Chloe nodded. "But all this has me thinking more about that loan and how legal it is."

"I've been making payments on it, and Paul Massey said…" Baily let the words trail off. "Massey was a fucking criminal, selling drugs for the cartel. And maybe he had a stake in me going under." She stopped pacing and plopped into the chair with a sigh. "And maybe my brother knew that."

Fletcher stepped behind her, pressed his hands into her shoulders, and gave them a good squeeze.

"That doesn't make sense," Decker said. "If there was a competing cartel running drugs in this town, that cartel would've wanted you to stay in business. They would've done whatever it took to make sure that happened." He turned to Fletcher, catching his gaze. "Including telling Baily the loan was legal, and she needed to continue paying on it."

"Paul always sent business to Baily," Fletcher said. "He was supportive. But considering he was born and raised here, that wasn't a shocker."

"Before we learned he was a drug smuggler and a murderer, outside of his animosity towards Audra and her return, and perhaps the fact he could be an arrogant asshole, he was always trying to lend a helpful hand. Always slipping me a big fat tip." Baily glanced over her shoulder. "But he did so with that slimy kind of look that I never missed. It wasn't like Silas, who does it with a sweet half smile and a bit of guilt, knowing how prideful I am. No, Paul made me wonder if he expected me to pay him back."

"I barely knew the guy," Decker said. "But if he worked for the cartel, I'm sure he expected some kind of return on his investment, and if that day had ever come, he would've found a way to remind you of all he'd done."

"Sounds like you know these types well." Chloe glanced between Decker and Fletcher.

"I spent my youth ducking and dodging them, only to learn that my arrogance in adulthood hadn't shaken them," Decker said with his gaze firmly planted on his feet. "As far as your brother goes. I didn't know the man, so I could be talking out of my ass." He lifted his gaze. "But, since he was married to Julie, and he married her young, it's quite possible he went into that relationship blind. That they waited until they knew they had him by the balls…pardon my expression…before they showed their hand and started controlling his actions through fear and manipulation. It's how they operate. I've seen people like them do it in my old neighborhood."

It was hard for Fletcher not to give Decker some respect.

Chloe lifted her phone. "I need to call Greer's cousin first thing in the morning and set up a meeting. I think both Fletcher and Baily should be present for that, and you need to bring all the loan paperwork and anything else that might help with that paper trail."

"We'll be ready." Fletcher nodded.

"Greer says he's good," Chloe said. "If there's something connecting the Barbaros to the loan, your accounts, or anything tied to this town, he'll find it."

"Anything else we need to discuss?" Fletcher asked.

Decker inched closer, tapping his knuckles on the

table. "I have an idea. It's risky, but I think it's better than pulling me out of the equation altogether."

"I'm listening," Fletcher said.

"Right now, the plan is for me to disappear. But what if you have me go through with the bid?" He held up his hands. "I mean that only in terms of right to the point of the actual auction. I draft the plans, make the calls, and talk to Mueller and the investor to keep up appearances. If they think I'm still doing their bidding, they'll stay out of my way. Then at the town meeting, I'll kill the proposal. I can do it publicly or quietly. That's up to you. But we can turn the tides before they even know they're drowning."

Baily crossed her arms. "If you do that publicly, you'd become a target."

Decker nodded. "I know. But I kind of already am. And doing it this way buys us time. If I go dark on them now, we don't know what they might do. But if I play along...maybe you all can figure out the pieces that you don't have."

Fletcher leaned back. "That's a hell of a gamble, but I kind of like the odds better."

"They already know I'm on the edge," Decker said. "They've threatened me, my company, my reputation. They want me to play ball or get crushed. They know I don't like to lose. I'm good at my job. My weakness has always been three things. Fear of being dirt poor again. My reputation. Nothing worse than being a no-good loser. And being a criminal like my family.

They've hit me with all three, and they believe I'm crumbling."

"Why are you doing this?" Baily asked. "Because just a few weeks ago, you were willing to date me to get intel and give it to those assholes."

"Because life—and being in this town—has taught me a few things." Decker tapped his chest. "I've been poor, and I've survived. My reputation has taken big hits before, and I can rebuild it if I'm honest and true. I'm not a criminal. I never have been, and I won't let them turn me into one. But the one thing I've never had before…ever." He waved his hand. "Is this—community. I want to be a part of it. I know it's not something I can just walk into and expect to be trusted or welcomed. But this is how I can first, right what I've done wrong. And second, help where I can. Let me."

"Your plan keeps us with an open line to Tessa and to the Barbaros outside of putting Baily in the middle by having her reach out to Julie and playing that angle," Fletcher said.

"Agreed," Chloe nodded. "But we still may want to do that." She stood, tapping on her screen. "Fletcher, you need to get with the boys about how to work the auction angle and make sure Decker's plans are good enough that they'll be entertained and won't cause suspicion from anyone."

"I wanted to speak with Fletcher about that." Decker reached across the table and lifted the stack of papers he'd brought. "I've been working on two sets of plans. One on my computer. Those, Tessa has seen. They're good. Actually, they're great—but not for a town like this. It's too upscale. Too yacht club vibe. But these?" He waved and whistled. "I've been sketching offline and by hand. Very small town. Very fisherman vibe. I can work with you guys to create exactly what you're looking for and what this town needs."

"You sound quite confident," Fletcher said. "But if we screw it up, it's not just your neck on the line—it's the whole town."

Decker cracked a crooked smile. "Then we don't screw it up. We fight like hell and beat those assholes at their own game."

"Those are fighting words." Fletcher nodded. "And Calusa Cove and Mitchell's Marina aren't going down without one."

CHAPTER 12

The steady click of her pen was the only sound in the marina office besides the distant whirl of a trolling motor and the occasional cry of a gull. Baily stood behind the counter, thumbing through invoices and rental logs, trying to ignore the knot forming at the base of her neck. The numbers didn't lie—things were tight. Tighter than they'd ever been, even with allowing help from Fletcher and his friends.

She glanced at her cell. No new texts from Fletcher, and that made her nervous, especially since he'd been meeting with the boys and Decker for a super-secret meeting at the B&B about the plans for the old Crab Shack.

Of course, she was also waiting for an update from Chloe regarding this Enzo lawyer-person and when that meeting would take place. It felt like she was in a holding pattern, waiting either for someone to tell her they had an answer or for another bad thing to happen.

The door opened, and in strolled Trinity, rubbing her little baby bump. "Hey there. How are you today?"

"It's not the worst day." Baily stepped from behind the counter to hug her friend. "What brings you by?"

"Keaton left his favorite hoodie on his boat, along with one of my bags with some towels." Trinity shrugged. "Sometimes, my ultra neat freak husband can't remember the head attached to his shoulders."

"Bingo brought the bag, but there wasn't a sweatshirt that I saw." Baily pointed to the corner by her office door. "He's cleaning the boat as we speak."

"You're letting him clean boats while on the clock for you?" Trinity asked. "Now I feel a little guilty, but in a really weird way. Not so much for Bingo, because he needs the money, but like we're somehow taking advantage of you."

Baily laughed. "There isn't much for him to do right now, but I still need a body here. So, I told him if he doesn't have homework to do, he could wash the boats he's contracted to do. However, if something I need comes up, he's got to shift gears."

"That's mighty nice of you."

"When I was a kid, my dad used to let me double dip like that as well." Baily leaned against the counter. "Bingo's a great employee. He's an excellent student. I'm going to miss him when he leaves for college in the fall."

"Have you replaced him?"

Baily shook her head. "Technically, I haven't even advertised the position, but everyone knows it's going to open up. I've talked to a couple of his friends, but no one can give me the hours he can during the school year. So, either I've got to hire two kids, or one adult."

"You'll figure it out." Trinity smiled, rubbing her belly. It seemed as if that was all she did these days. "And we'll be around to help out when we can."

"I know. I appreciate all that you do as it is."

"What are friends for?" Trinity paused the circular motion and glanced down. "Give me your hand." She raced around the corner, grabbed Baily's hand, and placed it firmly on her lower abdomen. "I'm constantly feeling this little rascal, but Keaton's only felt it once, and that was last night. It was just a little… Feel that?"

Baily jerked her hand back like she'd been burned. "Yeah." She blinked. "Holy cow."

"I know, right? It's like the movie *Alien*, and it's growing inside me."

Baily burst out laughing. "I would expect Audra to describe her kid as a monster, but not you."

Trinity shrugged. "It's so strange. I mean, I'm ready for the parenthood part. I can handle breastfeeding, diapering, and being puked on. But this part? It's so strange. I mean, my boobs are massive. My ankles are swollen. I've gained ten pounds already. That part I don't care about, but everything seems so foreign. Keaton thinks I'm losing my mind."

"You are." Baily grabbed Trinity by the forearms and kissed her cheek. "But it's why we all adore you."

"Now, you sound like Audra." Trinity glanced at her watch. "Speaking of which, I need to head over to the B&B and pick her up. I talked her into doing a registry for the baby." Trinity wiggled her finger under Baily's nose. "And you and Chloe are in charge of the shower."

Baily rolled her eyes. "Yeah, I've been informed."

"I'll see you tonight for the bonfire." Trinity waved her hand over her head before disappearing out the door. Sometimes that girl was too much.

Baily sighed, leaned against the counter, and went back to the numbers. She'd promised Fletcher a bottom line for what she needed to run the marina through the winter months, ignoring the payment for the loan.

Static crackled through the two-way radio mounted on the wall behind her.

"This is Mitchell's Runabout Three," came a panicked voice, male, maybe mid-twenties. "We're dead in the water, just west of Marker 14. Boat won't start."

Baily stood instantly. "Copy that, Runabout Three. This is Baily at Mitchell's. What happened? Can you describe what you've done to try to start the engine?"

"Engine turned over, sputtered, then died. Tried

again. Nothing," the man said. His name was Nolan, and he and his girlfriend had rented the boat early that morning. It was the only rental still out.

"Check your kill switch and make sure the gas line valve's open. Then give the bulb a good couple of squeezes before trying again."

"We already did. Nothing," Nolan said. "Won't even turn over anymore. I tried everything I can think of."

Baily sighed. Christian had recently serviced all the boats. They should be fine. *Should be* were the operative words. They were old. The boats were in good shape and would last a long time. But the engines? Well, she could only rebuild them so many times before they plumb died on her. This could be that time. "Can you give me your location?"

"I'm guessing we're about twenty-five minutes from the docks. We're near that big cypress bend."

"All right. Sit tight. I'll come get you." She grabbed the airboat keys from the hook, slipped her cell into its waterproof case, and slung it over her shoulder.

She stepped outside, locking the door to the marina, and turning the sign that read: *At the docks. Be right back.* She strolled down toward Keaton's shiny new center console fishing boat. "Hey, Bingo," she called.

"Yeah?" He popped up from the stern, all sweaty and soapy.

"I have to go rescue the rental." She shook her head and rolled her eyes. "The door to the marina is locked. The sign's on the door. I don't expect anyone but Silas, Hayes, and Fletcher. They will need to gas up the Everglades Overwatch boats."

"The ones at the dock, I've already done. Bill is waiting for them when they return from giving tours."

"I'm gonna be lost without you when you go to college."

"I doubt that," Bingo said. "I just have to hose down these engines and dry off the covers. Once I'm done, I'll head into the marina."

"You've got your keys?"

"Sure do."

"See you in about an hour." She turned and headed toward the last dock. The one that was falling apart. The one that she wouldn't let a customer walk down if it were the only dock on the premises.

The airboat was old—a rust bucket—but she kept the maintenance up on it, just like the rest of the boats she owned.

She fired up the engine and eased out from the dock, heading out of the canal and into the Everglades. God, she loved being on the water. Sadly, she didn't get out on it enough. Too many things needed to be done around the marina, and there weren't enough employees to do it.

Lifting her chin, she enjoyed the warm air smacking against her skin. The sun lowered in the sky, but it would be hours before day gave way to night.

She gave the airboat a little more gas.

It barely crawled forward.

She tried again. It gave barely a sluggish glide. Then came the faint gurgling. Shifting her weight, she glanced down—water sloshed at her boots. "Shit." She released the lever brought the boat to idle, and before lifting the hatch to check the bilge.

Full of water.

She flipped the switch. Nothing. She tried again, but the pump wasn't running.

She lowered her body, lying in the water seeping in through the hull, which also didn't make sense. The boat was taking on too much water...too fast. Quickly, she stuck her hand inside the hatch, found the hose, and tugged. Holding it in her hand, she blinked. "What the hell?" The hose wasn't just severed. It was cut. Not frayed. Not worn.

Someone had taken something sharp to it and sliced through the rubber. She didn't need to be a detective to figure that out.

Her stomach dropped.

She turned and sat her ass back in the captain's chair. She didn't have much time. She hit the lever, but the engine sputtered then died. She twisted the key, but it didn't turn over.

Nothing.

The gas gauge taunted her. "No. No. No." She fisted her pants. She kept this boat gassed up at all times in case of emergencies. It was the only boat she didn't rent. The only one that was always at the docks.

She reached for the radio. But it didn't hiss or crackle, which was odd. She pressed the mic.

Nothing.

That's when she noticed the wiring—sliced, frayed at the base. This wasn't wear and tear. It was deliberate.

Pulling her cell from its protective wrap, she checked the service bars. Barely one. She tried Bingo's number. It failed. She tried again. Same thing. She was in that weird dead zone spot right in the mouth of the Everglades.

Panic prickled across her skin.

She grabbed a flare from the emergency kit, but the container was empty.

"This can't be happening," she whispered, scanning the horizon. The Glades stretched in every direction, the sawgrass endless, the water black and bottomless.

And then she saw them—gator eyes. Low, steady, moving closer.

She didn't scream. Yelling didn't help. She stood slowly, trying to keep her balance as the boat dipped lower.

She waved her arms, hoping to catch the sun's reflection, praying someone—anyone—was out there.

A motor buzzed faintly in the distance.

Then again—closer.

She turned, heart racing.

An airboat rounded the bend, and at the helm was Silas, sunburned and wide-eyed. He spotted her instantly and cut the motor with a hard skid, gliding in.

"Hey, Baily... Oh crap. Jesus. You're about ready to sink," Silas said.

"No shit." She took the hand he offered and climbed onto his skiff.

"What happened?"

"Sabotage," she said, trying to keep her voice steady. It waffled between fear and rage. "Radio's fried. Bilge pump line's been cut, and I think there's a hole in the hull. Tank's empty. I check this boat every couple of days. I didn't check it today, though."

"That boat's going down fast," he said. "Don't think we can tow it."

"Wonderful. I'm not going to be able to afford to replace that, Silas."

"I know." He looped an arm over her shoulder and eased her onto the bench. "I'll radio Fletcher and Hayes. They're about thirty minutes past Boone Bend."

"I've got a rental in trouble," she mumbled. "They're between here and Boone Bend. They said they were floating dead in the water by Cypress Island." She lifted her feet and rested them on the console. "We need to let Bingo know what's going on, too."

"I got you." Silas lifted the mic off the handle.

"Gatoreater, Gatoreater, Gatoreater, this is Rodfather, come in."

"This Gatoreater, go ahead, Rodfather," Fletcher's voice cut through the thick swamp air like butter.

"Don't be alarmed, but I've got Baily with me. Her boat was taking on water. It's actually about to be a salvage vessel," Silas said. "Also, one of her rentals is going to need a tow. They should be around the Cypress bend."

"Rodfather, this is Flame Tamer," Hayes said. "I'm coming around that bend right now. No one's there. Not a single boat. Especially not one of Baily's. As a matter of fact, I saw one of her boats take the loop around the south island half an hour ago. They should be south of you. If they were having engine trouble, with the tide going out, they could've floated in front of the canal opening by now."

Silas snapped his gaze at Baily.

"Hayes, take the starboard loop," Fletcher said. "I'll take the port. Silas, get Baily back to the marina. We'll see you soon."

"Copy that." Silas rehooked the mic and pressed the throttle down.

She glanced over her shoulder and stared at the sinking airboat as Silas turned them back toward the marina. "Silas," Baily started, "I'm gonna ask you a strange question, and I want an honest answer."

"Of course."

"Do you think my brother was capable of destroying my dad? Of burying me and him so deep in debt that it would take a flipping miracle to save us?"

"That depends on which Ken we're talking about." Silas raised a brow. "Because the Navy SEAL hero Ken couldn't have done that. Nor could've the little kid who used to run around these parts barefoot with a frog between his fingers and smile so wide it was contagious. But the Ken that whispered in dark corners of the street where the lights were broken, or in the back of the bar, with the likes of Benson, yeah, that Ken could lie, cheat, and steal if he needed to. And the Ken who married Julie?" Silas let out a long breath, running a hand over his white beard. "Well, that Ken was the kind of man who believed money talked and dollar signs mattered more than family and hard work."

"Wow," she said softly. "Have you always thought that, or is this new, and you're telling me now because I asked?"

Silas squeezed her shoulder and kissed her temple. "I had my doubts and reservations about Ken when Victor went missing because of the way he treated Audra. But hell, I wasn't much better when that fiery redhead up and left this town."

"That doesn't answer my question."

"No. I haven't always believed that about Ken," Silas said over the hum of the engine. "As time has ticked by, and strange things have happened in our quiet little town, I've started thinking about every little thing. Every tiny detail. Especially after reading those things written in Tripp's journal. I started remembering things about Ken. Things that just don't add up. I've told all of this to Dawson and Fletcher."

"Why not me?" She stared straight ahead, focusing on the horizon. On the approach to the marina.

"I didn't want to add to your stress, but also, it's all things you already know. Things about how he treated you, or the way his wife just changed him. Or maybe he was already different before he left."

"I'm starting to think I didn't know my brother at all."

"I hate to agree with that statement," Silas said. "But think about how Fletcher and the boys feel about that. I know he was your brother. Your flesh and blood. But you didn't go into battle with him. It's a mind-fuck for sure."

"It sucks." She leaned her head against Silas's shoulder. But it didn't stay there long. "Hey. That's my boat and the couple that rented it are nowhere in sight." She pointed her finger wildly.

"I see that." Silas navigated his boat toward the docks. He pulled into his slip.

She tied off the stern and jumped. "Bingo? Bingo, where are you?"

"He's over here," Keaton called, waving by the gravel path.

She took off running down the dock and up the path. "What the hell…" She skidded to a stop. "What on earth happened?" She stared at Bingo, who sat on his ass, an ice pack pressed to the back of his head.

"I'm so sorry," Bingo said. "That couple? They pulled in, and I was confused, so I started asking questions. I guess they didn't like them because next thing I knew, Keaton here was smacking my face and waving something under my nose."

Keaton knelt beside Bingo. "Dude. You've got a bump on the back of your head the size of a golf ball, and when I got here, you were face down in the dirt." He helped Bingo to a standing position. "I think this guy should get checked out."

"I'm fine," Bingo said.

"You were knocked unconscious, and we don't know for how long." Keaton held him as the poor boy wobbled.

Baily raced to his other side, wrapping her arm around his waist. "At least go to the station house and let one of the EMTs take a look at you."

"That's what I was going to suggest." Keaton nodded. "Silas? Do you mind taking him?"

"Not at all." Silas stepped around them, heading toward the parking lot.

"You can take my truck. You both will be more comfortable." Keaton opened the passenger door and helped Bingo up and inside the cab.

Baily took a step back and wrapped her arms around her middle. The day's events soaked into her bones. It was no longer about the boat. She could eventually replace that. It was just a hunk of metal. A thing.

But she could have died out there.

And Bingo had been attacked.

This wasn't about money. It was about control—power—and ultimately, she was in the way. She was collateral damage.

Keaton's truck engine roared to life. Silas waved as he backed out, turned, and maneuvered onto the main drag.

"You okay?" Keaton rested a gentle hand on her shoulder.

"Bingo's lucky you came when you did," she whispered, blinking. "Why did you come back? Trinity collected the things you left on the boat."

"Bingo sent all of us a text message." Keaton arched a brow. "He was concerned about the fact you'd gone out to rescue a boat that came in less than ten minutes after you left, and the couple swore they never made an SOS. It just felt off to him, and he didn't know what to do."

"He's a good kid, that one. Smart, too."

Keaton pressed his hand on the small of her back, guiding her back toward the docks. "Did you know he's going into the ROTC program when he goes to college?"

"I did." She nodded. "He's become very enamored by all of you and wants to be a SEAL."

"It's not an easy road." Keaton chuckled. "We've seen him lifting weights, training at the gym, and running every morning, but we had no idea. I told him that we're more than happy to answer questions and help him anyway we can."

"He's a humble and proud kid."

"I think this town breeds everyone that way."

Baily paused at the edge of the lower docks, where Everglades Overwatch kept their boats. Fletcher and Hayes had pulled in and were currently helping their guests off their vessels.

But that didn't last long. At least not for Fletcher, as he made a beeline for Baily while Hayes continued with the final few moments of their tour.

"Hey, you." He tugged her to his chest, pressing his warm lips to her temple. "I'd ask if you were okay, but that seems like a stupid question considering we passed by the boat. Only the very top of the center console was visible from the water line."

She rested her head on his shoulder. "I remember when my dad bought that hunk of junk. I was maybe all of five."

"He took me and Ken out in that boat the day he brought it home. We went fishing for hours and caught absolutely nothing, but it was the best day ever." He tilted her chin with his thumb. "This changes things, and I can't have you fight me on being alone. Someone didn't want to just scare you. They wanted you dead."

"I thought about that, and it doesn't make sense," she said softly, but with a slight tremble to her voice. "My will leaves everything to you."

He jerked his head. "I didn't know that."

She shrugged. "I didn't know what else to do after Ken died. I thought about leaving it to my nephews, but that meant Julie would have control, and I figured she'd sell it. I didn't want that. I knew you'd try to keep it for them. Or at least make an—"

He hushed her by pressing his mouth over hers in a sweet kiss. "The problem isn't who you're giving the marina to in your death, it's who controls that loan, because it might not matter."

CHAPTER 13

THE UNSEASONABLY WARM Florida evening clung to Baily's skin like a damp second layer as she stepped onto the back porch of Hayes and Chloe's house. Normally, the winter months were a welcome respite, with the lack of humidity and the potential for a cool breeze floating in off the ocean.

However, even if snow floated from the sky, nothing could dull the temperature rising in her bloodstream.

A glass of iced tea sweated in her hand, the faint clink of ice cubes breaking the silence as she joined the others already seated beneath the string lights that stretched from post to post overhead.

The porch overlooked a patch of land between two other rentals, just outside of town. Across the street, Harvey's cabins and the familiar silhouette of Dawson and Audra's B&B were nestled between two large live oaks. And in the distance, just behind the tree line, was the edge of the Everglades.

She eased into one of the chairs and did her best to shed the heavy weight of her problems, as if she were a snake shedding its skin.

To her left, Fletcher draped his arm across the back of her chair, his palm just barely brushing her shoulder. He smiled, leaned in, and kissed her cheek, soft and sweet. He could be so kind. So gentle. So loving. She cherished that part of Fletcher. Especially now when her world felt as though it had spun out of control and there was no way to stop it.

To her right, Dawson leaned against the railing, his thumbs hooked into his front pockets, his sharp gaze scanning the horizon like he half-expected trouble to walk out of the trees. But that was typical of Dawson. Always on high alert. Hazard of being police chief.

Enzo Hudson sat at the table. He wore a crisp white, button-down shirt, which he'd rolled to his forearms. He tapped a thick manila folder against the wood with steady fingers. He'd shown up at Chloe's five minutes after Baily and Fletcher, with an all-business attitude, ready to jump into whatever he'd found.

Baily appreciated that, but everyone needed—or wanted—a moment to pour drinks, make the introductions, and get settled.

"I started pulling more boxes from closets in my

parents' house," Fletcher whispered. "We can go through them later."

"You really think we'll find more things like that notebook from my dad?" she asked.

"I have no idea. But my folks did tell me that Ray was acting strangely right before his heart attack. Not to mention my mom kept everything. There could be more clues, and I can't shake the feeling that whoever tore through your apartment and rifled through your desk at the marina was looking for something specific."

"I can't imagine what that might be." She lifted her glass and sipped, staring off toward the Everglades. So many secrets hidden in the murky water. Too many betrayals lurking in the past.

"Okay," Enzo said, his voice as smooth as silk but with a current of steel beneath. "Not that I'm in a hurry, because I've got all day, but I've been hyperfocused on this ever since I started. So, are we ready?" Enzo lifted his black-rimmed glasses and pushed them on his face, glancing around at everyone with a glimmer of excitement in his eyes.

"I take it you found something interesting." Fletcher waved his hand.

"You could say that." Enzo tucked the pen behind his ear and lifted a stack of papers. "I've reviewed the loan documents, which by themselves are sketchy. So, I reached out to a forensic accountant and gave him access to the financial information that I had, and…" Enzo's words trailed off as he shuffled papers around.

Baily held her breath, tightening her grip on the glass. "And?"

"First things first." Enzo offered a small, reassuring smile. "The loan is trash. Illegally constructed, likely unenforceable if push ever came to shove, with the exception that you've been making payments."

"What exactly does that mean?" Baily asked. "Because it sounds like they could make me pay."

"Technically, no. They can't." Enzo peered over his cheaters. "But predatory loans like this, ones buried behind shell companies, are designed for people like you not to ask questions. They expect you to be fearful of losing everything. They promise that you won't, but then when the loan is called in, and you can't either pay off the principal or make the payments, they decide they can no longer carry the loan. They figure you'll never consult with someone like me, because you can't afford it, aren't smart enough to ask the right questions, or by the time the loan is due, you're too beaten down to care anymore. But if you do, the problem is you've been making the payments, which does give them some legal rights even though the loan by itself isn't legal."

"That doesn't make sense," Dawson said.

"If this were to go in front of a judge, and the people behind it weren't criminals, a good attorney would argue that for seven years, you valued the loan enough to make payments. My argument would have to be that your dad didn't understand what he was getting into, and that might be hard to prove."

"What about the fact we don't believe her dad ever received the loan in the first place?" Fletcher asked.

"Yeah. That's a new twist, though I have seen it before. Usually, it's when a company or person plans on taking over a business quickly," Enzo said.

"It's possible, if the Barbaros are behind this loan, that they had every intention of calling it in sooner," Dawson said. "But we're not sure why they would've done that. It would've shown their hand. It would've put Ken in a tough spot. And then, there's the whole drug cartel issue, putting whatever their end game is at risk."

Enzo took off his glasses, set them on the table, and leaned back. He didn't appear more relaxed. As a matter of fact, Baily wasn't sure this man knew how to relax, but he did have kind eyes and a gentle demeanor. "I've had some interaction with Barbaro Manufacturing." He rubbed his jaw. "It was a couple of years ago, and the circumstances were a little different. A family living in Miami had lost everything when their son moved to Delaware and invested their life's savings into a small business under the urging of someone inside Barbaro Manufacturing. It was difficult to prove that one of the Barbaros gave this kid a bogus loan. The paper trail wasn't this tight. And I'm not licensed to practice law in Delaware, so I had to find a firm willing to take the case—pro bono."

"What happened?" Chloe asked.

"Unfortunately, the kid decided to end the legal suit," Enzo said. "My lawyer friend in Delaware believes this young man was pressured. Threatened. My buddy kept an eye on him and his business for a while."

"What kind of business?" Dawson asked.

"It's a small restaurant in the harbor, but in reality, it's a money laundering business and a front for drugs." Enzo arched a brow. "Possibly something bigger, but he couldn't be sure. The kid went missing about a year ago."

"Jesus," Baily muttered. "Do you think they could've been putting that kind of pressure on my brother?"

"Anything's possible." Enzo took off his eyeglasses and shoved them back on his face. "His in-laws could've been banking on his ability to push your dad and you into selling. Or the idea that when the funds didn't come through, it would force your dad to default quickly."

"I don't get that part," Fletcher said. "In the notes I have from Ray, it appeared that Ken kept telling his dad to hold on and wait. That the money was coming. And I guess Ray made the payments, so they couldn't force his hand?"

"That's correct, and if Ken told him to do that, then Ken might've saved the marina from being taken over years ago," Enzo said. "My forensic accountant buddy and I have seen this kind of thing before. No deposit record for the full amount. No wire. No traceable disbursement through any formal institution." Enzo sighed. "I've studied those notes and examined the timeline. It does appear that Ken played both sides of this. Or he could've been waiting to tell your dad it turned out to be some Ponzi scam. That even his in-laws were taken, and they lost a cool million or something—but that never happened, so that makes me wonder a few different things about Ken."

"You say all this like it's an everyday occurrence," Baily mumbled.

"It's not," Enzo said softly. "But it happens. These people are good at being fiscally creative. And even better at tugging at the right emotional strings of their victims. I'm sure the Barbaros were beating Ken up with something, and in turn, he knew what to say to get your dad to trust him. I just wish I knew if Ken was actually stuck in the middle, like it appears, because your dad made the loan payments on money he never received, or if the Barbaros just weren't ready to take over the marina for some reason."

"There was another cartel doing business in this area back then," Dawson added.

"My dad trusted Ken when he took out that loan." Baily lifted her tea to her lips, wishing it were whiskey.

Chloe leaned forward, her hand resting on

Hayes's knee. "So, what does this mean for Baily? Legally, anyway."

"You can tell them to shove it," Enzo said. "But if you really wanted to, you could go after them. File suit. Hit them for fraud and predatory lending. But first, we need to send them a letter."

Fletcher let out a slow exhale. "And what does that look like?"

"Depends on whether the company is legitimate or not. If they are," Enzo said. "It would be a long, messy, expensive process. They'll drag their feet, file counterclaims, and try to bleed you dry through paperwork alone. But you'd have a case. A damn good one."

"But it doesn't matter, because it appears it's not about the money. But the land. The Everglades. The professional appearances," Dawson said. "And you said it a few minutes ago, they can make people disappear."

Baily rubbed her forehead. "What if I don't pay them? Just… ignore them. Let them come at me." She blinked, glancing around at her friends. "I mean, they've already tried to sink my boat with me in it. Maybe that was a warning. Maybe they knew Silas was right around the bend. Who knows? But what if we change the rules of their game?"

"That's a real option," Enzo said. "I doubt they're gonna try to foreclose or seize the property. They'd have to show documentation they don't actually have. It's risky—because they might go scorched earth. But if we wait and let them try, we might force their hand and get a look at who's the face behind the curtain, who might give us insight."

"Are you sure you're just a boring old corporate lawyer?" Chloe said. "Because that's some real FBI agent speak." She lowered her chin. "Greer said you had chops, but I had my doubts."

Enzo chuckled. "Yeah. Greer. She's a good one. And she tried like hell to get me to join her at Quantico. But no. A gun and a badge aren't the world for me. I've got a wife and two kids. I prefer the battle zone of boardrooms and mounds of paperwork. It's not bloody, but it can be messy."

"You say that like you get off on it," Fletcher said.

"I kind of do." Enzo nodded, tapping the paperwork. "The next payment is due before the town meeting regarding the Crab Shack. I would think they'd have someone in town watching. Maybe they'll rely on Decker, but I'm guessing they'll send someone else. My suggestion would be not to make the payment. Ignore any phone calls or notices. As a matter of fact, anything that comes regarding the loan, send it to me and let me handle it."

"I can't afford you," Baily said.

Once again, Enzo got rid of the black-rimmed glasses. This time, he stood and leaned against the wooden railing and looked out toward the B&B. "I'm a really good lawyer. I don't say that to be an arrogant asshole. I'm saying that because I have to assess cases based on a couple of different criteria." He turned. "The first one, is it winnable? I always take those. They're no-brainers. Now." He wiggled his finger. "Even those, sometimes, I lose. But in general, if a case is the kind that I can either make a good deal for my client or waltz into the courtroom like I own the place, I take it. However, I hate those cases."

"Why?" Baily asked.

"Because they're boring." Enzo let out a dry laugh. "They pay my bills. They'll put my girls through good colleges, and they're the bread and butter of my law practice. But they don't have meat." He rubbed his neck. "The second criterion I look at is twofold. Do I believe my client, and do they have a case? Now, winnable and believable are always the perfect duo. But they don't always go hand in hand. The law isn't always about right or wrong. It's about justice, and sometimes, that means I take a case where it's not about my billable hours. It's about making sure those who did a very bad thing…get what they deserve."

"You can't do this for free," Baily said.

"I can." Enzo nodded. "And I will." He smiled. "I take on one pro bono case every year or so. I haven't had one in eighteen months. Consider yourself having just won the lottery."

Fletcher shifted beside her. "But now you're suggesting she bait them. Give them time to act and respond."

"I am." Enzo nodded. "But they won't be prepared for her to challenge them. For her to know they can't take the marina. Not without a fight. And we'll fight."

He pointed to Dawson, then Hayes. "Don't forget they'll also be looking at the Crab Shack property. They'll think that's in the bag, right?"

Dawson nodded. "I like this plan. Makes them play their next move, and we'll see it coming."

"She could get hurt, Dawson," Fletcher said.

"She almost drowned yesterday. You think they're going to stop if we play nice?" Hayes asked.

Baily looked down at her tea, and the ice had nearly melted. "How long before they do something?"

Enzo shrugged. "I bet they'll come at you immediately after you miss the payment. They need to put the pressure on if they're gonna invest in this town."

"The Barbaros know we're all here," Fletcher said. "If she doesn't pay, they know she's got protection. Friends. Eyes everywhere."

Dawson scratched his jaw. "Which is why we need to do this Decker's way."

Baily raised a brow. "You trust him now?"

"I trust he wants out of the Barbaros' grip," Dawson said. "And he's useful. He's still got family in Miami—cousins who've done time, some of them tied to loan enforcement ops. He knows how they handle things when borrowers push back."

Chloe stood and grabbed her phone off the table. "He's in his cabin. I saw the lights on earlier."

"I'll call him," Dawson said, pulling his phone from his pocket and tapping the screen. He pressed the cell to his ear.

Everyone sat in silence for a moment.

"Yeah. He's on his way over." Dawson pointed, chuckling. "Look. Here he comes."

"There's a part of me that feels bad for that man," Hayes said. "We all know I was the quiet loner of the group, but I've never been alone in this world. I kind of feel like that guy doesn't have anyone. I did some research into his family and damn. He wasn't kidding about all that."

"Nope," Fletcher said. "I want to trust him, but he doesn't make it easy with those stupid, expensive boat shoes and that SUV. I hate those cars." He sighed. "But the man is putting himself on the line for us. For Baily. That's something."

It sure was.

A few moments later, Decker crossed the yard with a loose jog, his ball cap turned backward, and a suspiciously amused expression on his face. She'd never seen him wearing an outfit like that, or even looking that relaxed, which was odd.

But it was as if a weight had been lifted.

"You rang?" he called, hopping onto the porch like he'd done it a hundred times.

Dawson waved him over. "Have a seat, you're officially part of this circus."

"Oh, goodie. I've always wanted to be a clown." Decker plopped into the chair next to Enzo. "Is there beer in that cooler?"

"Beer, soda, water. Pick your poison and help yourself," Hayes said.

Decker leaned forward, snagged a cold brew, and

cracked it open. "So, who's this, and why am I being summoned? Not that I mind. I was starting to go cross-eyed."

"I'm Enzo. I'm Baily's lawyer." Enzo gave him the short version. The bogus loan, the shell company, the lack of documentation. Everything.

"What do you think?" Fletcher asked at the end of Enzo's tale.

Baily wanted to either hurl or go swim with the gators.

Decker reached into the cooler and grabbed another beer. He took a long, slow draw. "When I was a kid, they strong-armed my uncle into laundering money through his fish bait store." Decker sighed. "I say *they* because I didn't have a name. There are a couple of cartels that do business in Miami. A few loan sharks. A few stray drug runners. Arms dealers. You name it, we've got it. I just wanted to keep my nose clean, but my uncle said the name out loud."

"What name did he use?"

"Valenia Barbaro," Decker said softly. "He only said her name once and it was more like a whimper than words. He was terrified of her. I was maybe five, but I remember because in my stupidity as a small kid, I wondered why he'd be so afraid of a woman. But then, when I was eleven, something happened. I don't know what. All I know is that my uncle came to the house and told my old man that he'd screwed up. Next thing we knew, he'd been arrested for dealing arms. It was a big raid. Strange thing though, I'd been in that back room where they found the guns the day before, and there hadn't been any. I told my dad. He told me to never mention that again. He told me the people my uncle had been involved with were bad people and that I needed to learn to lie low."

"You know a lot of people they apply that kind of pressure to?" Fletcher asked.

"I wouldn't say a lot. A few family members. And I saw things while living there, but I tried to make myself blend in."

"You don't do that now," Dawson said. "You stand out."

"I know." Decker nodded. "But once I started making my own money, which I had believed I'd done pretty much on my own, I thought standing out was a good way to keep people like that away. I didn't need them, and I thought that showed. I've since learned my lesson."

"Tell us how they operated in your neighborhood." Dawson snagged a beer and took a healthy chug.

"It's very different from how this will go down," Decker said. "They apply pressure first—but it's slow and subtle—a few broken windows, some veiled threats. Maybe a fire if that doesn't work." He looked at Baily. "But if you don't flinch, they'll try to buy you out again. Or ruin you legally."

"What do you make of Ken and his relationship with all this?" Enzo asked.

"He sounds a little like my dad," Decker said. "Caught between a rock and a hard place. I mean, Ken married Julie Barbaro, the girl who holds the keys to the kingdom. He might not have known that when he said, 'I do,' but I'm sure he was given a quick lesson right after the honeymoon. And then a few tests of loyalty." Decker raised his hand. "If I'm being totally honest here, it sounds like the Barbaros went after Ken, knowing he had a tendency for the illegal."

"I take offense to that," Baily said. She shouldn't defend her brother. Not anymore, but he was still her flesh and blood. Decker hadn't even ever met the man. He had no right.

"I didn't mean to." Decker set his beer on the railing. "But take my uncle, for example. He cut corners all the time. And he dealt drugs in high school. The people running my neighborhood did their homework. I wouldn't be surprised if they'd stayed away from me, knowing I was a strait-laced kid, looking to get out."

"And then they hit you where it counted," Enzo said. "Got you where it hurt the most. The thing you worked so hard to build—business and reputation."

"Jesus, these people are horrible." Baily leaned closer into Fletcher. "But they've underestimated me because they should've counted on the fact that I don't give up. That the marina means more to me than anything. I'm not going to bend over and hand it to them."

"They know that because they've been patient,"

Decker added. "More patient than with most things. They've played the long game, so it's not just the marina. It's Calusa Cove. For them, Ken was the key to that. But I suspect they didn't anticipate Ken's Navy SEAL buddies retiring here. I'm sure that's why the pressure is much more subtle. I bet it's why they're using me." He crooked a finger. "All the more reason to let me walk into that town meeting with a dummy set of plans."

"Oh, we're gonna let you do that," Fletcher said.

Baily folded her arms. "Do you think they'll make another move soon? Another shot at destroying the marina, like when they stole gas? Or maybe, this time, blow up my car?"

"Don't joke about shit like that." Fletcher took her hand and squeezed it.

Decker took a long pull from his beer. "I doubt it. They sank your boat. They're gonna watch and see if you use money to buy a new one or pay off the loan. After that, they're gonna toss legal bullshit at you."

"And that's where I come in because I'll throw it right back at them." Enzo inched across the deck and gathered up all the paperwork.

"Sounds like we've got a plan," Dawson said. "Let's see who comes knocking."

Baily stared at Fletcher, who didn't say anything for a long moment, just kept his gaze fixated on the horizon, his jaw tight.

"What's going on?" Baily reached for his hand.

He looked at her then, his eyes dark with worry.

"We do this together. But I swear to God, if someone tries to hurt you again—"

"They won't get the chance," she said, squeezing his hand. "We've got too many people watching."

And as the sun dipped below the tree line, casting long shadows across the porch, no one said a word. But every one of them knew—this wasn't over.

Actually, it had just begun.

CHAPTER 14

THE TRAIL behind Cypress Ridge wound like a lazy snake through the dense brush, the late-afternoon sun casting golden shards through the canopy overhead. Fletcher moved slowly, boots crunching along packed earth and pine needles, clipboard in hand, surveying a downed tree reported near mile marker six in Calusa Cove Park.

This was the part of his job that he loved. The quiet, peaceful, rich beauty of the land that surrounded the Everglades. The hours he could walk in silence and be connected to the earth. As a kid, he hadn't truly grown to appreciate this spot. While he'd loved living here and had only a few regrets, he hadn't fully come to understand what it all meant. Perhaps no one had until they'd lived a little and seen a little heartache. It took searching the world for something that had already lived in his heart to see what had always been a part of him. To know what had always grounded him in ways many couldn't understand.

The Navy and being a SEAL had taught him honor, duty, and what being loyal really meant. It had given him brothers. A family he chose. A family who, no matter what, had his six. It had brought him full circle, giving him perspective he couldn't have ever gained anywhere else.

Sometimes, that saddened him because it meant he had to accept that he and Baily had had no chance back then. It hadn't been their time. He'd needed the space to grow and evolve, and while she'd been able to do all that living in Calusa Cove…he hadn't. He'd needed the distance.

He paused in the clearing. Birdsong echoed in the stillness. Too still, he realized. He frowned.

There was something wrong with the silence. He felt this thick weight of soundlessness. The unease of it. How it had an edge to it as if it were waiting for something to happen. He knew this sensation well. It had happened in battle all the time. He'd never welcomed it, but out there, while fighting for country, it had been a way of life.

But it didn't belong in Calusa Cove.

He squatted, scanning the area and reaching for a broken limb blocking the path, when the crack of a rifle split the air. A searing pain tore through his upper arm, white-hot and blinding. He dropped instantly, the world tilting as he slammed shoulder-first into the ground, sending leaves scattering.

"Shit—"

Blood soaked through the sleeve of his Parks and Rec shirt. He dragged himself behind the trunk of a long-dead sabal palm, adrenaline slamming into his bloodstream like a freight train. He took in a slow, shallow breath. The shot had come from the northeast, from a high location, and he'd been damn lucky he'd moved when he had or that bullet might have landed in the back of his head.

Testing whether the shooter was still there—and in the same location—he shifted, rustling the leaves, but staying behind the trunk.

Another shot cracked overhead—clean, precise. A sniper.

He pulled out his cell, opting for that instead of his radio. Too much noise and the possibility the enemy was listening to his frequency. He pressed the phone to his ear. It rang twice.

"Hey man, what's—"

"Dawson. I've been hit," Fletcher whispered.

"Did you say hit? As in shot?" Dawson asked.

"Yeah. Sniper. Clean. Still there, in a tree maybe fifty yards away. I'm on the Cypress Ridge Trail. North fork. I'm bunkered behind a tree between Marker Six and Seven. Closer to Six, about a half a klick from the bend. Need backup."

Crack. Bark exploded above him, spraying splinters across his face.

"Jesus," he muttered, pressing his hand hard over the wound on his arm. It wasn't too bad—the bullet went through, clean—but it burned like hell. His fingers trembled as he reached for his sidearm. Just in case.

A full two minutes passed.

"I'm en route. Patrol car had a damn flat. Taking my personal vehicle. ETA eight minutes. Texted Hayes and Keaton. Hayes is on the way. Keaton's with Decker. Told him to stick by his side. Stay down. Stay sharp. And watch your fucking back."

Fletcher sucked in a slow breath and kept low. He needed to think like Hayes, the sniper of the group. They were patient people in the field. They could lie on their bellies, propped up on their elbows, eyes peering through a scope...for flipping hours, and not bat an eyelash. Everyone thought it took a unique personality style to be a demolitions man on a team? No. It was the sniper who stood out as the odd duck.

Sweat slicked his brow. His ears strained for movement, but the shooter—if military trained—would be able to stick this out for a very long time.

Five minutes ticked by. Three more to go, and Dawson was never late.

Eight minutes was a long time under fire.

He tapped his phone with bloodied fingers, heart hammering, and dialed Baily.

She picked up on the second ring. "Hey! I'm with Chloe and Silas. We are waiting for Hayes before we—"

"I just needed to hear your voice," Fletcher said, barely above a whisper. "You okay?"

There was a pause. "Yeah. I'm fine. We're fine. Why? Fletcher, what happened? You sound…off."

"I'm up on the trail. There's been an…incident. Gunfire." God, he shouldn't lie to her, but he didn't want her freaking out. Not yet anyway. "Dawson and Hayes are on their way, but I needed to know you were safe."

A sharp inhale. "Fletcher…"

"Stay where you are," he said. "Stay with Chloe and Silas until I say otherwise. Please."

"I will. I swear. Just—just be careful. I…I…I love you, okay?"

He closed his eyes, the words hitting him harder than the bullet. "I love you, too."

The line disconnected.

It wasn't like they hadn't said those words to each other a million times. However, it had been years since they'd tumbled from her lips. Years before, he'd felt the weight of their impact.

Years since that part of his world had been put back together.

Another few minutes crawled by before the crunch of boots sounded over breaking twigs.

Fletcher sucked in breath, held his weapon, and shifted. He peered over the tree trunk, scanning the area.

Nothing. No movement. Only the sharp sound of an owl. Only it wasn't a real one.

Dawson.

Fletcher responded with his own owl noise. A few more repeated.

Hayes.

The gang was all here. But they had a job to do.

Find the fucking sniper.

Unfortunately, Fletcher was the sitting duck. His job was to do nothing but wait.

He craned his ear, listening to every little noise. Even the stillness told him something.

Crack. Pop.

Movement and gunfire. Just one round.

Thud.

Then boots. Dawson's voice called out, "Fletcher! Talk to me!"

"You're going to fucking pay for that," a deep male voice said.

"You shot our friend first," Hayes said, with the kind of pride dipped in a sense of humility that he'd always had when he hit his target. "I think the law might be on our side."

"Here," Fletcher called, lifting his hand enough to wave. All the energy he'd stored in his muscles left like a bird taking flight.

Dawson crouched beside him seconds later, already assessing the wound. "Damn. You weren't kidding."

"Just a flesh wound."

"Right, because a bullet going in one side of your biceps and coming out the other end isn't a big deal." Dawson lifted his gaze, waving a hand. "At least

Hayes didn't kill the asshole, so now I get to have some fun and question him."

Fletcher grunted. "I want to be there."

"I can let him stew in a cell while you get that cleaned out and stitched up." Dawson took off his jacket, ripped off a piece of his shirt, and tied off Fletcher's upper arm.

"Hey," Remy called. "Tully and I did a sweep. We didn't see anyone else. Thanks to a rainy winter, we did see tracks. One set. Leading right to the tree where Hayes took out the shooter. That's it, other than Fletcher's tracks."

"Good. Now go read that jerk-off his rights and haul his ass to the station. I'm gonna take this guy to the hospital."

"You got it, boss," Remy said.

Fletcher dropped his head against the tree trunk.

"You're looking a little pale there, buddy." Dawson applied more pressure to the wound. "Should I call an ambulance?"

"No." Fletcher sat up taller, taking Dawson's hand, and with some effort, he stood. His legs were wobbly and his brain foggy. But he'd had to deal with far worse and walked a longer distance to receive help.

Dawson's phone buzzed. He checked the screen. "It's Keaton." He answered with a clipped, "Yeah?"

Fletcher couldn't hear the words, but he saw Dawson's expression tighten as they moved as swiftly as Fletcher could handle down the path.

"What?" Dawson paused mid-step. "You've got to

be fucking kidding me." Another long moment stretched. "Okay, heading there now with Fletcher. See you soon." Dawson hung up and turned. "Decker collapsed while eating a burger at Massey's Pub. Keaton was there with him. Said one minute he was eating dinner, pretending to argue with Keaton, just in case someone from that damn boat parade was a plant, the next he was gasping for air like his lungs stopped working. EMS got him stabilized, but they're running tests."

"He's too young to have had a heart attack," Fletcher said, ignoring the throb in his arm. "Not to mention, someone tried to drown Baily and kill me with a stray bullet. What just happened to Decker can't be a coincidence."

"That's what Keaton believes. He said it looked like Decker was choking on nothing. Couldn't breathe. Skin flushed. No obstruction. He suspects poison. His father-in-law's girlfriend is running some tests…off the books."

"That's nice of Emily. She's a good person and a great doctor." Fletcher eyed the parking lot.

Dawson opened the passenger side of his new, fancy SUV, which had a big, old-*dad* vibe to it. "Add in my flat tire, which I bet when I take a good look at it, either someone simply let the air out or slashed it, and I'd say the Barbaros are escalating their timeline."

"Or they're feeling pressured." Fletcher tugged at the tourniquet that Dawson had made. "But they're not hitting the mark with these attempts, and they knew Ken. They'd have to know we don't scare that easily."

Dawson pressed the start engine button, turned the knob, shifted the car into drive, and pulled out of the lot. "Maybe it's not about scaring us anymore. The damage to the hull of Baily's boat was extensive. I'm surprised she got as far into the Glades as she did." Dawson shifted his gaze. "These people are coming in for the kill."

"That's not too smart."

"It is if they believe the language on the loan is buried. That no one knows about it." Dawson drummed his fingers against the wheel. "Baily never discussed that with Julie. Barely brought it up with Ken because she'd been so fed up with his bullshit. Hell, the only reason we knew was because she finally realized we were on her side. Like Decker said a while ago, Julie believes Baily's still pissed at the lot of us, and Decker played into that when he spoke to Tessa. But what I don't get is why take out Decker? He's their guy."

"They lost faith in Decker. Wouldn't be surprised if next week if we walk into that town meeting blindsided by a new guy. With new plans." Fletcher shook his head, letting out a long breath. "They've moved on to whatever their Plan B is."

"Well, then we need to get the town to move up their meeting." Dawson slammed his fist on the steering wheel. "I know just the guy to go to the committee and ask for the meeting to be changed."

"Silas," Fletcher said.

"Yup." Dawson nodded. "He'll plead that the town needs to heal from the mess Paul and Dewey created. Silas will get them to hear us, and the Barbaros won't be the wiser."

"Especially since Decker's the only one who showed any interest." Fletcher nodded. "Good idea." It wasn't much. It was barely a plan. But it was a beginning, and that was something.

* * *

"Thanks, Silas." Baily jumped from Silas's beat-up old Jeep. Her heart thumped in the center of her chest hard and fast. Her palms were sweaty, and her mind raced with a million thoughts, and not a single one was good.

"I should walk you in," Silas called. "Fletcher wanted eyes on you."

"I'll be fine. But you can text Fletcher and let him know I'm here." Her sneakers hit the pavement, and she jogged toward the emergency room bay doors, growing breathless. She needed to take up something other than walking. That didn't constitute exercise, no matter what anyone said.

The hospital hallway reeked of antiseptic and overcooked coffee. Fluorescent lights flickered overhead, casting pale shadows across the linoleum floor as Baily stormed past the nurses' station, her shoes clapping against the tile. She barely registered the soft murmur of voices behind curtains or the squeak of rubber soles. Her entire focus narrowed to the door at the end of the hall—Room 212.

That's the message she'd received from Dawson, along with a brief description as to why Fletcher needed to be seen by a medical professional.

She shoved the door open without knocking.

Inside, Fletcher sat on the edge of the hospital bed, shirt off, his left arm wrapped in blood-soaked gauze. The doctor, Emily Sprouce, in navy scrubs and a focused scowl, leaned over him with a curved needle and suture. Her gloved hands moved with quick, practiced efficiency.

Baily's breath caught at the sight of him. His skin was pale beneath the overhead light, and a smear of dried blood ran along his jawline like a cruel reminder of how close she'd come to losing him.

"You got shot?" Her voice cracked like a whip in the air-conditioning. "And you didn't think to tell me when you called. Or that the sniper was still sitting in some tree, waiting for you to poke your head out so he could kill you."

Fletcher turned, startled. "Bailey—hey, I—"

"You got shot, and I find out from Dawson in a flipping text message?" She stepped farther into the room, arms crossed, eyes blazing. "You called me from the woods, and you didn't say a damn thing?"

Fletcher flinched. Not from pain because Emily had just pulled the final stitch. He opened his mouth, but Emily held up a hand, glancing between them.

"I'll give you two a minute," she said quietly. "The sutures are done. No major damage. Just don't rip them open, getting yelled at." With a knowing smile, she peeled off her gloves and slipped from the room, closing the door behind her.

Baily didn't move until the click of the latch settled. Then she dropped her arms and stepped closer, her anger giving way to something far heavier. "What if you hadn't been lucky? What if you hadn't made that call, and I hadn't gotten to say those words? What if that bullet had hit something other than your biceps? You could've died, Fletcher, and you made light of it."

Fletcher met her gaze, a tinge of guilt flickering across his face. "I didn't want to scare you. Not when I knew Dawson and Hayes were coming. But I did need to know you were safe and I wanted to hear your voice. Selfish of me, I know."

"You don't get to protect me by shutting me out," she said, her voice softer but laced with a fierceness she hadn't expected from herself. "We're in this together. That means I get to be scared. I get to be mad. I get to know when the man I love is bleeding out in the woods."

"Bleeding out is a bit dramatic." He reached for her hand. She took it.

"Don't try to diffuse this with humor," she whispered. "You're not Dawson. He's the funny one."

"I'm sorry," he said. "It wasn't about shutting you out. It was instinct. Habit. I didn't even think—I just… I wanted to hear your voice. Make sure you were okay. And if you by chance heard what was going on out there, you'd know in that one instance, I was okay, too."

"But it's bigger than that, isn't it?" She brushed her fingers over the bruised skin around the gauze, her touch feather-light. "You called me, so I'd be the last thing you heard. In case you didn't make it out. In case Dawson and Hayes didn't get there, and that sniper got a second shot off. Because you never got those kinds of chances in the military."

His silence said everything.

Tears burned at the corners of her eyes, but she blinked them back. Instead, she leaned in and pressed her forehead to his. "I'm glad you called. I'm glad I got to say those words. But don't you ever keep information from me again. It's not fair, and you wouldn't appreciate it if I did it to you."

"I won't," he whispered. "I swear."

Their lips met—brief, tender, aching. A kiss that said more than words ever could. When she pulled back, he smiled faintly. "I missed this. Missed you. I do love you."

"I know," she murmured. "You're not getting rid of me again. Even if you try."

"I wouldn't mind hearing those words again. Seeing your face while your voice tickles my ears."

"Oh, my God. Now, you're trying to be romantic. Not you're thing either. That's split between Keaton and Hayes." She eased onto the gurney, lacing her fingers between his, feeling his warm skin. He was everything, and she'd spent the last few years pushing him away because she'd been too afraid to risk her heart.

Only, her heart already belonged to him, and life and love was one big risk.

"Oh, come on. I'm not that pathetic, am I?" He looped his good arm around her waist.

"You're a sweet, kind man, but you're not Mr. Romance. More like Mr. Practical, and I adore that about you." She rested her head on his shoulder. "I love that you think a romantic dinner is grilled fish that you caught, I cleaned, and a cheap bottle of wine down on the dock while we wave to Silas as he trolls by."

"Nothing better than watching the sunset over the Glades with the prettiest girl in Calusa Cove."

"Now you're being a cornball."

"Yeah, I've never had good lines." He kissed her neck. "I've never had game, but I had something, because I had you."

"You've still got me." She pressed her palm against his cheek. "I love you, Fletcher Dane."

"Oh, my full name." He smiled. "I must be getting lucky—"

A soft knock broke the moment. Keaton poked his head in. "Sorry, but you guys might want to come next door. Decker's awake."

"I'd like to talk to him." Fletcher hopped off the bed, snagged his shirt, and took her hand.

She followed him and Keaton to Room 214, where Decker Brown lay in a hospital bed, propped up by pillows, an IV line taped to the back of his hand. His skin was clammy and pale, his usual bravado dulled by whatever cocktail the doctors had pumped into him.

"The doctors are still flushing his system, and he's on some good drugs since he's been in a bit of pain." Keaton leaned against the far wall, his arms folded tight, like he didn't quite trust the stillness.

Decker cracked one eye open and sucked in a shaky breath before letting it out with a swish and wheeze. "Keaton tells me you had some excitement, too." He lifted a crooked finger.

"You look like shit," Fletcher said.

Decker managed a grin. "Thanks. I'd say you do, too, but you manage to make getting shot look sexy."

"Don't say things like that to him. It'll go right to his head." Baily stepped to the foot of the bed. "They said poison?"

"That's what the docs are telling me." Decker reached for the water on the tray.

Keaton raced to his side, giving him a hand. "Emily's running off-the-record labs. But his throat closed up fast. Skin flushed. No signs of obstruction. Classic signs of something synthetic. Fast-acting."

"I was mid-bite," Decker said, voice hoarse. "One minute, I'm arguing with Keaton about who pays for dinner to keep up appearances. Next thing I know,

I'm gasping for air like someone shoved a pillow down my throat."

Fletcher's jaw tightened. "This isn't simple escalation. Dawson and I believe they're gonna try to blindside us with a new developer at the meeting."

"That thought has crossed my mind since I've been lying here," Decker said, eyes sharpening despite the medication. "They know I've been stalling. Feeding them crumbs. They think I'm a loose end. But I don't get why they tried to kill you."

"I've been thinking about that." Fletcher shifted his gaze, catching Baily's. "It's all about creating an environment of fear. But also, if they take me out, in their minds, they're removing everything Baily has that matters outside of the marina, making it easier for her to walk away."

"They don't know me very well." She folded her arms across her chest. "All that would make me do is dig my heels in deeper. This is my home. It's all I've ever known, and it's all I've ever wanted. If they thought hurting the people I love was one way to get me to cave, well, they're fools."

"Don't mistake their miscalculation of who you are as being foolish." Decker lowered his chin. "Their plans are always layered. This has been years in the making. The Barbaros use people. Hell, they use their own. I'm sure Julie had no say in any aspect of her life."

"Are you suggesting she went after Ken?" Keaton asked.

"Oh, I am." Decker nodded. "Just like Tessa came after me. And I'm sure Damon and Valenia had all sorts of information on Ken to make sure that Julie knew just what to say and how to act to get his attention. I doubt he knew what hit him until it was too late."

Baily's chest tightened. "That's so cold and calculating."

"That's the kind of people they are," Decker whispered. "But I'm not playing their game. I'm all in. I want to take down every last one of those bastards. They used me. I'm sure they used Ken. And they need to be stopped."

Baily's heart pulsed in her throat. "And what if they bring in another sniper? Or a different kind of killer to Calusa Cove"

Decker scoffed. "Let 'em. They missed their shot. I'm still here. And I've got names. Records. I took a risk and reached out to my cousin back in Miami. He sent me a list of businesses linked to their laundering operation. You gave me a seat at the table, now I'm gonna help you blow this whole thing wide open."

"Dawson has that list." Keaton nodded grimly. "Chloe called Buddy. She did it quietly. He's sending an old friend of his. Someone we know. Someone who works for the Aegis Network to stand guard. But we've got to work out a plan and move fast because I wouldn't be surprised if the Barbaros are closing in."

Fletcher looked to Baily. She knew that look. It

was the look that told her he couldn't sit still. "I told Dawson I wanted to be part of the interrogation of the sniper," he said softly. "It was me the man tried to take out."

Baily hissed, clenching her fists at her side. "Do you think that's a good idea?"

"Nothing like rubbing his face in the fact he failed at his mission." Fletcher inched closer, resting his hand on the small of her back. "I need to hear what this guy has to say."

"Hondo's got a few days off, and he's keeping a watchful eye at the B&B," Keaton said. "I'm going to stay here with Decker until the guy from the Aegis network gets here, so why don't you drop her off at the B&B, and she can hang with Audra?"

"I wouldn't mind spending time with her." Baily nodded.

Fletcher pulled her close again, pressing a kiss to her temple. "All right, let's head out." He turned, resting a hand on Decker's wrist. "Call me if you need anything. And you can come stay at my place to recover when they release you."

"Thanks. Keaton offered the same." Decker gave a weak smile. "Does this mean we're friends?"

"Don't push it." Fletcher laughed, shifting his gaze toward Keaton. "Keep me posted."

"Will do."

She took Fletcher's hand and stepped out into the hallway. "I feel like I should call Julie or something."

"Maybe, but not until I'm sitting right next to you,

and we've got a better handle on what we're going to do next." He kissed her softly. "I get the feeling things are going to happen quickly, especially if we're able to push up the town meeting, and our bid on the Crab Shack is accepted."

"They're going to bring the war here, aren't they?" Baily shivered.

"Sweetheart, unfortunately, we're already fighting it."

CHAPTER 15

Fletcher stepped into the station house and was immediately greeted by a smile, followed by a frown and a wiggle of a finger.

"What the hell, Fletcher?" Anna, Dawson's secretary, learned against the counter. "I was told there was an incident, but I wasn't given the bloody details."

"Bullet went in." He tapped the front of his biceps. "And came out clean on the other side."

"You've always been able to downplay any injury." Anna shook her head. "I bet Baily didn't appreciate that."

"Nope." Fletcher chuckled. "She nearly bit my head off."

"So, the two of you are…back together…for good?" Anna asked with a twinkle in her eye and a half grin.

"That's my plan," Fletcher said. "If I can manage not to screw it up again."

"At least you're willing to admit you're the one who mucked it up to begin with."

"I might be a little dumb in the romance department, but I'm not a fool." He pointed down the hall.

Anna nodded. "Dawson's waiting for you."

"Thanks." Fletcher made his way down the corridor.

Dawson stepped from his office. "How's the arm?"

"Fine." Fletcher rolled his shoulder, wincing slightly. "Spent a few minutes with Decker. He's no worse for the wear, but Emily's gonna keep him a day or two."

"I'm so glad he's going to be okay."

Fletcher nodded. "He's all fired up, though. Ready to take on the Barbaros, and I can't blame him. I want this shit to be over. For Baily to have some peace. Her life has been hard for too long."

"We'll get that for her." Dawson waved a hand, then tucked a folder under his arm. "Let's go have a chat with this asshole."

Fletcher followed Dawson into the interview room. A stillness settled over him, reminding him of darker days.

The room was quiet.

Too quiet.

The kind of quiet Fletcher hated—thick, oppressive, unnatural. The walls felt closer with every second that ticked by. Dawson sat across the metal table from their shooter—a wiry man in his early forties with the leathery skin of someone who'd spent too much time in the sun and too little time around people. His brown eyes were flat, unreadable. His hands were cuffed to a metal ring bolted to the table, but he didn't fidget. Didn't twitch. Didn't blink.

Fletcher leaned against the wall, his arm still throbbing beneath fresh gauze as a reminder. Not that he needed one.

The bastard had waited in the brush, watched Fletcher hike up the trail, and then pulled the trigger. If Fletcher had taken one more step to the right, the bullet wouldn't have grazed his arm. It would've gone straight through his neck.

But the man hadn't missed.

Not entirely.

Fletcher wondered if he'd aimed for the arm on purpose.

Dawson tapped a pen against the tabletop with a rhythm that bordered on irritating. Which, Fletcher knew, was the point.

"So," Dawson said, his tone casual, as usual. It was Dawson's style. Not much rattled the man, and if it did, he rarely let it show. At least not with a suspect. "We found your perch. You built a nice little nest up there. Perfect view of the ridge. A little off the main path, but not too far for a clean shot. You a hunter, or just enjoy creeping in the woods with a rifle?"

Silence.

The man stared ahead, unmoved and unfazed.

"What's the matter? Cat got your tongue? Or did the Barbaros tell you to keep your mouth shut?"

Nothing.

Fletcher shifted his stance and stepped closer. "You know, I was trying to figure out your angle. You could've killed me. You didn't. Which means you weren't trying to. Which means you're either not a murderer, or you were sent to deliver a message."

Dawson clapped his hands once, loudly, making the man blink. "That's it, isn't it? You were hired to send a message. A simple one. Scare the pretty girl. Put the town on edge. Stir up a little chaos. Then sit back and watch what we do in the wake of all that chaos."

Still, the man said nothing.

Dawson leaned in. "The thing is, my friend here doesn't scare easy. And neither does the woman you were trying to rattle. So, you might want to consider talking before the Barbaros decide you're a liability for not finishing the job because we both know what happens to liabilities."

That got a twitch of the eyes.

Just a flicker, barely noticeable. But it was there.

Fletcher took a step closer and opened the folder Dawson had placed on the table. He pulled out the folded photo Dawson had printed off. It was a wide-angle shot from the park ranger's trail cam. The man in the photo, aiming a rifle. Clear as day. He slapped it on the table. "What's your name?"

The man stared at the photo.

"You talk to us," Fletcher said, voice low, steady. "Or we let your employers think you already have because we have friends in high places who can find out who you are, and we can deliver our own message. Which would you prefer?"

The man's lips parted. "I'm not afraid of you," he said.

"Okay." Dawson rifled through the folder until he found an image of the Barbaros. "But you should be afraid of them. Afraid of what they'll do to you or your loved ones. Now you can cooperate with us, and we'll protect you. Or we can feed you to the wolves. It's your call."

The man shifted his gaze between Dawson and Fletcher. "You're right. It wasn't a kill order."

Dawson shot Fletcher a look. "Progress. Now tell me who gave you that order. I need you to say it."

"A man I only knew as Oliver. Said he worked for the Barbaros. Said the woman had been causing problems. That hurting her wasn't the goal. I was to make her feel vulnerable. Unsafe. That hurting him would make her weigh her options more carefully as the Barbaros moved ahead with their plans."

Fletcher clenched his jaw. "You could've missed. I wasn't standing still. You could've hit something vital."

The man nodded. "But I didn't. I'm good at what I do. I waited for the right time. Only mistake I made was following orders by sitting around and watching because Oliver failed to mention that the parks and rec guy would call for the police chief and some trained military sniper guy." The man rubbed his thigh. "I still need medical attention."

"The EMTs took a look at that." Dawson waved his hand. "Flesh wound. Barely a scratch." Dawson crossed his arms and leaned back. "What about the poison?"

He blinked, jerking his head back. "I don't know what you're talking about."

"The hit on Decker? The man enjoying lunch at Massey's Pub," Dawson said. "How do you explain that?"

The man shook his head slowly. "I didn't have anything to do with that. They never said a word about any other guy I was supposed to deal with. Just the parks and rec man. The Barbaros... They don't let the left hand know what the right one's doing. Layers on layers. You're just a cog in the wheel."

Fletcher leaned forward. "Why take the job? You don't strike me as the kind of guy who takes orders easily." Not that he had any insight into this guy, but he thought he'd take a stab in the dark. It couldn't hurt.

The man exhaled, long and slow. "Because they have my brother over the coals. I do this for them, and they let him off the hook."

Dawson's tone hardened. "What's your brother's name? And while we're at it, we still don't know yours."

"My name is John. My brother's Mark Jensen.

He's not a part of any of this. Just a mechanic from Jacksonville. Doesn't even own a gun."

"What do the Barbaros want with Mark?" Dawson asked.

John closed his eyes for a long moment before blinking them open. "A couple of years ago, they loaned him money. I was still in the Marines. I didn't know, or I would've told my brother to tell those assholes to fuck off. But they come in all sweet at first. Promise you this and that. Then they have you sign on the dotted line, only you don't have a flipping clue as to what you're actually signing, and next thing my brother knows, he's laundering money for these people. And strange packages are being delivered. Turns out, they're drugs."

Fletcher's pulse ticked faster. He turned to Dawson. "So, what you're saying is if you did this favor for them, your brother gets his shop back, free and clear."

"That's what they said." John nodded.

"And you believed them?" Dawson asked.

"No. Not really. But what else was I supposed to do?" John asked. "Besides, if I didn't do it, they told me they'd turn on Mark. Set him up to take a fall, and off to prison he'd go. My little brother couldn't handle something like that. He's a good man, a little soft, and prison would break him."

Dawson rubbed the back of his neck. "You just stepped into a minefield, pal. You want to help your brother? Start talking faster. Every detail. Names.

Contacts. Where you stayed last night. You give us enough, we'll forget about you taking a shot at my friend over there, and we'll help you get your brother out alive and with his shop intact."

The man hesitated, gaze darting to Fletcher, then Dawson. He looked tired. Like a man in too deep to swim but not quite ready to drown.

"How do I know this isn't bullshit to get me to lay over?" John asked.

"You don't." Dawson arched a brow. "But it's either me or the Barbaros. Time to pick a side."

"Fine. I'll talk," he said finally. "But I don't know much, except what little my brother's filled me in on how they operate."

"I might be a small-town cop, but I know people in high places." Dawson stood, gathering the paperwork. "For your safety, I'm going to need to keep you here." He pulled out his keys and uncuffed John. "I'm gonna call in a friend who's ex-FBI. She'll come and have a little chat with you, and I expect you to tell her everything. She'll get eyes on your brother and make sure nothing happens to him while we set up our sting operation here."

John leaned back, rubbing his wrists. "I haven't a clue as to what they have planned for you. I only know they're coming, and if they don't hear from me today, I'm scared as to what they'll do to my brother."

Dawson nodded, glancing at his watch. "If they have eyes on the town, they'll know we took you into custody. They'll also know I'm, for the most part, a rules man, so you'll get your one call. You'll make it to them, with me listening and guiding you as to what to say." He waved his finger. "You don't fuck me over, and I'll make sure you walk out of here free as a bird."

"Thanks, man." John blew out a puff of air. "I only did this to save my brother's ass. We're all each other's got."

"I understand that." Fletcher opened the door and stepped out into the hallway, Dawson one pace behind. "Do you trust he won't screw us?"

"I have no idea." Dawson threaded his fingers through his hair. "But we've got to let it play out, and we've got to do it fast. Silas got the town to move the meeting up. They're going to hear our plans and our bid tomorrow. They still believe Decker is on his own, and I'm not about to correct them on that. But Silas asked the committee not to make a stink about it for fear that some other big company would try to make a play. He told them everything that's been happening and how he's concerned it's all sabotage."

"And what did the committee have to say about that?" Fletcher asked.

"For the first time since Audra's dad went missing, no one in this town is crying conspiracy theory." Dawson arched a brow. He glanced at his cell. "Chloe, Remy, Tully, and I will handle things here. Why don't you go back to the B&B and stick close to the girls? Trinity's there, too. Hayes will meet you. Keaton's gonna stick by Decker."

"We need Decker's input. We can't do this without him."

"You can always FaceTime. But I don't think it's a good idea for everyone to waltz into that hospital."

"You're probably right about that." Fletcher nodded. "Let's touch base in a couple of hours." He turned and headed down the hallway, waving a hand over his head at Anna. Pushing open the door, he let the warm Florida air smack his skin as he sucked in a deep breath. He tilted his head and stared at the darkening sky.

"What the hell did you get us all into, Ken?"

* * *

Baily twisted the corkscrew into the wine bottle, the soft pop echoing through the warm, lived-in quiet of Fletcher's kitchen. A soft golden glow spilled from the undercabinet lights, reflecting off the glass of the wine she'd already poured and the neat row of snacks she'd set up—apple slices, sharp cheddar, and a small bowl of pretzels. Nothing fancy but comforting. Familiar.

Except for the three boxes taunting her from the table. Fletcher had brought them down from his bedroom closet earlier. They were all labeled with his name in his mom's bold handwriting, nice and neat.

She turned, doing her best to ignore them and the past, reaching for the whiskey glass Fletcher liked best. It had a small chip near the base from where he'd dropped it last year. He refused to throw it out. Said it added character. But the reality was...it had been his father's, and Fletcher struggled to toss anything that had belonged to his parents.

She understood. She really did. But sometimes, it wasn't about holding onto things.

Things could be replaced. Memories couldn't. Fletcher held himself accountable for not being there for his parents. For not being there when they'd died. But there had been no way of knowing that the end would come in a fiery car crash. It hadn't been his fault. Nor had it been theirs.

It had been an accident due to poor visibility during a torrential downpour on a night that had destroyed more than two lives. That storm had taken many.

Behind her, she heard him move—bare feet on hardwood, the faint brush of fabric as he leaned against the doorway.

"You trying to seduce me with snacks and whiskey?" he asked, voice low and teasing.

She turned and grinned. "If I was, it'd be working."

He crossed the room in three long strides and slid his arm around her waist, resting his good hand against the curve of her hip. "You're all I need, Baily," he murmured into her hair. "Snacks are just a bonus."

She tilted her face toward his and kissed him, slow and soft. "You keep talking like that, and I might actually forgive you for keeping a bullet wound from me and give you a little peace and quiet right here in this kitchen."

He tossed his head back and laughed. Hard. "Do you have any idea where I got the phrase *peace and quiet* from?"

"I'm scared to ask, and honestly, I'm a little disgusted that I just referenced a blowjob by using it. I mean, really. It's a little rude if you ask me. It's like saying the only time you get any peace and quiet around here is when my lips are wrapped around your—"

"Oh, my God." He pressed his hand over her mouth. "Do not say it. You've been hanging around Audra too much."

"Is that where you got it from? Because coming from her, it's almost funny."

He rested his chin on her shoulder. "No. And I can't believe I'm going to even say this because it's kind of gross. I once heard my parents use it to reference the same thing. I believe they had code names for all sorts of sexual acts they didn't want their son knowing about. Or maybe they didn't want me to know they were kinky old people."

"We did catch them in a compromising position in the boat…and in the car." She chuckled. "Your parents were so adorably in love."

"That they were." He took the glass she handed him and lifted it. "To us, finally getting it right this time."

"To us," she echoed, clinking her wine glass to his.

Her heart swelled. They were finally on even ground again, standing side by side. She sipped, staring into his unwavering gaze.

He set his glass aside, then took hers and did the same thing. "So, shall we go through one of those boxes?" He waved his hand toward the kitchen table and arched a brow.

Shifting her gaze, she sighed. "Do you really think we're going to find anything other than memories from your childhood?"

"We might not, but it could be fun to rummage through." He took her hand and led her across the room.

She took a seat as he opened one of the boxes, pulling out his senior yearbook, setting it aside, then digging his hand in and finding a small box of letters.

"Oh, my," he whispered. "These are all from you." He waved the stack of envelopes. "I can't believe my mom stuffed them in here. All of them are addressed to the first Naval Base I was stationed at."

"Some of those letters are super embarrassing." Her cheeks flushed. "I hope your folks didn't read them. In my early letters, I got a little sexually graphic."

"I know, and I always enjoyed them, but would have to hide them from my friends." He laughed, setting them aside and pulled out more pictures and a few trophies before moving on to the second box. "You once described in great detail how you wanted a repeat session of sex on my parents' boat."

She dropped her forehead to the table and groaned. "I can't believe some of the things I wrote to you back then."

He pulled her from the chair and crushed her to his chest, kissing her heard. "I'm thinking I want to defile this room again. Or maybe a different room."

"We've probably had sex in every room in this house." She wrapped her arms around his shoulders, careful not to graze his wound. "I thought for sure your mother finally caught us when we tried it in the laundry room. Why on earth did we think that would be sexy?"

"I'm not sure we did." He smiled. "I believe it started out as my mom scolding me for bringing in half of the swamp and telling me to undress in the mud room and put my stinky clothes in the washer. Then you strolled in…and gave me ideas."

"You're the one who had ideas because I didn't even say hello before you had my sun dress up to my waist."

"That's what happens when you go commando." He arched a brow.

She shrugged. "It was easier because you always had sex on the brain."

"So did my girlfriend." He tugged her tight to his chest and kissed her good and hard. It was the kind of kiss that told her she wasn't making it out of the kitchen without him stripping her of half her clothes if she wasn't careful.

Not that she cared.

She loved him, and she wasn't going to fight it anymore. She couldn't figure out why she'd been fighting it so hard for so long. They were meant for each other.

He slipped his hand under her shirt—

And then came three crisp raps at the side door. They weren't loud, but they were sharp.

They both froze.

Fletcher cocked his head. "I'm not expecting anyone," he whispered.

"Neither am I."

He pushed from the counter and stepped around the island. Baily followed, walking barefoot on the cool wood floor, while snagging her wine glass as she passed it. If she wasn't going to have her fill of Fletcher, she was going to have her fill of wine.

As Fletcher reached the door and flipped the lock, she caught a glimpse through the side window.

Her breath caught. "No way," she managed, clutching her chest.

Fletcher cracked the door open, his body angled like a shield. "Julie? What are you doing here?"

Julie Mitchell—if she was still going by her married name—stood on the stoop, a soft pink sundress hugging her frame, blond hair swept into a sleek knot. She looked put together, as she always did. An effortlessly calm, easy, and graceful, as if she were meant to line the pages of *Better Homes and Gardens* or something.

Hard to believe she was the daughter of a ruthless

criminal. A killer. Well, perhaps her father hadn't actually done the murdering, but he hadn't had any trouble sending a man to sit in a tree and take aim at Fletcher.

Baily took that personally.

"Hi," Julie said, with that same rehearsed smile Baily had grown to loathe. "Sorry to drop by unannounced."

Fletcher didn't open the door further. "I'm shocked you're even in town."

Julie glanced past him and locked eyes with Baily. "I was in Orlando with the boys—took them to Disney. Figured while they stayed with their grandparents for a couple of days, I'd take a little solo trip. Clear my head. And, well…talk to Baily. I see she's here. Mind if she and I chat for a moment alone?"

Fletcher glanced over his shoulder.

"It's fine," Baily said, with a nod. "Let her in, but alone isn't happening. This is Fletcher's home, so he stays."

"Maybe we can go somewhere else and grab a glass of wine for old time's sake." Julie stepped inside like she belonged there. Her gaze scanned the kitchen, noting the wine, the snacks, the casual intimacy. She blinked slowly. "I was a little surprised to see the two of you…in a lip lock. I thought those days were over. I mean, the last time we spoke of you and Fletcher, you told me you'd get back with him over your dead body."

Baily folded her arms. "What do you want, Julie?"

"I thought we could talk." Julie looked between them, feigning innocence. "I didn't realize the old family house was... sold. I stopped by, and well, let's just say me and the new tenants were a little shocked."

"Oh, come on." Baily's voice rose. "You knew I sold it. We talked about it, and it became one of those things you used as one more reason why I should sell the marina after Ken died."

Julie gave her that wounded look she used to give when Baily would dig her heels in about something Ken didn't approve of. "I knew it was on the market. But I didn't think you'd actually go through with the sale. It was your family home, and you were always going on about family legacies and such."

"I had no choice," Baily snapped, frustration bubbling from her gut.

Fletcher stepped closer, brushing her hand lightly. A silent cue for her to remain calm...steady. But her anger flared. It burst to the surface like a rocket hurling through the clouds.

Julie's gaze landed on *him*, then lingered. "So, this is real? You two...back together?"

Baily didn't flinch. "It has always been real. We just needed some time and space."

Julie gave a slow nod. "I see." She shifted her purse on her shoulder. "Oh, what's this?" She ran her fingers over the yearbook on the table. "Are we going through things from the past? Anything in here from Ken? I'd love some things from his childhood."

"Those are all my things," Fletcher said, stepping between her and the table. "Nothing there that would've been Ken's or interest you at all."

"Okay." Julie narrowed her stare. "Baily, can we go somewhere?"

"No," Baily said. "I'm good right here. Unless you plan on allowing me to visit with my nephews."

"I told you I didn't bring the boys. I thought this would be better, just the two of us. They're having a great time with their grandparents. No idea I even came to see you. It's just not the right time, you know?"

"Why now?" Fletcher asked, voice neutral. Guarded.

Julie shrugged. "Because I've been thinking about the past. The future. About everything. I saw the article about the drug bust with Paul Massey. Then there was the serial killer…" Her voice dropped to a hushed tone. "This place isn't safe. Not for Baily. Not for children. Not for anyone. Not with what's been happening."

Baily's fists clenched. "So, you're here to what? Gloat? To remind me that you don't want me to have a relationship with my brother's children?"

"No," Julie said, her voice soft. "I'm here to offer you a place in our lives. If you moved…to Delaware… we could have a real relationship again. The boys could have their aunt. You'd be near family. And you'd be safely away from all the wreckage of Calusa Cove. This place has never offered anything but destruction. Ken never wanted anything to do with this town. It's why he left. It's why he so desperately wanted you to sell. He was always so worried about you. About what this place might do to you."

"That's bullshit," Baily said, disbelief thick in her tone. "You want me to abandon everything I love, know, and cherish. And for what?"

"It's not like that. At least not in those terms. What I want is for you to have something more than what this place can offer. I want you to have a future. I want you to have a relationship with Ken's boys. I want you alive," Julie said sharply. "You being here… you won't survive. My boys ask questions. Questions I can't…won't…answer. And your brother, well, he didn't want them to be a part of this place."

"They're my nephews," Baily's voice cracked. "And you've kept them from me long enough and for no real good reason."

Fletcher squeezed her arm. "Calusa Cove isn't the problem, Julie. Ken never saw it that way. That was your influence."

"No," Julie said. "Ken walked away when he joined the Navy, and he never wanted to come back. Ever. He told me that time and time again."

Baily blinked hard, breathing through the anger. "I'm not leaving, Julie. This is my home. I'm not scared of what's coming. You are."

Julie's jaw tightened. "You're making a mistake. A big one."

"Is that a threat?" Baily asked.

Julie raised her hands. "God, no. I'm just saying that you're drowning here, and that's apparent. All I want is for you to be part of our lives. But that can't happen if you're going to stay in some crime-ridden world."

"That's the most ridiculous thing I've ever heard," Baily said. "I made a mistake when I let you twist Ken's memory and control who got to be in your sons' lives. But I'm done playing by your rules."

"The only rule I'm making is controlling the fact that my boys will not be part of this backward town." Julie turned to Fletcher. "You're okay with her staying? With the danger this place represents?"

Fletcher's eyes stayed steady. "Baily's stronger than anyone gives her credit for, and Calusa Cove is a small town with lots to offer. You're the one making it ugly."

Julie's expression turned stony. "Well, I tried." She took a breath and smoothed her dress. "I hope you don't regret it, but I can't let my boys be part of this legacy."

And with that, she walked out.

Fletcher closed the door. The click of the latch felt final.

For a long beat, silence reigned.

Then Baily hurled her wine glass into the sink. It shattered with a satisfying crash. "Son of a bitch," she yelled. "She just showed up here like she owns the place. Like she's in control. Like we're the criminals."

Fletcher crossed to her, wrapped his arms around her. "Let it out, sweetheart."

"I will never let her take this from me," Baily said, voice raw. "I will fight. I will burn every last piece of their scheme to the ground."

"I know you will," he whispered against her hair. "And I'll be right there with you."

She closed her eyes, breathing him in. Re-grounding. Reclaiming her fight. Julie hadn't broken her.

She'd lit the fuse. And Baily Mitchell was ready for war.

She lifted her gaze. "Let's go through those boxes. Let's find the smoking gun."

CHAPTER 16

FLETCHER PACED in the parking lot. His pulse raced as if he were charging onto the battlefield. In some ways, it felt as though that were the case. He paused briefly, scanned the area, looking for anyone—especially Julie—lurking in the shadows.

He saw no one but locals. No one but the people who belonged.

And for some reason, that made him nervous.

"You need to relax," Hayes said as he strolled across the gravel, hands in his pockets like he didn't have a care in the world. "We've got this."

"You didn't get a visit from Ken's widow the other day." Fletcher leaned against his truck. "Julie came in all smiles and judgments. Dawson called around, seeing if he could find out where she stayed, but there's no record of her at any hotel in a fifty-mile radius."

"I'm not surprised. She hates this place." Hayes

raised a hand. "And I know Dawson had Chloe pull in a few favors, but there's no record of her or the Barbaros staying at any Disney property either."

"So, where the hell are they?" Fletcher couldn't shake the feeling that someone was watching them, like a sniper in a tree. "They can't be far."

"Chloe looped in her old partner, Buddy. He's got his contacts in Virginia, working on getting a visual on all of them."

"Dawson said one of the Sarich brothers—Logan, I believe—from the Aegis Network is up there as well, poking around."

"Dylan Sarich confirmed that." Hayes nodded. "He's lurking around here somewhere. Good men, all four of the Sarich brothers. Logan will get a lead on the Barbaros, and we'll get a better read on what they're doing by the end of the day, I'm sure." Hayes patted Fletcher's good arm. "We're all on edge about what's been happening. The events are calculated, but even the attempt on Decker's life wasn't meant to kill."

"What do you mean?" Fletcher stood tall.

"Emily got the toxicology report back, and there wasn't enough poison in Decker's system to kill him. There was just enough to put him in the hospital for a few days." He waved his hand as Keaton pulled into the parking lot. "Emily released him to us late last night. She really didn't want to, but Dawson explained the situation. We hired a retired orderly from the hospital who's a retired combat medic…the one that you know…the one you set up to walk Trinity out the door after she'd been shot. Figured between him and Dylan, we'd have all of our backs covered."

"Yeah, the orderly from the hospital is Pete Kidd. He's a good man. He'll take good care of Decker, and he's also not the kind of dude you want to mess with. He's the protective kind, and back in the day, when he was in high school, he used to work at the marina."

"I got the feeling he was a little protective of Baily."

Fletcher laughed. "He thinks of her like a little sister."

"So, not jealous?"

"Of Pete?" Fletcher let those memories flood his brain. Pete was a couple of years older. He'd been a quiet guy. Kept to himself. Didn't have a lot of friends. Did his job and kept his nose clean until he'd left for the Marines. His attachment to Baily had never rubbed Fletcher the wrong way, but it certainly had gotten under Ken's skin. That might have had more to do with the fact that Pete also had protective feelings for Audra and often didn't like the way Ken had treated her. Tried to tame the fire right out of that girl. "Nah. Pete never had any interest in Baily that way. We all grew up together, and when things changed between me and Baily, Pete just wanted to make sure I treated her right and made that clear." Fletcher chuckled. "He lectured me harder than her dad had, but if I'm being totally honest, Pete never liked Ken much."

"Why?" Hayes asked.

Fletcher shrugged. "Pete never really said. I did ask him after Trinity was shot, and again when we found the journal. I wanted to know if he knew about Ken dealing drugs, or anything else, even though he left when we were sophomores."

"And?"

"He knew Benson was dealing, and because Ken hung out with Benson sometimes, it made him suspicious, but he didn't know for sure," Fletcher said. "Pete told me he caught Ken in a couple of lies. Stupid little things around the marina that didn't make sense. Stuff like he'd said he'd done something his old man had told him to do, but he hadn't. And then there was Audra. Pete really didn't appreciate some of the things Ken said to Audra, especially about her dad."

"I've heard that a few times now, but you've never commented on it."

"That's a hard one because Victor was a crazy old coot. Right before he disappeared, he had some wild conspiracy ideas. Stranger than normal. His mind was going, and while most understood that, Ken often had a short fuse about it."

"Some of those theories Victor rambled about turned out to be true," Hayes said.

Fletcher nodded. "But others were just nuts. It was hard for us to watch Audra defend her father in one breath, and the next, tear him apart with that sharp tongue of hers. Looking back now, listening to Audra share some of things Ken had said to her, or even me, especially that month before we left for boot camp, I can see how he was really pushing the narrative that Audra's dreams, and what she believed to be true about that night, were her just being like her dad…crazy. And that's not true." He threaded his fingers through his hair. "I feel bad about that now because even though Audra could be dramatic, she wasn't nuts, and we all turned on her based on what Ken put in our heads."

"Do you honestly believe Ken could've known that Paul and his son killed her dad?"

"With everything we're finding out about my best friend? Yeah." Fletcher swallowed the bile that smacked the back of his throat.

"It's like we never really knew him at all," Hayes said softly.

"I thought it was Julie who had changed him." Fletcher let out a long, slow breath. "But now I wonder if he was always a secret keeper. Always a manipulator. Always a liar. And I just never saw it."

"Hey. None of us did." Hayes rested his hand on Fletcher's shoulder. "Don't beat yourself up. Besides, we wondered if he was keeping things from us. We could see something behind his eyes, like something was eating at him, especially the last year of his life. For all we know, he was caught between a rock and a hard place his entire life." Hayes lowered his chin.

"Massey could've been holding something over his head when he was a teenager. Everyone who knew he'd been dealing said they thought he'd stopped. But we don't know what he had to do to get out. And we don't know the circumstances under which he really met Julie because that doesn't track."

"I can no longer make excuses for him, and it sucks that he's dead because I can't even confront him." Fletcher pushed from the vehicle. "Keaton's waving frantically. We should head in."

Fletcher nodded and moved slowly across the parking lot. His heart hammered in his chest. Winning this bid wasn't just about him and his buddies opening another business. It wasn't just about their livelihood. This was about Calusa Cove. It was about the people and what their community represented.

The town meeting room in Calusa Cove's modest municipal building smelled faintly of pine cleaner and old paper. Rows of folding chairs had been lined up with military precision, their metal legs scraping softly as residents shuffled into their seats. Overhead, fluorescent lights buzzed with a faint whine, lending a sterile glow to the room that clashed with the tension humming beneath the surface.

Fletcher stood near the back, arms crossed over his chest, scanning the space. The turnout was bigger than expected. Locals from every corner of the Cove had shown up—some curious, others concerned. He spotted Silas leaning against the far wall near the fire exit, eyes narrowed, looking like a snake ready to strike at the first hint of danger. Chloe, Trinity, and Audra sat together in the second row, heads close, whispering behind their programs. Keaton was near the aisle, stone-faced, while Hayes stood by the window, his stance deceptively casual.

And in the back corner, hunched slightly and pale, sat Decker Brown with Pete. Decker looked like hell—pale, drawn, still weak from the poisoning—but his eyes were sharp. Determined. He gave Fletcher a faint nod, and Fletcher returned it. This afternoon, everything needed to change.

Mayor Ruth Talbot, a stern woman with a no-nonsense haircut and a louder-than-necessary voice, banged the gavel. "Let's come to order. The first and only item on the agenda: finalizing the redevelopment of the Old Crab Shack parcel."

A few committee members—Marge Elder, who ran the Cove's historical society; Tony Whittaker, the owner of the gas station; and Glen Morris, a retiree who never missed a town vote—flipped open their binders. They all had expressions that couldn't be read. Not a furrowed brow. Not a cracked smile. Nothing.

"The committee received two proposals," Ruth announced, glancing up. "But I've just been informed that one of them is being withdrawn."

All eyes turned toward Decker. He stood, slowly, using the back of the chair for support. "I'm officially pulling my bid from consideration. I...believe the other plan better serves the town's interests."

Ruth blinked. "Mr. Brown, you're certain?"

"Absolutely." He looked toward Fletcher. "And I'm offering my services as a contractor for the project, if accepted."

A low murmur swept through the room.

Ruth gave a curt nod. "Very well. That leaves the proposal submitted by... Parks and Recreation Director Fletcher Dane and associates."

Fletcher stepped forward, unfolding a large rendering of the proposed site plan. "We're proposing a dockside restaurant that incorporates the existing foundation of the old Crab Shack. The design keeps the original footprint but adds additional docks, a covered patio, and an outdoor stage. It'll be a place where residents and tourists alike can bring their catch, have it cleaned and cooked on-site, and enjoy live music from local talent on weekends. It will create jobs, and it won't take away from the landscape that's been in place for decades."

Tony scratched his beard. "So, it's not some corporate chain?"

"Not even close," Fletcher said. "This stays local. The people, the food, the music—it all comes from Calusa Cove."

Marge adjusted her glasses. "The exterior? It keeps the same waterfront feel?"

"Absolutely," Fletcher confirmed. "Nothing flashy. Wood siding, muted colors. Even the signage will reflect the old-style charm. It's all in these plans."

Glen Morris gave a low grunt of approval. "Sounds better than that monstrosity they wanted to build a few years ago."

Hayes stepped forward, handing out copies of the permits and zoning applications. "All the documents are in order. Our lawyer, Enzo Hudson, filed them this morning."

"Hudson?" Marge looked impressed. "Doesn't he have a cousin that's an FBI agent or something?"

"Former agent and now a sheriff in Oregon," Keaton added. "Her name is Greer, and she worked with Chloe a few years ago."

More murmurs.

"And you boys are willing to pay the town the full asking bid?" Glen asked with his glasses lowered to the tip of his nose.

"We are," Fletcher said. "All the financials are in order. The bank has approved a building loan. All we need is the town's approval."

Ruth looked around the committee. "Unless there are objections, let's take a vote."

All hands went up. Unanimous.

"Motion carried," Ruth said. "Congratulations, gentlemen. The Crab Shack property is yours. We'll fast-track the permitting process."

The moment the meeting adjourned, the crowd began to dissipate. Fletcher slipped outside, where the night air felt thick with salt and humidity.

Dawson, Hayes, and Keaton joined him near the sidewalk, the streetlamp casting a golden halo around them.

"Well," Hayes said, clapping Fletcher on the shoulder. "That went better and faster than expected."

Keaton nodded toward Decker, who emerged from the building with the help of Pete. "He stuck the landing," Keaton said. "The plans he drew up for us and all the permitting he handled really made the difference.

"Yeah," Fletcher muttered. "They're nothing short of amazing. I really like them."

"Agreed." Dawson crossed his arms. "Decker plays like he's going forward with the development. We let the word slip to John. The Barbaros will think they've lost control of the land and that Decker turned on them."

"And Baily?" Keaton asked. "Her payment is due today."

Fletcher exhaled. "She doesn't pay a dime. Not with what Enzo uncovered. I'm sure by tomorrow, they'll show their hand by calling in that loan. In the meantime, she and I will continue to go through boxes, hoping to find something."

Hayes looked out toward the dark horizon. "This town's been through enough. Let's finish this."

Fletcher nodded. "Time to bring this fight to us and do it our way."

CHAPTER 17

The marina office smelled like sun-bleached paper, diesel fumes, and worry.

Baily sat at her desk, trying to pretend she wasn't counting the minutes to the end of the day. The morning had started off deceptively quiet—no suspicious boats, no broken equipment, no late-night fuel thefts. Just a stack of invoices, an overworked coffee pot, and a new knot in her stomach that she couldn't untangle.

For the first time since her father had passed, she'd missed a payment. Not once had she been late with that damn loan. Sure, she'd postponed things like the mortgage, but she knew the lender at the bank. Known him her entire life. She could call him on the phone, make a deal for a partial payment, and he'd get off her back for a day or two. She'd take a hit with a late fee for her phone. She'd worked out deals with other business associates because they knew at the end of the day, Baily would always hold up her end of the bargain.

However, because she had no idea who owned that loan, she'd never once messed with it. Never once taken a chance.

The only good news had been that Fletcher and the boys had won the bid for the Crab Shack. That was something. However, she knew that would trigger a chain reaction with the Barbaros. They'd wanted that land, and they'd lost. Worse, they'd been betrayed.

By Decker. By John.

But she'd been betrayed by her own brother. That was worse. Fletcher kept telling her that maybe Ken had been stuck between a rock and a hard place. Maybe there was something they all didn't know. Fletcher was so caught up in the idea that he'd been painstakingly going through the rooms of his parents' house, one by one, searching for anything. He'd become obsessed.

She wasn't so sure anymore.

She reached for the old ledger she kept as a backup—just in case their digital system failed. Habit, she supposed. Or superstition. She stared at it for a long moment, thinking about the good old days. The days when she hadn't a care in the world. The days when all that had mattered were sunsets with Fletcher while she'd waited for her parents to fall asleep so she could sneak into Fletcher's bedroom.

But even those days had been filled with Ken

scheming. He'd always been looking for ways to skirt doing his chores around the marina. He'd complained about having to work for free, but the reality had been that their father had paid them in other ways. They'd been able to use the marina boats anytime they hadn't been rented out, and there had always been at least one readily available.

Money might've always been tight, but they hadn't really wanted for anything. At least she hadn't. But Ken? He'd wanted the world. He'd always itched for what he didn't have. A bigger, better boat. A fancy car. Money in his pockets.

Her cell rang. She snatched it up and pressed it against her ear. "Mitchell's Marina, this is Baily."

There was a pause, followed by a soft crackle of static, then a man's voice—sharp, efficient, slightly amused. "Miss Mitchell, this is a courtesy call regarding the pending balance owed on your marina loan."

Her spine straightened. Her heart hammered in her chest. Her breath hitched. "I've already submitted documentation to the holding company. We've initiated a dispute—"

The man cut her off from her well-rehearsed speech that Enzo had given her and that she'd practiced with Fletcher all morning. "You're in default. Payment was due yesterday, and if you read the fine print, there is no grace period. As of the close of business today, you owe the entire balance in full. If you do not make this payment, the deed to the marina belongs to the holding company."

Her fingers tightened around the receiver. "I've spoken to a lawyer, and that's not legal."

The man laughed. "Our contracts are legal, standard, your father signed it, and you've been paying. The law is on our side, so if you want to keep your marina, you'll make that payment. Otherwise, you're in default and you'll either have to pay the entire thing or lose it."

"There's no signature from me on a default trigger," she said, voice rising. "And the holding company has been unresponsive to a formal inquiry."

"Then I suggest you stop wasting time with formalities." His tone dipped—still smooth, but with a sharp edge now, like glass beneath silk. "You pay, or you forfeit the marina. Simple."

"I—who the hell are you?" she snapped. "What company do you represent?"

"You don't need my name. You need cash." Another pause. "And maybe a little common sense. Your place? It's not worth the trouble you're courting. Walk away while you still have a choice."

The line went dead.

Baily stared at the phone like it might explode.

Then she was on her feet, moving on instinct, shoving open the door. Warm, humid air swept over her like a wave. The early morning haze hadn't yet lifted, and the sky had that gray, watery glow that warned of a late afternoon storm.

She scanned the marina yard, eyes locking on Fletcher. He was crouched near one of the airboats, tightening a bolt with a socket wrench, sleeves rolled up, muscles flexing as he worked. His bandaged arm did not appear to hinder him at all.

"Fletcher!" Her voice cracked.

He turned instantly, standing and striding toward her, the concern already etched into his face. "What is it?"

She handed him her phone. "Just got a call. Someone demanding payment in full, or I lose the marina by the end of the day. Said I'm in default." She blinked. "I shouldn't have come and found you, but I was just so stunned."

"It's okay," he said softly. "Is this the number that's on the bill?"

She shook her head. "I don't know, and I don't know who it was. He wouldn't give a name. Just threats wrapped in fake professionalism."

Fletcher took the phone and tapped the screen. "Got it." He snapped a screenshot, sent it to himself, and then pulled out his own cell. "I'm sending this to Dawson. He'll trace it."

"Do you think it was one of the Barbaros?" she asked quietly.

Fletcher looked up, his expression hardening. "Could be. Hang on, it looks like Dawson is texting back." Fletcher tapped his toe and exhaled. "Okay. Dawson said the number for the shell company you provided earlier routes through a dummy network.

This one? Well, it's not that. It might give us something real. He's gonna dig deeper, but it'll take some time to do that."

Baily crossed her arms, hugging herself against the weight of it all. "They're not playing games. This is real, and they're gonna take my marina."

"No," Fletcher said. "They can try, but as Enzo said, they don't have a legal leg to stand on."

"But if I fight them on this, they'll…they'll…"

Fletcher curled his fingers around her biceps. "They want you scared. That's what this is."

"It's working," she whispered. "I'm really frightened. They tried to drown me. They shot you, and they poisoned Decker. What's next?"

"I won't let them take your marina or hurt you."

"This is bigger than Massey's operation. We know that," she whispered. "And in some ways, it's worse than how Dewey terrorized this town. My brother was in on this. He knew what they were planning. My own brother, Fletcher. He betrayed me. He betrayed all of us." She looked out over the docks, the quiet water stretching toward the horizon. Boats bobbed, ropes creaked, and somewhere nearby a gull screamed.

This was her home.

"We're going to beat them at their own game," Fletcher said softly. "I need you to trust me."

"I do," she whispered. "And the Barbaros, they'll have to rip this place out of my cold, dead hands because I won't let them win."

* * *

Fletcher paced the narrow strip of floor in his guest room, the carpet worn thin from boots and restless nights. He'd emptied the closet, tossing out old linens, dusty boxes, a stack of mismatched throw pillows that had no home, and still—nothing. Just air, walls, and silence that pressed too heavily on his shoulders.

He couldn't shake the feeling.

Something was here. Something Ken had left behind.

The bastard had been on his porch more times than Fletcher could count, even during years when he should've been visiting his own family. And then there was Ray—that damn notebook he'd handed over like it was nothing. Like it hadn't taken years off his life.

He sank to his knees, running his hands along the baseboards. Nothing. No scuff marks. No loose panels. He dragged a hand through his hair and blew out a frustrated breath.

Behind him, Baily's voice drifted in from the doorway. Soft. Cautious. "Fletch…maybe you should take a break. You've been at this for hours." She'd not only lost any faith that they'd find something, but she no longer believed her brother had possessed a single ounce of dignity or loyalty.

Fletcher held out a shred of hope because in all the years he'd served with Ken, one thing had always held true—Ken had always had his six. He'd never failed to save his ass. He'd always been right there in the line of fire, ready and willing to take a bullet for each one of his teammates.

Ken had been a different man on base than when Julie or her family had been lingering in the background, pulling his strings, telling him what to do, how to act, even what to say half the time. But there'd always been something lurking in Ken's eyes. Something that Fletcher hadn't ever quite been able to put a finger on. At first, he'd thought it had to do with Audra and how that had all gone down. Then he'd figured it was Julie and how she just hadn't taken to Navy life and the boys.

But it was deeper. Darker. More dangerous.

"I can't," he muttered, not looking at her. "I know I'm missing something. Ken... He wouldn't have left us to drown in this mess without a breadcrumb. Not if he was who I thought he was."

She stepped inside. "You mean the man who lied to us? Hid all of this? The man who let my father sign a bogus loan and then make payments before he even got the check? The man you thought had good intentions, but screwed us all, even in the wake of his death?"

He looked up, jaw tight. "Yeah. That man. But I also remember the one who sat on that dock with me after my parents died and made sure I didn't fall apart. The one who swore he'd always have my back."

Baily knelt beside him. Her fingers brushed his.

"Then maybe it's not in here. Maybe it's in a place that mattered more to both of you."

Fletcher blinked, his mind ticking back.

Summer afternoons.

Cold sodas and warm bait buckets.

Girly magazines hidden where no mom or little sister would look.

The bait boxes. "My nightmare," he whispered.

"What?"

"My fucking dream. He told me where to look right before he died." He jumped to his feet and grabbed her by the forearms. "I can't believe I didn't put this together before."

"What are you babbling about?"

Tears burned the corner of his eyes. "Right before Ken was killed, he said these words: *Take care of Baily. And when she really needs help, you'll find it behind the bait...*" Fletcher blew out a long breath. His pulse thumped in an uneven rhythm. "That's all he got out." Thick emotion caught in Fletcher's throat. "But whatever Ken knew about what his in-laws were doing, or about that loan...it's in the garage." He bolted down the hall, heart thudding hard enough to rattle his ribs. The garage door groaned open, sunlight streaking through the high windows in shafts of dusty gold. The old tackle bench sat untouched, flanked by crates of gear and rusted tools. He hadn't touched those bait boxes since the day he'd buried his dad. He'd promised himself every weekend he'd muddle through, and then stuff would happen, and they'd sat there, collecting more dust.

A few times, he'd managed to make his way out to this spot. He'd stood in the middle of the garage, stared at all the things, and it was as if he'd been frozen in time. He worried, if he touched a single one of his father's tools, it would be like destroying his dad's memory. Silly, but that's how it had made him feel. This house…the things in it…were all Fletcher had left of a childhood he'd always valued.

Always cherished.

And yet, he'd chosen to walk away from it as if it hadn't held the key to his soul.

Sucking in a deep breath, visions of his dad moving around his convertible, working on the engine, like it was a fine piece of machinery, instead of a constant reason for his mom to pick a fight. Fletcher chuckled.

"What?" Baily shouldered against him, leaning into his body.

"I was just remembering how my mom would needle my dad about that damn Mustang, but she loved that stupid car as much as he did."

Baily ran her sweet hand up and down his spine. "They drove it everywhere." She shook her head. "Your dad got so mad when you broke the top. He grounded you for like an entire month."

Fletcher smiled. "Yeah, but we had fun fixing it together." He swiped the tear that dropped from his eye. "It's almost fitting my folks died in that car." He moved toward the old bench, knelt, and yanked the storage bin aside. Behind it, wedged between the wall and the back of the bench, was a weathered wooden box. The kind his dad had used for backup gear, always labeled but never locked.

His hands trembled as he pulled it free and pried it open.

Papers. Stacks of them filled the space, but none of them belonged to Fletcher.

Or his parents.

"What is all this stuff?" Baily mumbled, leaning over his body, hands pressed on his shoulders.

"That's a very good question." On top, sat a journal, leather-bound and cracked at the spine. He flipped it open, his breath catching when he saw the handwriting. "I believe this was Ken's."

"Oh, my God. What is it doing out here?"

"Ken and I used to hide shit out here when we were kids. Treasure maps back in elementary school. Chewing tobacco in middle school. Girly mags when puberty hit." He sank onto the cold concrete floor, the first page already tearing into his chest. "You need to hear this," he managed with ragged breath.

I never wanted any of this. Not the secrets. Not the deals. All I wanted was to go to college. To get out of this town and to take Audra with me. But I saw something I shouldn't have. Did shit I shouldn't have. And now I'm screwed. Massey said he'd destroy me. Said he'd make sure I never get into the Navy if I didn't make Audra believe her dad went missing and she was mistaken about what happened. He had pictures of me selling drugs. Said he'd give those to the Navy. I figured I could talk my way out of that, but then Massy said he'd make sure Audra was the next to go missing. That he'd finish what he started. He all but admitted he killed Victor. What's worse, when I was sitting in that hospital room, while Audra was talking to Tripp, Massey appeared out of nowhere. He shoved doctored pictures of me out there in the Everglades, pushing Victor over the side of that boat. Massey's a real piece of work, and now I'm screwed. I've got to get Audra out of here.

Fletcher's stomach turned. He blinked. "What was Ken thinking?" He glanced over his shoulder.

"I have no idea, but at first, he did push Audra hard to leave town. It was all he talked about right before he left," Baily said. "He'd become so desperate, it was strange."

"I agree."

"Keep reading, please." Baily eased to the floor, sitting across from him, twirling her hair, like she used to do when she'd been younger and deep in thought.

I can't believe it. I met a girl. Name's Julie. She's nice. But she doesn't want anyone to know about us. Well, there isn't really an us because, for starters, I'm still a little hung up on my high school sweetheart. Although that ship has most likely sailed, especially since I haven't a clue as to where Audra disappeared. I haven't told Julie about her. Don't think I will either. Don't think Julie and I will last. She wants to keep us a secret, and

I'm keeping one hell of a secret from Fletcher and Baily. It sucks."

"Are there dates in these entries?" Baily asked.

Fletcher nodded. "That one was from about one year after Victor disappeared. Which doesn't track with when he said he met Julie."

"I know. That would've been two years after Victor died." Baily inched closer, leaning against the bench, stretching out her legs. "What's next?"

"Two related entries. One from right before he went to meet with Audra and one right after," Fletcher said with an ache in his chest.

I got a weird call today from Massey. He told me that he knows where Audra is and that he needs me to go see her. Like I wouldn't want to do that. I've been worried sick about her. But here's the kicker. He wants me to make sure she doesn't return to Calusa Cove. Okay, yeah. I don't want her to either. I want her here with me. But that wouldn't bode well with the new girlfriend. So, what am I to do? Well, Massey made that easy for me. He reminded me of all the crap he's got hanging over my head. All the ways in which he can make my life miserable, like sending me to prison for shit I didn't do.

Fletcher cleared his throat. "The next entry is dated four months later. But that tracks with when we came back here to visit."

"That journal has been in this garage the entire time?"

"Appears so." Fletcher nodded.

"It kills me that I broke Audra's heart...again. But it's

better this way. Better for her. Safer for her. She'll figure life out. She's got fire and grit. I have to believe that. Paul, his son, and whoever they're working for—it's bigger than I could've ever imagined. I'm glad I got out. Now, I wish I could get my sister out. But she's about as stubborn as a mule and stuck to my dad like glue. She won't even leave for Fletcher, and I know she loves him. Maybe I can help get the marina on stable ground so it's not bleeding money anymore. Make their lives would be easier. Julie and I've talked about that, which is funny because her family is so rich, her biggest hardship is worrying about what color sports car to pick for her twenty-first birthday.

"He sounds lighter in that entry," Baily whispered.

"I agree." Fletcher nodded, glancing up. "This is right before he started bringing Julie around, and we all commented on how he started having a spring to his step again. We thought that maybe it had to do with getting over Audra. I always thought that was hard on him. It's not like he didn't love her."

"He did love her." Baily rubbed her hands on her thighs. "That's why some of this is so hard. I feel like there were times my brother acted like the man I always knew, but then at other times, like a total stranger."

"We all thought that of him." Fletcher flipped a page and scanned a few of the entries. The next couple were mostly about Julie. How sweet and kind she'd been. How much fun they'd been having. How alive he felt, but how it bothered him that she struggled with the team. That she didn't want to spend time with the team. They were his brothers. His family. His lifeline.

Fletcher smiled, tapping his finger against his chest.

Further in—another entry, years later—but this one wasn't very rosy.

Julie and her family aren't who I thought they were. I've been trapped since the wedding. They own me. I don't know what to do. I stopped writing things down because I've been so afraid. But this needs to be documented. I need to figure this out. I can't tell the guys. Not yet. I know I can trust them. It's not about that. They are loyal. True. And they have my six.

But I've fucked up royally. And oddly, it all dates back to when I first sold my first dime bag of weed for Benson. What an idiot I've been. Now, if I want to be a dad to my own boys, I've got to feed my dad bad tips for the stock market. Worse, now they have me pushing a predatory loan on him. It's going to bleed him, my sister, and the marina dry. I tried to push money back, and I told Dad to keep paying the loan even when they said not to. But they caught me. I figured I'd end up in some massive custody battle I couldn't afford, but no, instead, they showed me a picture of Audra. A recent one. They told me they'd finish what Massey started.

Fletcher gritted his teeth. Tears burned.

"Oh, my God. They were using his children and his love for Audra to…to…that's just disgusting," Baily said softly.

"I understand why Ken kept his distance from us

now. Why he struggled to look us all in the eye." Fletcher squared his shoulders. "Because if he had, he would've broken down and told us, and he didn't feel as though he could. Not without putting his kids or Audra at risk."

"I guess I can't hate him anymore."

Fletcher let out a sarcastic chuckle. "Oh, there's some animosity swirling around in my gut still." He cocked a brow. "Ken should've trusted we would've had his back. That we would've protected the boys, Audra, you, your dad, and this fucking marina. But he didn't, and I'm sorry, but he was being a little selfish from the beginning, all because he didn't want anyone to know he'd been dealing drugs for the likes of Paul Massey."

"Can you blame him?" Baily asked.

"A little bit." Fletcher nodded. "Why don't I continue?"

I've made a decision. The Barbaros are going to think I'm all in, and then I'm gonna burn the place down. I don't care if I go down with them. At least my sister won't. They already took my dad from me. The guys don't respect me like they used to, and I don't blame them. I lost the only woman I've ever really loved years ago. But I can do this for my boys. Hopefully, they'll see that their dad, in the end, was brave enough to do what was right.

"Jesus, that's a profound statement," Baily said.

"That was two years before he died." Fletcher flipped the page. "Holy shit."

"What?"

"Listen to this."

I was able to shuffle all the money that was meant for the marina—for my dad and Baily—into an offshore account. I learned from my in-laws how to create dummy LCCs and shell corporations, so the money's hard to find and his name won't be easily found on the accounts. But it's there, and all of it can be found in the box I left at Fletchers. When the time is right, I'll come clean, and my sister and my boys won't ever have to worry again.

"I'm not sure I understand," Baily whispered.

"It sounds like he hid money for you." Fletcher threaded his fingers through his hair. "Only one entry left, and it's dated a few weeks before our last deployment." He glanced up. "I didn't know Ken visited you then."

"He didn't. Not that I know of."

"Strange because that's the only way he couldn't have gotten this last entry in here," Fletcher said. But as he was learning, there was a lot about his friend he hadn't a clue about.

I've been collecting evidence. Little things here and there. Financials. Records that came across my desk as they taught me the business. Notes I've taken on how they streamline things. How they muscle people. Pressure people. Find their weak spots and exploit them. Though I don't have a lot on that. My role is the money. The books. I've always been good with numbers. They want me to sweet-talk people with investments. Jesus. I'll be walking into small towns, all smiles and unicorns, to quote my sister, and getting people to invest in bogus shit. Then, the

Barbaros take over everything. It's crazy. And they've been doing this for years. Well, they're not doing it to my town. Baily has been keeping up with the payments. I hate that she has to do that, but soon, I'll be able to help her come out from under that. We don't talk much about things and when we do, we fight. I need to ask her questions about stuff, but it's not because I'm needling her. I need to know how to protect her through the storm. Because it's coming. Sooner rather than later.

The journal ended abruptly. But the information inside the box didn't.

He pulled out folders. Receipts. Wire transfers. Ledgers with fake names and flagged invoices. A hard drive. USB sticks.

Photos.

Documents tying the Barbaros to laundering, drug runs, and even arms deals. Fletcher's pulse pounded in his ears. "I've got to call Dawson. Get him, Chloe, and maybe even Enzo over here." He handed Baily a few things to rifle through.

"I can't believe that for three years, we've been sitting on this stuff. That it's been right under our noses," Baily said. "I wonder what would've happened if Ken hadn't died."

Fletcher found a file marked Legal. He opened it and gasped. "I think this might give you some insight into that." Inside were the early makings of divorce papers…Ken's divorce papers. A signed will…dated only a few weeks before the deployment. A letter to a lawyer outlining Ken's wishes to leave his wife, file for custody of the kids, a note stating that if something happened to him, his death should be considered suspicious, and that they should look at his wife and/or in-laws as suspects, and finally, his re-enlistment papers…signed.

"Oh, my God." Fletcher held the last piece of paperwork in his shaking fingers. "He told us he was done with the Navy. But these are signed. Ready to be processed. He was going back in…with us."

Baily took the folder, thumbing through all the other documents. Her forehead scrunched. Her lips pursed. "There's a sticky note that says if they find out I'm leaving, they'll kill me."

Fletcher stared at the box. At the pieces of his friend.

A man who had betrayed them.

A man who had been a prisoner.

A man who had tried to make it right.

His eyes burned.

"This is what they must've been looking for," Fletcher whispered. "He might've screwed up, more than once. But he was trying to fix it." He leaned back against the bench. "When that mission ended, we were all supposed to come here for a little R & R. Even Ken had agreed, much to Julie's dislike. He even mentioned he had something he wanted to discuss with all of us. Dawson had been the first one to roll his eyes, believing it was just Ken with another one of his, *Oh, be happy for me. I'm leaving the Navy, and I'll be wearing a suit from now on*, pep talks. Hayes thought maybe Julie was pregnant again, and Keaton was being a dick by suggesting that Ken wanted all of us to invest in some new business he was going to start under the Barbaro name. But none of us would've expected this." Fletcher waved his hand over the mounds of paperwork. "This had to have taken him years to collect. He put his life on the line. He risked everything to…make this right. But he never got the chance. He died, and I couldn't save him."

"Don't do that to yourself, Fletcher. That wasn't your fault." She pointed to the box. "But this? Well, I do blame my brother. And while I want to forgive him because I can't imagine the hell, he'd been living for all those years, he brought this shit on when he decided to sell drugs. Or lie to Audra. Jesus, Fletcher. Think about what this is going to do to Audra when she finds out that Ken knew Massey killed her dad, but let her believe she was the one who was nuts?"

Fletcher set the files back in the box and stood. He helped Baily to her feet and cupped her face. "None of this is easy. Ken's not here to defend any of his actions, and I'm not making excuses for him. He had to live with his choices, and it's obvious to me how many of them were eating him alive. But now that we know, we have to act. Ken made a lot of stupid mistakes, but he just gave us all the knowledge and power we need to bury the Barbaros." He pulled out his cell and sent a text to Dawson, Chloe, and the rest of the team, informing them of what they'd found. "There's enough evidence here to put them away for life."

"What about Chad and Todd? What's going to happen to my nephews? Who will take care of them if their grandparents and mother are in prison?"

"We will," he said softly, tugging her to his chest.

"What?" She blinked, staring at him with confusion etched in her sweet eyes.

"You're a blood relative. We can petition the courts after all this plays out. We can raise those boys together. You and me."

"You're joking, right?"

"I've never been more serious about anything in my life." He kissed her softly. "I love you, Baily. I want to spend the rest of my life showing you just how much. Someday, I want to have kids. However, I'm certainly not opposed to helping you raise Ken's."

"That's putting the cart before the horse."

He looked down at the box again, and this time, when he closed the lid, it was with purpose. "Maybe. But those aren't empty words. I mean them."

"Scary, because I believe you."

"Good." He brushed his thumb over her lip. "You know, I've got my parents' rings up in my nightstand. You could put on my mom's engagement ring."

"Oh, my God. Fletcher Dane, you're not actually proposing to me, are you?"

"You've always told me I suck at being romantic."

"You do." She sighed. "And this really is the totally wrong moment."

"Are you saying that you'd say yes if I picked a better one and did the whole down-on-bended-knee thing?"

"I'm not having this conversation with you right now. *Especially* after we just learned all that." She pointed toward the police vehicle as it pulled into the driveway. "And certainly not with an audience."

Well, at least he knew he stood half a chance when all this was over because he was going to pull out all the stops. Baily wasn't getting away this time. Not while he had blood pumping through his veins.

CHAPTER 18

The scent of cinnamon and clove hung in the B&B kitchen like a comforting shawl, but Baily couldn't seem to relax. It had been forty-eight hours since they'd found the mounds of hidden paperwork. Two days since the FBI and DEA had taken over the case. Two days since Fletcher had told her that the end was close. However, it didn't feel that way.

Fletcher kept reminding her that it took a while to put together a sting operation, especially one this size. They didn't want to risk tipping their hand, and the Barbaros were already spooked at it was, considering they'd lost the Crab Shack bid. They hadn't harassed her about the loan in the last twenty-four hours.

Chloe took that as something completely different. She believed the Barbaros knew something was brewing and were perhaps preparing. But the question was, did they know they were about to be arrested for crimes so massive that it would put them away forever?

Baily sat at the oversized butcher-block island. Her fingers wrapped around a mug she hadn't sipped from in ten minutes. Across from her, Trinity rocked gently in her seat, a hand stroking the swell of her baby bump as if to calm both herself and the little life within.

Audra sat to her left, arms crossed, her eyes red but dry. The truth about what Ken had known had cut her to the core. No one knew what to say anymore. The quiet between them wasn't hostile—it was thick with shared disbelief. Days of tears, hugs, and common grief surrounded them like the fog hanging over the Glades.

"I always knew something was off about how Ken reacted to my dad disappearing," Audra said, palming her mug while staring into it like it had answers to questions only a dead man could bring. Her voice didn't shake, but it hit hard. "Ken's journals, they hint that he saw something."

"We don't know if that was something about your dad, or more about Massey's operation," Trinity said.

"It doesn't matter. Whatever it was, Massey used it to manipulate Ken. To terrorize him into doing whatever he needed. Ken was barely an adult. Only eighteen. I can only assume he tried to tell himself it was to protect me, but let's be real, he did it to protect himself just as much, and damn it, the whole thing...it hurts, you know?"

Baily reached for her hand. "I know. I wish I had something better than that to say, but I know. I waffle between forgiveness because of the piles of evidence he collected…the risk he took to gather it…the money he put away…and wanting to beat the crap out of him for putting all of us in this situation to begin with."

Trinity offered a sympathetic smile. "Before Ken joined the Navy, he should've trusted Audra to be strong enough to handle the truth. To deal with what he'd done. He should've gone to Tripp. He would've known what to do."

Audra nodded, lips pressing together in a hard line. "He always underestimated me. Even when we were kids. But I also don't understand why he never told Fletcher, Dawson, or Hayes what was going on with Julie and her family. Or why he didn't just give his dad the money. He bled that man dry." She set her mug on the table, pushing it aside. "He left Baily vulnerable for years, and he died before he could hand off the evidence."

The three women fell quiet again. Outside, the wind rattled the porch swing against the railing. The only other sounds were the low hum of the refrigerator and an occasional thump from the upstairs rooms.

"So," Trinity said, lifting her cell and tapping the screen. "Did Chloe give any indication of when the FBI, DEA, ATF, and whoever else is involved in this big sting operation is actually making their move?"

Baily huffed a dry laugh. "The fact that Chloe, Hayes, Keaton, and Fletcher all raced off to the station to meet Dawson, I'm guessing something either happened, or is happening as we speak."

"Enzo couldn't believe the crap Ken had collected." Audra sighed.

"He's been going through the documents for the shell corps and LLCs for the offshore accounts," Baily said. "Enzo said it's like a maze, and it's going to take a while before I'll be able to access any of that money. Some of it's also tied to the boys, and Enzo's worried about the legality of some of it, but as he follows the trail of deposits, it appears it all came from Ken's personal accounts. Direct deposits over the years, right from his income from the Navy."

"I hope for your sake it's all legit because the laundering information was more than enough to file charges against the Barbaros and so many others that work for them. But then you add in the detailed information about the way they bring in drugs, money, and people?" Audra shook her head. "Dawson was mortified. He sat at his desk for hours, just staring at the mounds of documents, near tears over it all."

"Keaton said it made Massey's operation look like a five-and-dime shop in comparison," Trinity said.

"Speaking of Massey," Audra added. "Dawson went to see him yesterday with Agent Pope and Buddy."

"I heard Massey's still not talking much." Baily

reached across the counter and snagged a piece of cheese. She wasn't hungry but knew her body needed fuel. "His lawyer is pushing hard for an immunity deal and federal protection. He's worried about other cartels."

"It's not the cartel he's worried about." Audra waved a finger. "It's the Barbaros, and he admitted that to Dawson. Pope told Massey that they can give him the same deal as Trevor, but he's got to roll over and give them everything. Turns out, Massey and his son Benson did what they could to keep the Barbaros out of Calusa Cove."

"That's interesting. Why would he do that?" Trinity asked. "I'd think the cartel is way scarier."

"Maybe in some ways." Baily nodded. "But Fletcher told me that Massey said he'd rather deal with the devil he knew. And that the bigger the operation, the more likely it was that he'd get caught."

"This might be a dumb question, but how'd he manage to help keep the Barbaros out?" Trinity asked.

"I guess there was this weird honor among thieves between the Mendoza Cartel and the Barbaros regarding certain territories." Audra leaned back and placed a hand on her growing belly. "The Barbaros respected the small towns that Mendoza's had a strong foothold in, but if property came up for sale, and the Mendoza's or their people didn't buy it, the Barbaros could."

"Did Paul know about the loan?" Trinity crinkled her forehead.

Audra nodded. "But not until after Ray signed it, which meant it was too late to do anything except make sure the marina stayed open and in business under its current ownership. Paul dumped as much money into the marina as he could."

"But his son didn't," Trinity added.

"His son had a side deal with the Barbaros." Audra let out a long breath. "One Paul didn't know about until just the other day."

"This is worse than a bad mafia movie." Trinity lifted her tea and sipped. "I can't wait for it to be over so we can go back to planning baby showers."

Baily glanced toward Audra. "How are you feeling? Still dealing with the morning sickness?"

Audra rolled her eyes. "Oh yeah. This kid is a relentless little sucker. I swear, I throw up more now than I did after the night we all did tequila shots."

"Oh, that night was the worst." Trinity groaned. "But I can't wait until I can have tequila again. I kind of miss it."

"I miss my independence. Dawson keeps fussing over me like I'm made of glass. And now, with this whole thing about Ken and the Barbaros, I swear he's about to duct-tape me to the couch."

Baily smirked. "You say that like it's a bad thing. Like you don't want *daddy* to tie you up."

Everyone burst out laughing—full on belly laughs

—and it felt damn good, even though they all knew the lightness of it wouldn't last.

And seconds later, their giggle fit was cut short.

The front door creaked open, followed by the sound of boots scuffing the new wood floor, and a second later, Dawson, Fletcher, Keaton, Hayes, and Chloe filed into the room. One look at their expressions and Baily felt her stomach knot.

"You're all wearing that look," Trinity said. "The one that says you've got news and we're not gonna like it."

Dawson nodded. "We do, and it's both good and bad."

Baily stiffened. "Well, don't leave us hanging."

Hayes leaned against the counter, arms crossed. "We'll start with the good. The FBI, DEA, ATF, and Homeland Security raided Barbaro Manufacturing in every city. It was a clean raid, well thought out. All the warrants were perfectly executed. It's done. Shut down."

"They found more than enough to put them away for life," Chloe added. "Drugs, weapons, illegal offshore accounts. And yes—evidence of human trafficking."

Audra choked on a gasp. "Good. I hope those fucking assholes rot in hell."

"The charges are massive," Dawson said. "It'll be a while before the case comes to trial, or even a possible plea deal, but there will be a reckoning, and there is no way out for them."

"And the bad news?" Baily asked. "Because that part sounded like it's all wrapped up in a nice, neat bow."

Keaton stepped forward. "Julie, Damen, and Valenia Barbaro have vanished. No one knows where they are. They weren't at any of the plants, offices, or their homes. It's like they saw this coming, and they ran."

"Of course, they did," Trinity muttered.

"The Feds believe they had outside help," Chloe added. "Which means they could be anywhere. But they'll surface. People like that always do."

Baily rubbed her hands together. Panic gripped her heart. "What about Chad and Todd? Where are they? What happened to them? They're just little boys, only eight and six."

Fletcher came to her side, taking her hand. "They were found safe. The Barbaros had a house in Naples. The boys were there with a nanny. CPS has them now, but I made it clear that you want to file for temporary custody."

Baily's eyes filled. "Thank God they're safe."

"It'll take a little time," Fletcher said gently. "But we'll bring them home—to us. It's where they belong."

"They're going to hate—"

Fletcher pressed his finger over her lips. "We'll deal with that one day at a time. For now, we need to focus on preparing to fight for them, for their arrival, and staying safe until the cops can find the Barbaros."

Audra stood, walking to the window. "So, what now? We just wait for the Barbaros to make their next move? To show up and start slinging bullets at us?" She turned. "They had pictures of me." She pounded her chest. "Dawson showed me, and I know exactly when they were taken. They've been watching me, which means they've been watching all of you." Her chest rose and fell, hard, with every breath. "I had no idea I wasn't safe all these years, but I'll be damned if I'm gonna sit around and wait for someone to start taking pot shots at me or anyone I love."

"And that's my wife," Dawson said with a sarcastic tone as he stepped beside her, wrapping his arm around her waist. "We kinda have no choice but to wait this out. However, we're not alone in this. Logan and Dylan Sarich are sticking around. They'll watch the town and keep their ears to the ground. Their organization is searching for them. So are the feds. It's an all-out manhunt. Not to mention that every news station is plastering their faces on the screen across the country. They won't be able to hide."

"We're not taking any chances," Hayes added. "Everyone needs to stay alert. Don't go anywhere alone. Check locks. Carry protection. Whatever it takes."

Trinity sighed. "Just once, I'd like to be part of a girls' night that doesn't end with a safety briefing—unless I can have a tequila shot."

Baily managed a small laugh, but her heart was

still heavy. As everyone began to scatter—Hayes pulling Chloe into the den, Keaton checking Trinity's blood pressure, Dawson raiding the fridge like nothing had changed—Fletcher leaned close and whispered, "You ready to head out?"

She nodded. "Yeah. Let's go home."

Because whatever came next, they were facing it together.

CHAPTER 19

THE SHEETS WERE TANGLED around Baily's legs like seaweed, damp with sweat and the weight of another dream that slipped through her fingers the moment her eyes opened. Her heart raced. The dark pressed in thick around her, and for a moment, she thought she was still trapped in a nightmare—until she realized the bed beside her was empty.

"Fletcher?" she whispered, voice raw from sleep.

No answer.

She sat up, clutching the sheet to her chest. Moonlight streamed through the open curtains, casting silver patterns on the hardwood floor. She spotted him, a silhouette by the window, one shoulder propped against the frame, arms crossed as he stared out at the Everglades, like he was trying to read a message written in the stars.

"Fletcher," she called again.

"Hey," he whispered, glancing over his shoulder,

his expression shadowed but soft. "I'm sorry, I didn't mean to wake you."

"You didn't." She stood and padded across the room, wrapping her arms around his middle and resting her cheek against his bare back. His skin was cool, the tension in his body unmistakable. "What's got you up?" she murmured. "Another nightmare?"

"Not this time. But there are too many ghosts out there," he said. "Too many what-ifs. I keep thinking about the boys. About what kind of life they've had. I wonder what they know. Or don't know. I worry about all the questions they're going to have and how we're going to answer them. When I got out of bed and looked out this window, I was reminded of all the times Ken and I played out in that yard as kids. How we'd catch snakes, and frogs, and torment you and Audra."

"There was a lot of tormenting going on." Baily smiled against his skin.

"I loved my childhood here and even when you and I were at our worst, I still thought…believed…I'd always end up back here someday, in this house, with you, and that we'd be sitting on that porch watching a couple of kids do all the dumb things we did. But now, I'm trying to envision what kind of life we can give Todd and Chad because it'll be so very different from what they've known. Neither of us has seen them since they were three and five. A lot can change in three years."

"That's some deep midnight thinking." Baily

kissed his shoulder and stared out at the ripples on the water. The swamp shimmered in the moonlight, beautiful and unknowable. Inviting and dangerous. The Everglades were both heaven and hell. And this was the only place she ever wanted to be. "We've made calls. We've done everything we can. Enzo said the lawyer's solid. But I just... I don't know if that's enough. I don't have anything, Fletcher. No money, no fancy legacy. Just a crumbling marina that, even after all this, might not still make it. Even if all that money Ken stuffed away manages to be legal, it should go to his boys for their future."

He didn't say anything right away. He just kissed her temple, then reached into the drawer of the nightstand, pulled something out, and then turned back to her. "We have everything because we have each other."

"You sound like your grandma." Baily smiled.

"She was a smart woman, and she always told me that people are more important than things. That the right partner in life mattered more than anything else because if you had that, you'd be able to make things happen. Look at our friends. Dawson and Audra, they're pure gold together, like two sides to a coin. And Keaton and Trinity are the poster children for why opposites attract."

Baily giggled. "And Hayes and Chloe are like a perfectly worn pair of boots."

"That's one way of describing them." He nodded.

"So, what's your weird metaphor for us?"

"We're like a river. We came together too fast, too soon. We split, gained strength, knowledge, and power, and then collided together at just the right moment to become one."

Tears burned the corner of her eyes. "Well, oh, my Fletcher Dane. You just might've hit your first romantic note."

"And at precisely the right moment." He lifted his hand. A diamond ring sparkled in the moonlight, elegant and simple, set in a band that looked strong enough to survive a hurricane.

She gasped.

"I was going to wait," he said. "Until things settled. Until we could breathe. But then I realized—we don't get guarantees, Baily. Not in this life. We only get the people we trust. The ones who fight for us."

He slipped the ring onto her finger, slowly and deliberately, as if anchoring her in place.

"Everything I have is yours. This house, the old Crab Shack, the airboats, every spare bolt in that shed. You've always had my heart. There's never been anyone but you in that space. We're better together. We always have been. In the shadows of these damn Glades, I will never stop being your lighthouse."

"Now, you're just being corny."

He shrugged. "I tried."

"Maybe a little too hard." With tears in her eyes, she lifted her hand and stared at the ring. "It's beautiful. Your mom loved this ring. She used to always tell me that someday, she'd take it off and give it to you to give to…" She let the words trail off. "I miss her."

"I miss her, too." He pressed his lips over the ring on her finger. "This ring was always meant for you. No one else. What do you say, Baily Mitchell? Will you marry me?"

She opened her mouth, but she didn't get the chance to speak.

A sound—sharp, jarring—echoed from downstairs.

They both froze.

Fletcher moved first, stepping away and grabbing the Glock from the drawer. He handed her a second handgun, smaller, but still deadly. "I know how much you hate these, but—"

"No, I'm good." She nodded. "I've been practicing with Audra, just like you asked me to."

"Stay behind me."

They crept down the stairs in silence, the creak of the old wood beneath their feet sounding like thunder in the otherwise still house.

The living room light was on.

Baily's heart jumped to her throat. They always turned that light off.

They rounded the corner into the open kitchen.

"Don't move." A man's voice. Cold. Familiar.

And there they stood.

Julie. Damen. Valenia.

And Bingo.

Bingo was on his knees, a split lip and blood at his

temple, with his arms yanked behind his back. A gun pressed to his head by Julie with her perfectly manicured hands.

Valenia stood behind her with a small duffel bag in one hand. Damen looked bored—like he was at a PTA meeting and not holding a young man's life in the balance.

"Nice place," Valenia said calmly, eyes flicking to Fletcher's gun. "But I'd suggest you put that down unless you want to clean up what's left of Baily's dockhand."

Baily's scream caught in her throat. The ring on her finger suddenly felt like a target.

"Not gonna happen." Fletcher didn't lower the weapon. His arm didn't even tremble. "Let him go."

Julie smiled—cold and calculating. "Let's talk about what you're going to do for us first."

Fletcher took one small step forward, angling his body as if to shield Baily's. She felt the shift in his energy—focused, fierce, utterly unafraid.

Where Baily was horrified—totally and unequally terrified. She'd been in situations before that any normal person would describe as harrowing. She'd come face-to-face with a six-foot rattlesnake. She'd killed pythons. She'd been one wrong step away from being taken out by an alligator. All things that happened in the Everglades, and people living there didn't bat an eyelash.

She'd even had to deal with old man Jenkins when he'd threatened Cooney and his chickens with a loaded shotgun. That was never fun and could always lead to being on the wrong end of a stray bullet.

But this? Watching her eighteen-year-old deckhand being held at gunpoint by her brother's wife? No. This was crazy town.

"Let the boy go. He's got nothing to do with this," Fletcher said. "And then we'll talk."

Julie tugged at Bingo's hair, jerking his head back and running the metal of her weapon against his neck.

Bingo's eyes grew wide, registering fear, but he didn't cry. He didn't whimper. He simply went rigid. Tense. Like fear gave way to anger.

"This one, he's loyal," Julie said. "Unlike my idiot husband." She shook her head. "My parents seriously miscalculated his loyalties." She smacked the weapon against Bingo's cheek. It cracked open his skin. Blood trickled out.

"Leave him alone," Baily cried, setting her gun on the counter with a shaky hand. "What do you want?"

"Two things." Valenia wiggled her fingers. "You give us the account information for the money Ken stole and stop your fight for custody of the boys. We have a plan for them, and no way are you part of it. If you don't do those two things, we kill this young man right in your kitchen, you two will go to prison for it."

Fletcher had the nerve to laugh.

"I'm so glad you find this amusing, son," Damon said.

"Don't ever call me, son." Fletcher kept his weapon aimed right at Damon's heart. "No one would ever believe either one of us would kill Bingo. Your plan is seriously flawed."

Valenia pulled out a folder from the bag, opened it, and set it on the counter. Inside were pictures… pictures of Baily and Bingo…together…looking intimate.

Baily gasped. "Those are fake," she managed.

"Not the point. It's enough of a deflection to cause a stir and an inquiry." Valenia smiled. "Such a shame, and it looks like you got engaged recently, too. Your reputation will be tarnished. Such a tricky thing for someone like you to come back from."

"You're disgusting." Baily glanced at Bingo, who hadn't moved, nor said a word. Just stared at Fletcher with a hardened expression.

"This isn't a very good plan," Fletcher said with an amused tone. "First, we don't have the money. It's not being released anytime soon."

"All we need is the paperwork for those accounts," Damon said. "Now turn them over. This is not a negotiation."

"We don't have them anymore." Fletcher shrugged. "And Baily's not giving up custody of her nephews."

"You're not getting my boys," Julie said. "Besides, these charges won't stick and my kids will be back where they belong soon enough. But until then, we need those documents, or I'll put a bullet in this kid's head."

Baily shifted her gaze to Fletcher. "Give them what they want," she managed. She couldn't let anything happen to Bingo. It didn't mean she'd stop fighting for her nephews, but this standstill needed to end.

* * *

"No," he said flatly, keeping his gun trained on Damen. "We're not giving you a damn thing. And you're not going to shoot him because the moment you do, you lose your leverage—and I put you down."

Julie's hand twitched on the gun. "You think you're in control here? You're not. You might get a shot off, but my mom, or dad will kill Baily. Is that what you want?"

Fletcher growled. He knew they'd do exactly that, but he had to play the game. "I think I've got nothing to lose. I've faced worse odds and walked away. You kill Bingo, and I guarantee you don't walk out of this house."

He needed time. Just a few more minutes to think… to find his way out. There was always an out. These people were desperate. Running on fumes. Backed into a corner with no way out and not thinking too clearly.

Behind Julie, Bingo's hands flexed. Barely noticeable, but Fletcher caught it. He also caught Bingo's eye movement. Quick, sharp. The kid was up to something.

Then, he showed a couple of fingers. Damn. He'd worked through part of the bindings. Good kid.

"Ken's accounts were already turned over to the authorities. That's out of our hands, even if we gave you the paperwork, if you tried to funnel money out —without Baily, they'd find you," Fletcher added. "You kill us, and they'll know it was you who did. We don't have any other enemies. So, if you want any hope of scraping together your little empire again, you're going to need someone alive to trade for. Someone who has the legal authority to touch those funds."

"That's why she's going to sign it all over." Julie smiled.

"Over my dead body," Fletcher said.

Valenia narrowed her eyes. "You're bluffing."

"I'm not, but you're welcome to test me." Fletcher held Valenia's gaze.

There was a flicker of doubt in her face. Bingo shifted again. Almost free.

Outside, a creak sounded. A shadow moved across the porch. Fletcher didn't look. Didn't need to. Dawson. Hayes. Keaton. He could feel it like the storm rolling in off the Glades.

Bingo made his move.

With a grunt, he lunged sideways, knocking Julie off balance. The gun fired—once—into the ceiling. Fletcher dove left as Dawson kicked the door in, followed by Keaton and Hayes with their weapons drawn.

"Down!" Hayes shouted.

Chaos.

Fletcher tackled Damen. The man threw a punch, but Fletcher absorbed it and drove his shoulder into Damen's gut, taking him down hard.

Keaton wrestled Valenia to the floor.

Baily dropped behind the island, yelling Bingo's name.

Julie scrambled for the gun, but Bingo kicked it across the tile.

Logan Sarich came through the back door next, followed by Dylan, both armed and furious.

It was over in less than thirty seconds, but it felt like forever.

Julie was pinned, screaming. Damen coughed up blood. Valenia—unconscious.

Fletcher turned to Bingo—blood ran down the kid's face. "You good?" he asked.

Bingo nodded. "Better now."

Fletcher turned and saw Baily rushing toward them.

They met in the center of the chaos, clinging to each other.

"We're okay," Fletcher whispered into her hair. "We're okay."

Baily held him so tightly he thought he might suffocate, but he didn't care. He wrapped his arms around her, crushing her to his chest as she cried.

"It's okay. Everything's okay." He glanced over his shoulder as Remy stormed into the house, a little late to the party. Chloe and her old partner, Buddy, were next, followed by a couple of EMTs.

Miranda Rights were read. Cuffs were slapped on wrists, the metallic click piercing the stillness.

He guided Baily outside and down toward the dock, her body limping along next to him. "Are you hurt?"

"I don't think so," she managed through mangled sobs.

"Let me check you over." He stepped away, brushing her hair aside, and did a quick check for bullets, cuts, and other damage. Thankfully, there were none. At least, none on the outside. But he knew it would be a while before Bailey recovered emotionally from this.

He cupped her face and kissed her gingerly. "You're okay. We're okay. It's over."

"It's not over for Todd and Chadd," she whispered. "It's only just begun for them." She blinked away a few more tears. "How do I explain all of this to them?"

"Carefully and lovingly."

The ground under his feet moved. He glanced over his shoulder. Dawson and Bingo made their way across the yard.

Baily was out of his arms in a flash, making a beeline for Bingo.

"Are you okay?" She rushed to Bingo's side.

"I'm fine," he said, giving her a big bear hug. "No worse for wear."

"I'm so sorry." She gripped the boy's shoulders.

"It's not your fault, and in a weird way, it was good practice for me if I'm going to be a SEAL." Bingo smiled. The kid actually smiled. "And I got to work alongside the men I admire. It was kind of cool even if I was really scared for a minute."

Dawson chuckled. "I was terrified for longer than that."

"Fear will keep you alive out there." Fletcher slapped Bingo on the shoulder. "You'll make a good sailor and a great SEAL."

"I hope so." Bingo nodded. "Four years of college first. That's the deal I made with the old man."

"ROTC's not a bad route to take." Fletcher gave the kid a bro hug.

"I don't think I can stay in that house tonight," Baily said after a beat.

"Audra and I have a room at the B&B. You and Fletcher are welcome to stay with us." Dawson glanced over his shoulder. "I better get back there. It's going to be a long night of dealing with this shit show. Feds, and all that. Not to mention, Valenia took a bullet. Might not make it, I'm told. Julie and Damen are bitching about all sorts of bad police work on this, but I'm not worried. They're going away for a very long time." He sighed. "I do need to take your statements, but we can do that in the morning."

"We'll be by at first light." Fletcher took Baily by

the hand and tugged her toward the parking lot. "Come on. Let's get out of here." In silence, they walked around the side of the house. He paused by his truck and pulled her into his arms. "I love you, Baily. Whatever happens next, we're in it together. No more secrets. No more betrayals. It's all out there, and we can weather any storm because we have each other."

"I think I actually believe that." She rested her head against his shoulder. "I just hope after everything, the courts will see we can make a good home for those boys because I'm worried Julie will fight that. We've learned that even convicted felons have rights regarding where their children are placed. They have other family members. Blood relatives on her side. It's not a done deal that we'll get the kids."

"No. It's not." Fletcher tilted her chin. "But we have something that most of her family doesn't."

"What's that?"

"A loving home in Calusa Cove."

CHAPTER 20

A MONTH LATER...

THE SUN HAD BEGUN to dip behind the mangroves, casting a golden hue over Calusa Cove that shimmered off the water and set the marina aglow. Twinkle lights strung between the pilings and porch railings sparkled like fireflies, and laughter carried across the dock where a small, mismatched group had gathered to celebrate something that had once felt like an impossible dream.

Her wedding.

Baily stood barefoot on the dock, holding a paper plate with a melting scoop of vanilla ice cream and a half-eaten cupcake, and watched as Chad and Todd darted between rows of chairs, laughing like they'd been here all their lives.

They hadn't.

It had only been a month. A single month since the night everything had shattered and then they'd begun to rebuild.

Valenia Barbaro was dead. Shot during the standoff, she'd bled out before EMTs could even try to save her. Julie and Damen were behind bars without bail, facing a slew of charges that included conspiracy, extortion, kidnapping, and a laundry list of federal offenses. The town of Calusa Cove, though scarred, had found its footing again. Just like she had.

She glanced across the dock. Fletcher was talking with Hayes and Dawson, drink in hand, grinning as he said something that made them all laugh. The ring on her finger still felt surreal. Heavy in the best way. Symbolic of everything they'd been through, of everything they were building now—together.

They'd married quietly at City Hall last weekend. Just the two of them, the boys, and Keaton as their witness. Trinity had cried anyway when they'd told her, and Dawson had insisted on a proper party—even if it was just a gathering of friends with a cooler full of beer, Trinity's famous deviled eggs, and enough seafood to feed the town.

Baily didn't need anything else.

Audra sidled up beside her, handing her a fresh glass of sweet tea. "You good?"

"More than good." She took a sip. "It feels...safe again for the first time in a long time."

Audra nodded, her eyes scanning the crowd. "You deserve this. You fought for it. For them."

They both looked over at the boys. Todd, older now and trying so hard to be grown, was helping

Keaton reel in a crab pot while Chad poked it with a stick and made disgusted faces.

"They're adjusting," Baily said softly. "It hasn't been easy. Todd has nightmares sometimes. And Chad asked me last night if their mom was going to come take them back."

Audra placed a hand on her arm. "What did you say?"

"I told him the truth. That she's in jail. That we don't know what the future looks like, but for now, they're safe. That Fletcher and I aren't going anywhere."

"And that was enough?"

Baily blinked back the sting in her eyes. "For now."

The money from Ken's offshore accounts had come through, legitimized thanks to Enzo's maneuvering. Most of it would sit untouched, locked away in trust accounts for the boys. College. Therapy. Whatever they needed to build futures untethered from their past. The marina would survive without it.

She heard Fletcher laugh again and turned to find him watching her now. He raised his glass in salute, his gaze full of the same promise he'd made weeks ago—that he would always be her lighthouse.

She walked toward him, barefoot and smiling, and was intercepted by Chad, who grabbed her hand and tugged. "Aunt Baily! Come see what we caught!"

It wasn't the first time he'd called her that. But it still hit like a wave to the chest every time.

"I'm coming," she said, ruffling his hair.

As she neared the end of the dock, Fletcher reached for her. "Hey, Mrs. Dane."

She blushed. "I'm still getting used to that."

"You'll get there." He pressed a kiss to her temple. "You've got that married glow."

"More like sunscreen and stress," she muttered.

He wrapped an arm around her waist, pulling her close as the boys showed off their haul to a very patient Keaton. "They're going to be okay, you know."

"I want to believe that."

"We've got temporary custody. That's a big step. If the court agrees Julie is unfit—which they will—then we'll start the adoption process."

"And if she fights it?"

"Then we fight harder. We don't back down."

She leaned her head on his shoulder. "I don't know if I have it in me to fight anymore."

He was quiet for a moment, then kissed the top of her head. "You do. You always have. But you're not alone anymore. You've got me, the boys, all of this. And when you're tired, I'll carry the weight."

A lump lodged in her throat.

"I love you," she said.

"I know."

They stood like that, watching the sun slip beneath the horizon, casting Calusa Cove in golds and blues. Music drifted from a Bluetooth speaker someone had placed on a picnic table. Chloe and Trinity danced barefoot, Hayes reluctantly pulled into the fray. Dawson and Audra were swaying by the grill. Even Silas had shown up, perched on the edge of the dock with a fishing pole, quiet and content.

A new chapter.

A new beginning.

Baily breathed in the salt air and squeezed Fletcher's hand. "Let's go dance before this night ends."

EPILOGUE

TWO YEARS LATER...

THE NEWLY REBUILT Crab Shack buzzed with life. String lights twinkled above, casting a warm, golden glow over the picnic tables and wooden deck that overlooked the calm water. The scent of grilled shrimp and smoked ribs mixed with salt and sea air. Laughter carried across the patch of land, and Fletcher felt every ounce of it settle deep in his bones.

Peace. Real, honest-to-God peace.

"This place came out real nice if I do say so myself." Decker Brown smiled, handed him a beer, and stared out toward the Everglades.

"I heard you're breaking ground on the old Dewey Hale lot next week." Fletcher sipped as he stood on the deck, watching as the townspeople and his friends gathered to celebrate his family. "That you plan on making Calusa Cove your home, and you have a girlfriend."

"All true." Decker smiled.

"Well, where is this lady? I need to meet her. The boys and I have to approve."

Decker laughed. "She's right over there." He stretched out his arm and pointed. "The pretty lady in the pink dress, chatting up Lilly and Hondo. Her name's Joanna. She started as my office manager last year, and now she's my kinda everything."

"I'm really happy for you." Fletcher clanked his glass against Decker's. "I know things got a little rough because it took some time before charges were brought against Tessa Gilbert."

Decker shrugged. "I'm a much happier man being a smaller company. I still get to do what I love. I found a good woman who loves me. And more importantly, I found a community that embraces me. I've never had that before. I like it."

"I can't believe I'm going to say this, but we like having you around, too."

Decker burst out laughing. "I'd better go be by my lady's side. She's a little shy, and I promised her that I'd guide her through the insanity of this small town." He nodded as he stepped off the deck, all smiles, but the slickness of his grin had long faded. Even his swagger had less of a kick and more of a small-town stroll. Hell, he'd even ditched the expensive shoes and stupid pants, trading them in for jeans and durable boots or a pair of flip-flops when appropriate.

All in all, Decker Brown had turned out to be a decent guy. Go figure.

And for the first time in a long while, Fletcher felt as though he could breathe. He had his team, and he had his family.

The boys were finally his and Baily's—permanently. The adoption had come through. It had been the final piece of a puzzle.

Baily stood near the edge of the deck. She glanced over her shoulder and smiled. It sucker-punched him every time.

He inched closer. "Hey, you," he whispered in her ear. "Enjoying yourself?"

"I could stand here and watch this for days."

"I know that feeling." He leaned back against the railing, a beer in one hand and his other arm draped casually around Baily's waist. She had their two-month-old daughter, Kendra, named in honor of her brother Ken, curled against her chest in a soft sling. Todd and Chad were chasing Dawson's son, Victor, and Keaton's daughter, Petra, around the fire pit with water guns, and somewhere in the chaos, someone had managed to get Hayes wet.

"You're lucky," Hayes grumbled, wringing out the hem of his shirt as he stepped up onto the deck. "I got ambushed by an eight-year-old and a toddler. That's got to break some Geneva Convention."

"Don't start crying just because you're outnumbered," Dawson said, handing him a dry towel. "Victor was showing mercy. He only used the little gun, and he warned you before he pulled the trigger, something Petra would never do. That little girl isn't afraid of anything, and she has no off switch either."

"Max projectile vomited all over me, and I still think that was less traumatic," Hayes muttered, lifting his six-month-old son in his arms from the pack 'n' play. Max squealed in delight, kicking his legs. Chloe came up beside him, her hand resting on her already growing belly.

"Round two's already in training," Chloe said with a sly grin. "Why I thought having two kids close together in age was a good thing, I have no idea."

Dawson raised his beer in salute. "And here I thought Audra and I worked fast, but you're due like the day before she is."

"I told Trinity we have some catching up to do, and she told me only if I planned on pushing that kid out," Keaton said, stepping into the circle with Petra on his shoulders. She clutched two fistfuls of his hair and made an approving noise as he bobbed slightly with every step. Trinity followed close behind, her hand resting protectively on her daughter's back.

"Petra says Fletcher needs more glitter in his beard," Trinity announced, giving Baily a wink. "I think Fletcher needs to shave."

"I totally agree." Baily gave Fletcher that look—the one that said the razor better come out if he had any chance of having a second kid.

"I'll take that under advisement—the one about the glitter," Fletcher said with mock seriousness. "Only if Petra leads the styling session."

"Put me down, Daddy." Petra kicked her legs. "Play with Sean!"

"Only if you promise to stop squirting him in the face." Keaton set her down, holding her by the shoulders. "He doesn't like that, and Uncle Foster will take the squirt gun away again if you do."

"Okay, Daddy." Petra wobbled down the stairs.

Dawson burst out laughing.

The Oregon crew had arrived earlier that afternoon. Foster and Mac stood near the base of the deck, with their son, Sean, hiding behind Foster's legs.

"That kid is a holy terror," Hayes said.

"I can't wait to have another one." Keaton chuckled. "Trinity's so afraid it will be another one just like Petra. Every time we talk about it, she's like, *How did we get the Audra of the group?*"

"Oh, I can see a lot of Trinity in that girl," Fletcher said as he glanced around at what had become one of the busiest places in town. He puffed out his chest with pride. He only wished his parents could've seen what he'd managed to do. How he'd filled this place with love and family.

Kash and Jordan sipped sweet tea by the bar while keeping one eye on Ember as she inspected the edge of the railing. Saylor was tucked into one of the rocking chairs nearby, her newborn Drew sleeping soundly in her arms. Greer, visibly pregnant, stood with her husband Chase, hands entwined.

Fletcher was grateful that all of Foster's team had

been able to come. While Foster was Keaton's cousin, they were all brothers-in-arms—bonded in a way others might never understand.

"It's like a damn baby boom." Keaton raised his glass. "And we need to feed my wife some of the water, because I want another one. She's the only one not pregnant."

"Bite your tongue," Baily said. "I'm not, and I don't want to be again for a bit, thank you very much."

Fletcher laughed. "It's like all the chaos had to give way to something better."

"You mean diapers and sleepless nights?" Dawson asked, raising an eyebrow.

Fletcher looked out at the water, watching as the setting sun lit the sky in strokes of orange and pink. "I mean family."

Baily leaned into his side, and Kendra stirred slightly. He glanced down at her tiny face—so much like Baily's it hurt—and felt that familiar tug in his chest.

"Hard to believe it's been two years," Jordan said, settling next to them.

"Harder to believe the Barbaros are locked away for good," Foster added. "Both got three life sentences each. No chance of parole."

"Good riddance," Chase muttered.

"They tried to burn the town down," Fletcher said. "Now this town's stronger than ever."

"It's a nice place to visit, but I still wouldn't ever

want to live here." Foster cocked a brow. "Too many eyes in the water."

"Speaking of eyes," Dawson said. "Where are Todd and Chad?"

"Plotting their next ambush, I assume," Baily said, just as Chad came barreling up the deck with a slice of cake in each hand. "Mom! Dad! Can we have seconds? Please? We ate all our dinner. All our vegetables, too."

Mom. Dad.

It never got old. Fletcher's chest tightened.

"That's fine," Baily said, ruffling his hair. "But don't smear that icing on your brother again."

"No promises!" he shouted as he raced to a table where a couple of his friends and his little brother were seated.

"Looks like they've adjusted quite nicely," Foster said.

"Better than I ever could've imagined." Fletcher watched the boys laugh with their friends. "It's taken some time. A few angry outbursts. Some tears. A lot of explaining and even more love. But the past is fading into the distance."

"They love it here. They love you," Baily said, tipping her head up. "About the only thing they fear now is if something were to happen to us."

A cheer went up from the far end of the dock as Bingo stepped up with a guitar, strumming a few notes before leading the crowd into a familiar country tune. His voice was stronger, more confident now. He'd grown into himself. College had been good to him, and in two years, he'd be leaving for the Navy. He'd stuck to his plan and was thriving.

Fletcher took it all in—their friends, their children, their home. The warmth in his chest didn't fade. He squeezed Baily's hand. "We did it," he said.

"No," Baily said. "We're just getting started."

And as Kendra stirred again, letting out a tiny sigh before curling back into her mother's warmth, Fletcher knew with each beat of his heart that this was just the beginning.

For the first time since Fletcher had returned to Calusa Cove, there weren't any secrets lurking in the murky waters. There weren't any pirates hiding in the shadows. No murderers hidden in plain sight.

And no more betrayals by those he loved and trusted.

There was just peace in the place he'd always called home with the woman he'd always loved.

Thank you for reading *Betrayal in Calusa Cove*. Please feel free to leave an honest review.

If you'd like to learn more about Jen Talty's Aegis Network, please check out:

THE AEGIS NETWORK
The Sarich Brother
The Lighthouse
Her Last Hope
The Last Flight
The Return Home

The Matriarch
Aegis Network: Jacksonville Division
A SEAL's Honor
Talon's Honor
Arthur's Honor
Rex's Honor
Kent's Honor
Buddy's Honor
Duncan's Honor
Garth's Honor
Hawke's Honor

RAVEN'S WATCH

RAVEN'S CLIFF BOOK #1

New York Times & USA Today
Bestselling Author

ELLE JAMES
&
KRIS NORRIS

RAVEN'S CLIFF

RAVEN'S WATCH

NY TIMES BEST SELLING AUTHOR

ELLE JAMES
KRIS NORRIS

PROLOGUE

JSOC MISSION... Undisclosed location

"Beckett."

Major Foster Beckett nodded at his copilot, Sean Hansen, before banking the Pave Hawk over as the next burst of machine gun fire whizzed past the chopper, lighting up the darkness behind them. "I know, buddy. This guy just won't give up."

He tipped the machine farther forward, picking up speed as he skimmed across the top of a ridge then dropped the bird down the other side. Barely missing a crumbling wall as it materialized out of the night.

One of his four teammates groaned in the rear cabin. Whether it was from the way Foster tossed the helicopter around or because they were on the verge of bleeding out, he wasn't sure. But if he didn't lose the bogey on his tail, it wouldn't matter.

They'd all be dead.

Sean made a wet, gurgling sound, and Foster nearly plowed the machine into the ground as he snapped his attention toward his buddy, wondering how it had all gone sideways so fast.

The damn spooks.

Once again, the CIA had screwed them over. Because Foster bet his ass the agency knew two of their agents were dirty. That they'd set up Foster and his crew as bait when their supposed rescue mission had turned into a shootout minutes into the return flight. Calm, cool extraction one moment, an all-out attack the next with Agent Stein and Agent Adams leading the charge. The one scenario his teammates hadn't counted on. Not when they'd been working with the bastards for the past six months. Men they thought could be trusted. Would have their backs. Discovering they were the ones selling intel...

Foster should have recognized the signs over the past few weeks. The beads of sweat along their brows. The slight twitch in their hands. Their increasing reluctance to look Foster or his buddies in the eyes.

And now, his brothers were paying the price.

He banked again, narrowly avoiding the next round of gunfire. "Hang in there, Sean. Once I lose this asshole, we'll be back on course."

Sean panted, lifting his arm and jabbing his finger

at the only nav screen still working — leaving a bloody smear across the surface. "Here."

Foster frowned, dodging up and over another ridge before following the hill around to the right. Hugging the surface to the point dirt and stones kicked out behind him in twin eddies. "I realize we're desperate but even I think that's crazy."

Not that it stopped him from altering his course. Heading for that speck on the map glaring at him from beneath the smear of blood. Rain splattered across the bubble, flashes of lightning giving him fleeting glimpses of the landscape. A bulging rock face on his right. A lone tower on his left. What might be his saving grace when damn near every other navigational aid was dead. Even his night vision had gotten damaged, leaving him with nothing more than that one flickering nav screen and twenty years' worth of experience.

Foster hit the winding gulley leading to the narrow opening going as fast as the aircraft could handle. More than it could handle based on how the controls vibrated in his grasp, the odd alarm chirping to life. He divided his attention between the screen and the walls quickly closing in on him, mentally counting down the distance.

He was about twenty feet back when he banked the chopper hard to the right, holding it steady as the sluggish controls fought to respond — definitely a hydraulic leak hampering the inputs.

The gap appeared in front of him like an abyss

spiraling into the rock. The utter darkness drawing them in. He hit the tunnel going some insane speed, the controls still shaking as the engine whined from the strain. Any hint of light cut out. Even the nav blinked off for a few moments before he shot out the other side, a welcomed flash of lightning saving him from flying the machine into the side of the cliff as it curved around in front of them.

He cranked the helicopter over, trying to get more distance between them and the opening when the chopper surged forward as the sky lit up behind him, the force of the explosion spinning the aircraft.

Flames erupted from the fissure, parts of the other chopper whizzing through the air. Something hit the back end, pitching them sideways as a shrill whine echoed through the cabin. It took a few moments to get the bird stabilized, the controls like lead weights in his hands, with the last impact claiming what little hydraulics he'd had left.

Sean coughed, splattering blood across the window as he met Foster's gaze. "Hooyah."

"I got lucky. Nothing more."

Sean shook his head, his mouth pursing tight as he tapped his chest pocket. "My letter…"

Foster grunted, wishing he could move his arm enough to punch Sean in his thigh. "No. No talking about that damn death letter we've all written. You're going to be fine. You just have to push through."

"Beck…"

"I mean it Sean. Don't you dare give up…" He

cursed under his breath, giving Sean a nod when his friend managed to reach out and leave a bloody handprint on his arm. "I'll get it to Cheryl. I promise."

Sean nodded, closing his eyes as a shudder raced down him, blood seeping through the bandages around his neck and ribs. He'd taken the brunt of the attack when Stein had opened fire, lunging over to cover Foster after Foster had gotten hit twice in the shoulder. Their pararescue medic and Foster's best friend, Chase Remington, had done what he could to minimize the bleeding once he and his other buddies had dealt with Adams and Stein, but it was obvious it wasn't working.

Foster huffed. "Stay with me, brother. I've got this baby turned around. I'll have you on the ground and into a surgical room within fifteen. Ten, if I can get more speed out of her."

Sean chuckled, the raspy sound fading into that eerie gurgling noise as his head lolled back and he slumped against the window.

"Sean! Damn it, Chase, I think he's coding."

Chase popped into view, his hands covered in blood. "I need a minute, Foster."

"Sean doesn't have a minute."

"Neither do Zain or Kash. I can only spread myself so thin."

"We're not dead yet, dumbass." Zain Everett — their SAR specialist, sniper and all 'round badass. Though it sounded as if he was even worse than Chase had hinted at. "Take care of Sean."

Chase pursed his lips, fisting his hands for a moment before vanishing then reappearing with an armful of supplies. He checked Sean's neck, looking back at Foster before applying more bandages and giving the guy a shot of something.

Chase turned to face him, mouth pinched tight. Eyes shadowed. Blood oozed from a gash on his forehead, more soaking the hem of his shirt. What looked like multiple hits to his vest.

Chase had been with Foster from the start. Had been the one constant throughout his career — until they'd met Sean, Rhett, Zain and Kash a dozen years ago. The six of them had fallen into sync on their very first mission, and they'd fought hard to stay together since.

Chase tugged on the tape holding Foster's shoulder together, muttering obscenities under his breath. "Your damn shoulder's a mess. I'm not sure how you're even moving that arm. Everything's shattered."

Foster would have shoved him off if he'd had the strength. Instead, he merely nodded toward Sean. "How is he?"

Chase glanced away, making it look as if he was getting more supplies out of his bag. "He's lost at least two liters of blood, and I'm out of saline and plasma."

"But if I get him back…"

"You just focus on staying conscious as long as possible. Try to get us as close as you can to the base. Okay?"

"Chase…"

"I'm just a medic, buddy. I can't raise the dead."

Foster looked over at Sean. He hadn't moved in the past few minutes, his skin so damn white he swore it was see-through. "No. It can't end like this. You have to do something. That should have been me. My blood. My sacrifice. He's got a wife. Kids. I have to…"

To what? Save him? Because Foster knew if Chase couldn't save Sean, no one could.

Chase packed more gauze around Foster's wounds, adding another layer of tape. "Let me check on the others, then I'll be back. Do what I can to help keep you awake."

"You worry about Zain, Kash and Rhett. I'll be okay."

"No, you won't." Chase cut him off. "You're bleeding through the clotting powder. Your face is nearly as white as Sean's and your good hand is shaking so bad, I'm surprised the damn chopper isn't vibrating through the air."

"My hand's shaking because I've lost hydraulics. Go. I'll shout if I'm gonna pass out."

"Right, because self-preservation has always been first on your list. Just, don't fucking die on me."

"Says the man who's bleeding worse than me. And yeah, I noticed. How bad are you hit?"

"Enough I'm extremely pissed."

Chase disappeared, Zain's groan sounding above the engines a moment later. The fact Foster hadn't heard their flight engineer, Rhett Oliver, utter so much as a sigh since his team had finally overpowered Stein and Adams meant the guy was either dead or unconscious. Just like their dog handler, Kash Sinclair.

The engine chugged, dropping the bird several feet before it stabilized. They couldn't afford to land. Not while they were fifty miles from safety with Foster's entire team struggling to hold on.

Which meant, milking every ounce of speed out of the aircraft. Taking it as close to the edge as possible without actually blowing the engines or killing the transmission. That fine line between all-out and too far. One he'd skirted on more occasions than he should be proud of. But the mission and his team always came first.

Not team. Family. That's what they were to him. Brothers. Men he'd kill for. Or die to protect. The only reason he'd made it through twenty years without losing his sanity.

His soul.

To think it would go down like this — betrayed by their own people. Lost on the wrong side of a volatile border. A fate he could alter if he rose to the challenge. Pushed past his limits.

Rain pummeled the bubble, the lone wiper barely keeping up. Not that he could see much with streaks of black cutting across his vision. But he kept that bird pointed north. Kept the machine on the verge of crapping out as he raced across the landscape, the wind and thunder following in his wake. Like Apollo chasing them with his chariot.

Was it getting colder? Darker? Or was Foster simply running out of time.

Chase's hand closed over his good shoulder, jerking him back from that numbing haze. "If you have to put her down…"

Foster shook his head, pounding the heel of his other hand against his temple in an effort to clear his vision. "Not… an option."

"Foster. Brother, you're barely holding on."

He shook his head again. Or maybe he'd only thought it. He couldn't tell. Could barely feel his fingers he was so cold. "How…"

Shit. One word. That's all he managed before his tongue got too heavy to form more.

"Don't worry about anyone else. That's my job. You focus on flying and not hitting the ground."

"Can't…"

Another one-word reply. And it cost him. Had more than just his good hand shaking. He wet his lips, forcing his eyelids open. Glancing over at Sean whenever he wanted to pack it in. Give up. Because if there was even a glimmer of hope he could still be saved…

Bile crested his throat, his eyes burning as he stared at the raging storm beyond the glass. The lightning hardly making a difference in his visibility, anymore. It was too late. He knew it. Felt it. From the way Chase kept shifting his weight, unable or unwilling to even place his hip on the edge of Sean's seat, to the utter silence from the other side of the cockpit, Foster knew Sean was dead. But Foster kept going. Clinging to the false hope that if he could stay awake — make it one more minute, one more mile — it wouldn't be in vain.

That he hadn't failed his brothers when they'd needed him the most.

That maybe one day, he'd be able to look at his own reflection and not see Sean's ghost staring back.

* * *

"I'M NOT sure what I was expecting, Foster, but damn. You look like shit. Though, the bandages do kinda go with the long hair."

Foster twisted toward the door, shaking his head at the man leaning against the frame. Hands shoved in his pockets, looking almost as haggard as Foster felt. Keaton Cole, Foster's cousin and the only family Foster had left, other than the men gathered in his room. His teammates.

His brothers.

Foster arched a brow, brushing his hair out of his eyes. A leftover from his time in Flight Concepts, when he was encouraged to look like anything but typical military. He gave Keaton a once-over, waving the length of him. "And yet, still a thousand times better than you, buddy."

"Oh, someone didn't get their pain meds, today."

Keaton sauntered in, grinning at Chase, Kash and Zain. "You're obviously taking fashion cues from my cuz, Remington, because you look just as bad, with Sinclair and Everett only slightly better."

Chase flipped Keaton off as he leaned back in the chair. "At least we have a reason, Cole. What's your excuse?"

Keaton chuckled. "Civilian life. Who knew it was crazier than the Navy." He crossed his arms over his chest, waiting until Zain and Kash had wheeled their chairs over to Foster's bed. "So, rumor has it you four might be considering your options."

Zain grunted, absently rubbing his knee. Or more accurately, the new hardware hidden beneath the bandages and stitches. Foster wasn't sure if Zain even realized he was doing it, but the pain and frustration bled through his usual facade. Testament to how much their last mission had cost them.

Foster knew his buddy was in agony. He'd heard the muffled shouts and hushed curses as Zain dragged his ass up and down the hallways several times a day. The price of reclaiming even a hint of his former mobility. Though, Foster knew Zain would push until he was only a slightly broken version of his former self.

Zain shrugged. "It's come up."

Keaton nodded, walking over and resting his hip against Foster's bed. "I feel that. Been where you all are, myself."

Which was an understatement. Keaton had been

through hell. Had suffered a similar loss on his last mission, when their covert op had gone off the rails and one of his best friends had been killed. While Foster didn't know the specific details, he knew Keaton. And based on the hollow look in his eyes — the tremor in his voice that was only now starting to ease — he'd experienced something truly horrific. Not that it had been the first time.

Keaton's fiancée had died in a plane crash a dozen years ago, shortly after he'd joined the SEALs. Foster had come close to losing the man back then, despite all Foster had done to try and help Keaton cope with the loss. But words and a shoulder were rarely enough compensation for the kind of scars that took more than time to heal.

Though, Keaton had more than paid Foster back when Foster's parents had been killed in a car accident a month ago. Foster and his team had been running those traitorous CIA assholes all over hell's backyard on one covert mission after another and he hadn't been able to extract himself long enough to head home. But Keaton had dropped everything and stepped up.

Foster would never forget that.

Foster shuffled back a bit, giving Keaton a thorough once-over. "I can't believe I'm saying this, but Florida looks good on you. You sound better."

Keaton sighed. "Getting there. Which reminds me... You should all come down for a visit. See the town. Get a feel for what we do. There's always room for guys like you."

Kash chuckled. "Are you suggesting we consider retiring to Florida?"

Keaton grinned. "Sunshine. Beaches."

"Gators. Mosquitos."

Zain swatted Kash across the chest. "And don't forget the pythons. I hear those fuckers grow really big."

Keaton rolled his eyes. "You've all been hanging around Foster for too long. The Everglades are fine."

"Sure, if you're looking to disappear." Chase pointed a finger at Keaton. "Permanently."

"Just, keep it in mind. Though, I suppose my dumbass cousin is trying to talk you all in to heading to Oregon, where there's nothing but gray clouds and rain."

"I'm not trying to talk them into anything." Foster shifted on the bed, not that it helped eliminate the pain throbbing through his shoulder. "But my parents did leave me that turn-of-the-century manor house they'd been renovating. Sounds like a good place to start."

Keaton laughed, nearly falling off the bed before he straightened. "You're going to fix up that old dusty inn? Are you all nuts?"

"Beats swimming with gators."

"You keep telling yourself that. Besides, Raven's Cliff is so small, you have to run to the next town to change your mind."

"And Calusa Cove is your idea of big time? I hate to break it to you, cuz, but it's just as small." Foster smiled. "And there're gators."

Keaton shook his head. "Still as stubborn as a damn mule. Though, I guess some things never change. Like us. Whether you're ready to face it or not, sooner or later you'll have to admit that we're all just hardwired differently. No way you'll be able to stay out of the fray for long."

Foster pursed his lips, Sean's gurgling rasp sounding in his head. Foster glanced over at the windows, hating the eerie apparition standing in the graying light. Blood still dripping from its neck and ribs as the ghostly image tapped its chest pocket.

It wasn't real. He understood that much. Just a by-product of the pain and anger and loss. Too bad that knowledge didn't make it disappear.

Keaton sighed at Foster's silence, looking over at the window then focusing on him, again. "Hey, didn't you mention something about an old JSOC commander of yours starting up a search and rescue organization there?"

Foster snorted. "Colonel Atticus Parker. Bastard's already called me twice. Wants to know when we're all signing up."

"And?"

"I told him I wasn't interested, but *no* isn't in the old man's vocabulary."

"Is this where we start a pool on how long it'll be before you've all been recruited?"

"About as long as it would for me to move down to the Everglades." Foster shifted again, but it only shot pain down through his ribs. "I don't suppose you'd do us a solid?"

Keaton laughed. "I already ordered a few pizzas. Just thought I'd stop in and visit while they were being made. I'll go grab them. Keep my seat warm."

His cousin headed for the door, pausing at the threshold. "Whatever you jerks decide, do yourselves a favor — stick together. Civilians really are crazy and knowing I still have my team watching my six is the only reason I've stayed sane." He made a finger gun at Foster. "That, and you, cuz."

"Just grab the pizzas before we all start puking."

"Your wish." Keaton headed out, leaving a strange void in the air. As if he'd taken most of the oxygen with him. Left nothing but uncertainty behind.

Foster cleared his throat, looking each of his buddies in the eyes. "I know we talked about calling it quits. Going to Oregon and seeing if a change in venue somehow fixes the broken parts the doctors can't splint. And there'll always be a place waiting there for you jackasses to hang your hat. But there's no pressure. Given some time and enough rehab, you all might—"

"Might what, Beck?" Kash shuffled in his seat. "Get the urge to jump back in the saddle? Put our lives in the hands of some traitorous agents, again? Because I don't know about Zain and Chase, but there's not a chance in hell I could go down that road, again."

Some of the color drained from Kash's face and Foster suspected he wasn't the only one reliving that night. Though, Kash had nearly lost his four-legged partner, Nyx, on the gauntlet run back to the chopper. Realizing she'd almost died in order to protect two traitors who'd then killed Sean and put Rhett in what might be a permanent coma had obviously affected Kash on a whole other level.

Kash sighed. "I'm not saying that staying on the sidelines is in the cards. But I'm ready to try something new. While I'm still alive enough to enjoy it."

Zain gave Kash's arm a pat. "What he said. We're all up for re-enlistment over the next two months. Seems almost poetic in the timing, if you ask me."

"Which is why we didn't." Chase dodged Zain's slap. "And you're not pressuring us, Foster. After everything that went down…" He swallowed, looking as if he might puke. "I think we could use a fresh start. Don't much care where that is, other than Florida. That's just wrong."

Foster nodded, a bit of the tension in his chest easing. "Then, it's settled. I'll contact the lawyer — get him to send over the papers he's been keeping for me. Just remember. I warned you all ahead of time that nothing exciting happens in Raven's Cliff. So, make peace with that. Things are about to get really boring."

Raven's Cliff Series
with Kris Norris
Raven's Watch
Raven's Claw
Raven's Nest
Raven's Curse

ABOUT JEN TALTY

Jen Talty is the *USA Today* Bestselling Author of Contemporary Romance, Romantic Suspense, and Paranormal Romance. In the fall of 2020, her short story was selected and featured in a 1001 Dark Nights Anthology.

Regardless of the genre, her goal is to take you on a ride that will leave you floating under the sun with warmth in your heart. She writes stories about broken heroes and heroines who aren't necessarily looking for romance, but in the end, they find the kind of love books are written about :).

She first started writing while carting her kids to one hockey rink after the other, averaging 170 games per year between 3 kids in 2 countries and 5 states. Her first book, IN TWO WEEKS was originally published in 2007. In 2010 she helped form a publishing company (Cool Gus Publishing) with *NY Times* Bestselling Author Bob Mayer where she ran the technical side of the business through 2016.

Jen is currently enjoying the next phase of her life... the empty nester! She and her husband reside in Jupiter, Florida.

Grab a glass of vino, kick back, relax, and let the romance roll in...

Sign up for my [Newsletter](https://dl.bookfunnel.com/82gm8b9k4y) where I often give away free books before publication.

Join my private [Facebook group](https://www.facebook.com/groups/191706547909047/) where I post exclusive excerpts and discuss all things murder and love!

Never miss a new release. Follow me on Amazon:amazon.com/author/jentalty

And on Bookbub: bookbub.com/authors/jentalty

ALSO BY JEN TALTY

Brand New Series!
The Secrets of Stone Bridge
A Vintage of Regret
A Harvest of Lies

Welcome to...Everglades Overwatch!
Secrets in Calusa Cove
Pirates in Calusa Cove
Murder in Calusa Cove
Betrayal in Calusa Cove

Safe Harbor Series
Mine To Keep
Mine To Save
Mine To Protect
Mine to Hold
Mine to Love

Check out LOVE IN THE ADIRONDACKS!
- *Shattered Dreams*
- *An Inconvenient Flame*
- *The Wedding Driver*
- *Clear Blue Sky*
- *Blue Moon*
- *Before the Storm*

NY STATE TROOPER SERIES (also set in the Adirondacks!)
- *In Two Weeks*
- *Dark Water*
- *Deadly Secrets*
- *Murder in Paradise Bay*
- *To Protect His own*
- *Deadly Seduction*
- *When A Stranger Calls*
- *His Deadly Past*
- *The Corkscrew Killer*

First Responders: A spin-off from the NY State Troopers series
- *Playing With Fire*
- *Private Conversation*
- *The Right Groom*
- *After The Fire*
- *Caught In The Flames*
- *Chasing The Fire*

Legacy Series

ALSO BY JEN TALTY

Dark Legacy
Legacy of Lies
Secret Legacy

Emerald City
  Investigate Away
  Sail Away
  Fly Away
  Flirt Away
  Anchor Away

Hawaii Brotherhood Protectors
  Waylen Unleashed
  Bowie's Battle

Colorado Brotherhood Protectors
  Fighting For Esme
  Defending Raven
  Fay's Six
  Darius' Promise

Yellowstone Brotherhood Protectors
  Guarding Payton
  Wyatt's Mission
  Corbin's Mission

Candlewood Falls
  Rivers Edge
  The Buried Secret
  Its In His Kiss

ALSO BY JEN TALTY

Lips Of An Angel
Kisses Sweeter than Wine
A Little Bit Whiskey

It's all in the Whiskey
  Johnnie Walker
  Georgia Moon
  Jack Daniels
  Jim Beam
  Whiskey Sour
  Whiskey Cobbler
  Whiskey Smash
  Irish Whiskey

The Monroes
  Color Me Yours
  Color Me Smart
  Color Me Free
  Color Me Lucky
  Color Me Ice
  Color Me Home

Broken Heroes Mended Souls
  Shelter for Danni
  Shelter for Shay

Fallport Rescue Operations
  Searching for Madison
  Searching for Haven
  Searching for Pandora

ALSO BY JEN TALTY

Searching for Stormi
Searching for Winslet
Searching for Odessa

DELTA FORCE-NEXT GENERATION

Shielding Jolene
Shielding Aalyiah
Shielding Laine
Shielding Talullah
Shielding Maribel
Shielding Daisy

The Men of Thief Lake
   Rekindled
   Destiny's Dream

Federal Investigators
   Jane Doe's Return
   The Butterfly Murders

THE AEGIS NETWORK
   The Sarich Brother
   The Lighthouse
   Her Last Hope
   The Last Flight
   The Return Home
   The Matriarch

Aegis Network: Jacksonville Division
   A SEAL's Honor

ALSO BY JEN TALTY

Talon's Honor
Arthur's Honor
Rex's Honor
Kent's Honor
Buddy's Honor
Duncan's Honor
Garth's Honor
Hawke's Honor

Aegis Network Short Stories
  Max & Milian
  A Christmas Miracle
  Spinning Wheels
  Holiday's Vacation

The Brotherhood Protectors
  Out of the Wild
  Rough Justice
  Rough Around The Edges
  Rough Ride
  Rough Edge
  Rough Beauty

The Brotherhood Protectors
  The Saving Series
  Saving Love
  Saving Magnolia
  Saving Leather

Hot Hunks

ALSO BY JEN TALTY

Cove's Blind Date Blows Up
My Everyday Hero – Ledger
Tempting Tavor
Malachi's Mystic Assignment
Needing Neor

Holiday Romances
    A Christmas Getaway
    Alaskan Christmas
    Whispers
    Christmas In The Sand

Heroes & Heroines on the Field
    Taking A Risk
    Tee Time

A New Dawn
    The Blind Date
    Spring Fling
    Summers Gone
    Winter Wedding
    The Awakening
    Fated Moons

The Collective Order
    The Lost Sister
    The Lost Soldier
    The Lost Soul
    The Lost Connection
    The New Order

ABOUT ELLE JAMES

ELLE JAMES also writing as MYLA JACKSON is a *New York Times* and *USA Today* Bestselling author of books including cowboys, intrigues and paranormal adventures that keep her readers on the edges of their seats. When she's not at her computer, she's traveling, snow skiing, boating, or riding her ATV, dreaming up new stories. Learn more about Elle James at www.ellejames.com

Website | Facebook | Twitter | GoodReads | Newsletter | BookBub | Amazon

Or visit her alter ego Myla Jackson at
mylajackson.com
Website | Facebook | Twitter | Newsletter

Follow Me!
www.ellejames.com
ellejamesauthor@gmail.com

ALSO BY ELLE JAMES

Everglades Overwatch Series
with Jen Talty
Secrets in Calusa Cove

Pirates in Calusa Cove

Murder in Calusa Cove

Betrayal in Calusa Cove

A Killer Series
Chilled (#1)

Scorched (#2)

Erased (#3)

Brotherhood Protectors International
Athens Affair (#1)

Belgian Betrayal (#2)

Croatia Collateral (#3)

Dublin Debacle (#4)

Edinburgh Escape (#5)

France Face-Off (#6)

Brotherhood Protectors Hawaii
Kalea's Hero (#1)

Leilani's Hero (#2)

Kiana's Hero (#3)

Casey's Hero (#4)

Maliea's Hero (#5)

Emi's Hero (#6)

Sachie's Hero (#7)

Kimo's Hero (#8)

Alana's Hero (#9)

Bayou Brotherhood Protectors

Remy (#1)

Gerard (#2)

Lucas (#3)

Beau (#4)

Rafael (#5)

Valentin (#6)

Landry (#7)

Simon (#8)

Maurice (#9)

Jacques (#10)

Raven's Cliff Series
with Kris Norris

Raven's Watch

Raven's Claw

Raven's Nest

Raven's Curse

Brotherhood Protectors Yellowstone

Saving Kyla (#1)

Saving Chelsea (#2)

Saving Amanda (#3)

Saving Liliana (#4)

Saving Breely (#5)

Saving Savvie (#6)

Saving Jenna (#7)

Saving Peyton (#8)

Saving Londyn (#9)

Brotherhood Protectors Colorado

SEAL Salvation (#1)

Rocky Mountain Rescue (#2)

Ranger Redemption (#3)

Tactical Takeover (#4)

Colorado Conspiracy (#5)

Rocky Mountain Madness (#6)

Free Fall (#7)

Colorado Cold Case (#8)

Fool's Folly (#9)

Colorado Free Rein (#10)

Rocky Mountain Venom (#11)

High Country Hero (#12)

Brotherhood Protectors

Montana SEAL (#1)

Bride Protector SEAL (#2)

Montana D-Force (#3)

Cowboy D-Force (#4)

Montana Ranger (#5)

Montana Dog Soldier (#6)

Montana SEAL Daddy (#7)

Montana Ranger's Wedding Vow (#8)

Montana SEAL Undercover Daddy (#9)

Cape Cod SEAL Rescue (#10)

Montana SEAL Friendly Fire (#11)

Montana SEAL's Mail-Order Bride (#12)

SEAL Justice (#13)

Ranger Creed (#14)

Delta Force Rescue (#15)

Dog Days of Christmas (#16)

Montana Rescue (#17)

Montana Ranger Returns (#18)

Brotherhood Protectors Boxed Set 1

Brotherhood Protectors Boxed Set 2

Brotherhood Protectors Boxed Set 3

Brotherhood Protectors Boxed Set 4

Brotherhood Protectors Boxed Set 5

Brotherhood Protectors Boxed Set 6

Iron Horse Legacy

Soldier's Duty (#1)

Ranger's Baby (#2)

Marine's Promise (#3)

SEAL's Vow (#4)

Warrior's Resolve (#5)

Drake (#6)

Grimm (#7)

Murdock (#8)

Utah (#9)

Judge (#10)

Delta Force Strong

Ivy's Delta (Delta Force 3 Crossover)

Breaking Silence (#1)

Breaking Rules (#2)

Breaking Away (#3)

Breaking Free (#4)

Breaking Hearts (#5)

Breaking Ties (#6)

Breaking Point (#7)

Breaking Dawn (#8)

Breaking Promises (#9)

Hearts & Heroes Series

Wyatt's War (#1)

Mack's Witness (#2)

Ronin's Return (#3)

Sam's Surrender (#4)

Hellfire Series

Hellfire, Texas (#1)

Justice Burning (#2)

Smoldering Desire (#3)

Hellfire in High Heels (#4)

Playing With Fire (#5)

Up in Flames (#6)

Total Meltdown (#7)

Take No Prisoners Series

SEAL's Honor (#1)

SEAL'S Desire (#2)

SEAL's Embrace (#3)

SEAL's Obsession (#4)

SEAL's Proposal (#5)

SEAL's Seduction (#6)

SEAL'S Defiance (#7)

SEAL's Deception (#8)

SEAL's Deliverance (#9)
SEAL's Ultimate Challenge (#10)

Cajun Magic Mystery Series
Voodoo on the Bayou (#1)
Voodoo for Two (#2)
Deja Voodoo (#3)

Texas Billionaire Club
Tarzan & Janine (#1)
Something To Talk About (#2)
Who's Your Daddy (#3)
Love & War (#4)

Billionaire Online Dating Service
The Billionaire Husband Test (#1)
The Billionaire Cinderella Test (#2)
The Billionaire Bride Test (#3)
The Billionaire Daddy Test (#4)
The Billionaire Matchmaker Test (#5)
The Billionaire Glitch Date (#6)
The Billionaire Perfect Date (#7)
The Billionaire Replacement Date (#8)
The Billionaire Wedding Date (#9)

The Outriders
Homicide at Whiskey Gulch (#1)

Hideout at Whiskey Gulch (#2)

Held Hostage at Whiskey Gulch (#3)

Setup at Whiskey Gulch (#4)

Missing Witness at Whiskey Gulch (#5)

Cowboy Justice at Whiskey Gulch (#6)

Boys Behaving Badly Anthologies

Rogues (#1)

Blue Collar (#2)

Pirates (#3)

Stranded (#4)

First Responder (#5)

Cowboys (#6)

Silver Soldiers (#7)

Secret Identities (#8)

Warrior's Conquest

Enslaved by the Viking Short Story

Conquests

Smokin' Hot Firemen

Protecting the Colton Bride

Protecting the Colton Bride & Colton's Cowboy Code

Heir to Murder

Secret Service Rescue

High Octane Heroes

Haunted

Engaged with the Boss

Cowboy Brigade

An Unexpected Clue

Under Suspicion, With Child

Texas-Size Secrets

Made in United States
Cleveland, OH
07 October 2025